ELIZABETH GILL
WHAT DREAD HAND?

ELIZABETH GILL was born Elizabeth Joyce Copping in 1901, into a family including journalists, novelists and illustrators. She married for the first time, at the age of 19, to archaeologist Kenn... Her second marriage, to artist Colin Gill, las... death, at the age of only 32, in 1934, following complications from ... surgery.

She is the author of ... mystery novels, *The Crime Coast* (ak... , *What Dread Hand?* (1932), a... *de Luxe* (1933), all featuring eccentric but perceptive ... detective Benvenuto Brown.

By Elizabeth Gill

The Crime Coast
What Dread Hand?
Crime de Luxe

ELIZABETH GILL

WHAT DREAD HAND?

With an introduction
by Curtis Evans

DEAN STREET PRESS

Published by Dean Street Press 2017

Copyright © 1932 Elizabeth Gill

Introduction copyright © 2017 Curtis Evans

All Rights Reserved

First published in 1932 by Cassell & Co.

Cover by DSP

ISBN 978 1 911579 21 2

www.deanstreetpress.co.uk

"Tiger! Tiger! burning bright
In the forests of the night,
What immortal hand or eye
Could frame thy fearful symmetry?

In what distant deeps or skies
Burnt the fire of thine eyes?
On what wings dare he aspire?
What the hand dare seize the fire?

And what shoulder, and what art,
Could twist the sinews of thy heart?
And when thy heart began to beat
What dread hand . . . ?"

From "The Tiger," by WILLIAM BLAKE

INTRODUCTION

THE DEATH OF Elizabeth Joyce Copping Gill on 18 June 1934 in London at the age of 32 cruelly deprived Golden Age detective fiction readers of a rapidly rising talent in the mystery fiction field, "Elizabeth Gill." Under this name Gill had published, in both the UK and the US, a trio of acclaimed detective novels, all of which were headlined by her memorably-named amateur detective, the cosmopolitan English artist Benvenuto Brown: *Strange Holiday* (in the US, *The Crime Coast*) (1929), *What Dread Hand?* (1932) and *Crime De Luxe* (1933). Graced with keen social observation, interesting characters, quicksilver wit and lively and intriguing plots, the three Benvenuto Brown detective novels are worthy representatives of the so-called "manners" school of British mystery that was being richly developed in the 1930s not only by Elizabeth Gill before her untimely death, but by the famed British Crime Queens Dorothy L. Sayers, Margery Allingham and Ngaio Marsh, as well as such lately rediscovered doyennes of detective fiction (all, like Elizabeth Gill, reprinted by Dean Street Press) as Ianthe Jerrold, Molly Thynne and Harriet Rutland.

Like her contemporaries Ianthe Jerrold and Molly Thynne, the estimable Elizabeth Gill sprang from a lineage of literary and artistic distinction. She was born Elizabeth Joyce Copping on 2 November 1901 in Sevenoaks, Kent, not far from London, the elder child of illustrator Harold Copping and his second wife, Edith Louisa Mothersill, daughter of a commercial traveler in photographic equipment. Elizabeth--who was known by her second name, Joyce (to avoid confusion I will continue to call her Elizabeth in this introduction)--was raised at "The Studio" in the nearby village of Shoreham, where she resided in 1911 with only her parents and a young Irish governess. From her father's previous marriage, Elizabeth had two significantly older half-brothers, Ernest Noel, who migrated to Canada before the Great War, and Romney, who died in 1910, when Elizabeth was but eight years old.

Elizabeth's half-sister, Violet, had passed away in infancy before Elizabeth's birth, and a much younger brother, John Clarence, would be born to her parents in 1914. For much of her life, it seems, young Elizabeth essentially lived as an only child. Whether she was instructed privately or institutionally in the later years of her adolescence is unknown to me, but judging from her novels her education in the liberal arts must have been a good one.

Elizabeth's father Harold Copping (1863-1932) was the elder son of Edward Copping--a longtime editor of the *London Daily News* and the author of *The Home at Rosefield* (1861), a triple-decker tragic Victorian novel vigorously and lengthily denounced for its "morbid exaggeration of false sentiment" by the *Spectator* (26 October 1861, 24)—and Rose Heathilla Prout, daughter of watercolorist John Skinner Prout. Harold Copping's brother, Arthur E. Copping (1865-1941), was a journalist, travel writer, comic novelist and devoted member of the Salvation Army. Harold Copping himself was best-known for his Biblical illustrations, especially "The Hope of the World" (1915), a depiction of a beatific Jesus Christ surrounded by a multi-racial group of children from different continents that became an iconic image in British Sunday Schools; and the pieces collected in what became known as *The Copping Bible* (1910), a bestseller in Britain. Harold Copping also did illustrations for non-Biblical works, including such classics from Anglo-American literature as *David Copperfield*, *A Christmas Carol*, *Little Women* and *Westward, Ho!* Intriguingly Copping's oeuvre also includes illustrations for an 1895 girls' novel, *Willful Joyce*, whose titular character is described in a contemporary review as being, despite her willfulness, "a thoroughly healthy young creature whose mischievous escapades form very interesting reading" (*The Publisher's Circular*, Christmas 1895, 13).

Whether or not Harold Copping's surviving daughter Joyce, aka Elizabeth, was herself "willful," her choice of marriage partners certainly was out of the common rut. Both of her husbands were extremely talented men with an affinity for art. In 1921, when she was only 19, Elizabeth wed Kenneth de Burgh Codrington (1899-1986), a brilliant young colonial Englishman then studying Indian archaeology at Oxford. (Like Agatha Christie, Elizabeth made a marital match with an archaeologist, though, to be sure, it was a union of much shorter duration.) Less than six years later the couple were divorced, with Elizabeth seeming to express ambivalent feelings about her first husband in her second detective novel, *What Dread Hand?* After his divorce from Elizabeth, Codrington, who corresponded about matters of religious philosophy with T.S. Eliot, would become Keeper of the Indian Museum at the Victoria and Albert Museum, London, and later the first professor of Indian archaeology at London's School of Oriental and African Studies. Codrington's "affection and respect for Indian culture," notes an authority on colonial Indian history, "led him to a strong belief in a mid-century ideal of universal humanity" (Saloni Mathur, *India by Design: Colonial History and Cultural Display*)—though presumably this was not to be under the specifically Christian banner metaphorically unfurled in Harold Copping's "The Hope of the World."

In 1927 Elizabeth wed a second time, this time to Colin Unwin Gill (1892-1940), a prominent English painter and muralist and cousin of the controversial British sculptor Eric Gill. As was the case with his new bride, Colin Gill's first marriage had ended in divorce. A veteran of the Great War, where he served in the Royal Engineers as a front-line camouflage officer, Colin was invalided back to England with gas poisoning in 1918. In much of his best-known work, including *Heavy Artillery* (1919), he drew directly from his own combat experience in France, although in the year of his marriage to Elizabeth he completed one of his finest pieces, inspired by English medieval history, *King Alfred's Longships Defeat the Danes, 877*, which was unveiled with fanfare at St. Stephen's Hall in the Palace of Westminster, the meeting place of the British Parliament, by Prime Minister Stanley Baldwin.

During the seven years of Elizabeth and Colin's marriage, which ended in 1934 with Elizabeth's premature death, the couple resided at a ground-floor studio flat at the Tower House, Tite Street, Chelsea--the same one, indeed, where James McNeill Whistler, the famous painter and a great-uncle of the mystery writer Molly Thynne, had also once lived and worked. (Other notable one-time residents of Tite Street include writers Oscar Wilde and Radclyffe Hall, composer Peter Warlock, and artists John Singer Sargent, Augustus John and Hannah Gluckstein, aka "Gluck"—see Devon Cox's recent collective biography of famous Tite Street denizens, *The Street of Wonderful Possibilities: Whistler, Wilde and Sargent in Tite Street*.) Designed by progressive architect William Edward Godwin, a leading light in the Aesthetic Movement, the picturesque Tower House was, as described in *The British Architect* ("Rambles in London Streets: Chelsea District," 3 December 1892, p. 403), "divided into four great stories of studios," each of them with a "corresponding set of chambers formed by the introduction of a mezzanine floor, at about half the height of the studio." Given the strongly-conveyed settings of Elizabeth's first two detective novels, the first of which she began writing not long after her marriage to Colin, I surmise that the couple also spent a great deal of their time in southern France.

Despite Elizabeth Gill's successful embarkation upon a career as a detective novelist (she also dabbled in watercolors, like her great-grandfather, as well as dress design), dark clouds loomed forebodingly on her horizon. In the early 1930s her husband commenced a sexual affair with another tenant at the Tower House: Mabel Lethbridge (1900-1968), then the youngest recipient of the Order of the British Empire (O.B.E.), which had been awarded to her for her services as a munitions worker in the Great War. As a teenager Lethbridge had lost her left leg when a shell she was packing exploded, an event recounted by her in her bestselling autobiography, *Fortune Grass*. The book was published several months after Elizabeth's death, which occurred suddenly and unexpectedly after the mystery writer underwent an operation in a West London hospital in June 1934. Elizabeth was laid to rest in Shoreham, Kent, beside her parents, who had barely predeceased her. In 1938 Colin married again, though his new wife was not Mabel Lethbridge, but rather South African journalist Una Elizabeth Kellett Long (1909-1984), with whom Colin, under the joint pseudonym Richard Saxby, co-authored a crime thriller, *Five Came to London* (1938). Colin would himself pass away in 1940, just six years after Elizabeth, expiring from illness in South Africa, where he had traveled with Una to paint murals at the Johannesburg Magistrates' Courts.

While Kenneth de Burgh Codrington continues to receive his due in studies of Indian antiquities and Colin Gill maintains a foothold in the annals of British art history, Elizabeth Gill's place in Golden Age British detective fiction was for decades largely forgotten. Happily this long period of unmerited neglect has ended with the reprinting by Dean Street Press of Elizabeth Gill's fine trio of Benvenuto Brown mysteries. The American poet, critic, editor and journalist Amy Bonner aptly appraised Elizabeth's talent as a detective novelist in her *Brooklyn Eagle* review of the final Gill mystery novel, *Crime De Luxe*, writing glowingly that "Miss Gill is a consummate artist. . . . she writes detective stories like a novelist. . . . [Her work] may be unhesitatingly recommended to detective fiction fans and others who want to be converted."

WHAT DREAD HAND?

What Dread Hand?, Elizabeth Gill's second Benvenuto Brown detective novel, expands the criminal canvas of her first mystery, *The Crime Coast* (aka *Strange Holiday*), by richly encompassing not only the painting but the theatrical milieu. The title itself makes a literary allusion, being drawn from William Blake's famous poem "The Tyger," an excerpt from which serves as the novel's epigraph. Its opening chapters take place in London, where playwright Martin Pitt's acclaimed new realist tragedy, *The Lily Flower*, is having its premiere. In attendance when the curtains open on this powerful new play are the novel's focal character, lovely, twenty-three-year-old Julia Dallas; Lord Charles Kulligrew, Julia's brilliantly gifted fiancé; kindly yet distracted professor Edward Milk and his opinionated spinster sister, Agatha, Julia's uncle and aunt; and Julia's friend Benvenuto Brown, the accomplished artist and amateur sleuth. The other key players in the intricate murder puzzle which develops out of that fatal night are the play's flamboyant producer, Terence Rourke, and its bewitching leading lady, Louise Lafontaine, who has "created a reputation for undressing on the stage almost as great as Tallulah's own." (This last is a reference to Tallulah Bankhead, the outré American-born actress who became a fixture on the London stage between 1922 and 1931 and had her portrait done in 1929 by the famed English portraitist Augustus John, a Chelsea neighbor of Elizabeth Gill and her esteemed painter husband, Colin Gill.) And just who exactly was the mysterious wizened, elderly man who made such an unnerving impression that night? "My God, what an exhibit!" exclaims Benvenuto Brown of this eerie individual. "Looks like a Spirit of Evil invented by Dürer."

Several chapters that follow take place in Chelsea, but soon the action moves to southern France, the setting for most of Gill's first detective novel, where the activities of the master crook known as "the Tiger" are scandalizing the public. How does this affair link up with the murder in London? Julia finds herself baffled by a succession of strange events, but Benvenuto Brown, by now an accomplished hand at amateur detection, is on the case, and readers can rest assured that he always gets his man—or woman, as the case may be.

Aside from its agreeable writing, intriguing characterization and beguiling plotting, *What Dread Hand?* is of interest for its portrayal of the complex relationship between Julia Dallas and her fiancé, Lord Charles Kulligrew, which seemingly draws, in my reading, on intimate circumstances from the author's own life. After the ending of her engagement with

Charles, Julia concedes to herself the man's many good, even great, qualities:

> "He was one of those people who seem unfairly endowed with a multitude of talents, any of which taken alone and fostered would have brought fame and fortune to an ordinary man. Oxford remembered him both for athletic prowess and a Prize Poem, while to the public he was famous for his book on his Aztec expedition."

Yet Julia ruefully admits to herself that she nevertheless is glad to be liberated from spending the rest of her life with him:

> "[I]t was true that she had liked and admired and even in a way loved Charles, she told herself, and that she would miss him terribly. But she could not pretend that her life was broke up, that she had lost everything she valued, could not pretend that every now and again a little demon inside her did not lift its head and say— 'You're free—you're free.'"

In her depiction of Julia Dallas's ambivalent relationship with Charles Kulligrew, was Elizabeth--or Joyce as she was known in real life—channeling the experience of her own breakup with the distinguished Kenneth de Burgh Codrington, whom she had married at the youthful age of 19 in 1921 and had divorced by 1927, when she wed a second time, this time to the painter Colin Gill? A correspondent with T.S. Eliot, Kenneth Codrington was a prodigiously talented expert on Indian material culture who became Keeper of the India Museum at the Victoria and Albert Museum, London in 1935, three years after the publication of *What Dread Hand?* and one year after Elizabeth's untimely passing at the age of 32, after a colorful and independent-minded life of incident and variety. How does Julia Dallas fare in *What Dread Hand?* Read on and see.

Curtis Evans

CHAPTER I
DRESS CLOTHES

JULIA'S NOSE detected perfumes by four different dressmakers as she stood awaiting her turn at the long mirror. What acres of flowers, she reflected, must be bottled for every London season. Her mind wandered to the flower farms of Grasse, mountain paths at sunset heavy with the scent of lavender, then returned with a start as she swept her skirt out of range of a jewelled heel. The summer night was hot, the cloak-room of the Metz was crowded, each mirror echoed an absorbed face intent on the activities of lipstick or puff, feathers fluttered in the air, and jewelled fingers plucked at flowing lengths of skirt. Pink ladies, yellow ladies, green ladies, elbowed their way past Julia as at last she took her place before the glass, and if for a moment she looked at herself with satisfaction, who shall blame her? The sleek white satin of her Molyneux gown gave her the distinction of a lily in a bunch of over-dressed carnations, and stressed the slenderness of her figure; bright chestnut hair crowned her rather high white forehead; slanting brown eyes held a suggestion of humour even while they looked in the mirror; and three freckles which persisted on her nose gave a faint air of the schoolroom to Julia at twenty-three.

Really, she thought to herself as she turned from the mirror, really I do look awfully like the future Lady Charles Kulligrew. And remembering how she had kept Charles waiting, she dropped a shilling in the saucer, threw a glance of sympathy at the kneeling attendant who was sewing up a damaged flounce, and went out into the foyer.

Yet her confidence, even the confidence of wearing a perfect frock, began to slide away from her as she walked across to Charles Kulligrew, standing at the foot of the staircase. It is absurd, she told herself hurriedly for the hundredth time, to be engaged for three months to this charming, intelligent and distinguished creature, to be quite sure that I know him really well and adore him—when he isn't there—and then, when I'm with him—She slipped her hand through his arm and started to talk, to conquer her growing shyness.

Lord Charles Kulligrew, who looked down at her, was chiefly remarkable at first glance for the attractive and penetrating eyes which unexpectedly humanized a face and figure suggestive of a nervous race-horse. Tall and dark, he walked with a limp, the result of a German shell splinter, and when he spoke his voice betrayed a slight but charming nervous hesitation. He was one of those people who seem unfairly endowed with a multitude of talents, any of which taken alone and fostered would have brought fame and fortune to an ordinary man. Oxford remembered him both for athletic prowess and a Prize Poem, while to the public he was famous for his book on his Aztec expedition. During the war he had served with great distinction in that most adventurous force, the Intelligence Service, but met with acute dismay any reference to his achievements in this as in any other walk of life. He had become engaged to Julia Dallas partly because he admired her beauty and her mind, partly because, knowing her from childhood, he had never found in her independence and high-handed gaiety the hero-worship and invitation which he saw in the eyes of other women. Now, to their mutual but unspoken dismay, the demands of a closer relationship seemed to have done nothing but obscure a light-hearted friendship— and, half unconsciously, they invariably tried to arrange some kind of a party when they were to meet.

"Sorry I've been such an age, Charles. Have you been amused? It's the most exciting kind of evening, isn't it? I've a feeling Martin Pitt's play is going to be a success. Did you get him for dinner? You've not told me who's coming."

"The party's to be small but distinguished," he smiled at her. "Professor Edward Milk, Miss Agatha Milk, Benvenuto Brown—and ourselves. I tried to get Martin, but he's dining early with Terence Rourke. We'll probably see them inside if they haven't gone back to the theatre already. Look—isn't this the Professor and Agatha?"

Framed in big glass doors held apart by two commissionaires, against the background of Piccadilly lit by the evening sun, they could see a taxi-cab from which two people were alighting. The first, a very tall and bent old man, seemed confused between an attempt to help his sister down and to extract money from beneath the folds of his long caped coat in one and the same movement. The lady who stepped with determination on to the pavement conveyed somehow, in spite of the warmth of the evening, an impression of frost-bite surrounded by tulle scarves and jet. As thin as her brother, she seemed but half his height, and he bent down to listen to her as they entered the hotel, nervously fingering his white beard.

"Tuppence would have been quite sufficient," she was saying. "I do wish you could remember, Edward, that ten per cent. is the correct reward for the lower classes." She unwillingly gave him over to the custody of an attendant who led him to the cloak-room, following them with her eyes like an anxious hen. Julia clutched Kulligrew's arm.

"Such a nerve-racking moment," she whispered. "Last time I went to the theatre with the Professor, he took off his dinner-jacket with his overcoat in the front row of the stalls, and sat down blandly in his shirt-sleeves." Her face crumpled with laughter, and they went forward to greet Agatha, whose thin lips softened into a smile as she saw them.

"My dear children, this is a pleasure. I fear we are late, but Edward could not arrange to leave Oxford until this afternoon. He will be with us directly—he is removing his coat."

"You're so wise, Agatha, not to brave the cloak-room— there's such a traffic block."

"I washed myself before I left our hotel, my dear." Agatha's tone swept all the face-powder out of the universe. Then, suddenly softening, "I'm glad to see you are wearing white. Young girls should always wear white."

"Doesn't she look charming?" said Charles, and Julia went forward to greet Professor Milk, whose mild blue eyes looked at her affectionately.

"O matre pulchra filia pulchrior," he said, and then, turning to Charles, "Most kind of you, my dear Charles, to ask us up to this little gathering. It is a rare treat for Agatha and myself." He beamed vaguely round at the company. "I confess myself greatly stirred at the prospect of seeing Martin Pitt's play. A most promising boy—most promising—"

Kulligrew nodded. "Pitt is a great man, Professor, and has never won the recognition he ought to have had. I hear the whole of London is turning out for him to-night. Now, shall we go in and have a cocktail? Benvenuto Brown is joining us, but he rang me up and said he might be a bit late—he's painting a portrait—so we won't wait for him."

Julia took the Professor's arm and led the way along the softly lighted corridor to where Mario stood welcoming his clients at the door of the restaurant. "Good evening, Miss Dallas—good evening, sir—the window table, isn't it, Lord Charles? This way." He spoke with the urbanity only born of many years' association with the most expensive kinds of food, and led the party with slow dignity through the crowded tables, while waiters melted out of his path. He stopped at a round table by an open window which gave on to the Park, and as a final honour rearranged with his own hand one of the green orchids in the centre bowl. They sat down and Julia threw a grateful smile at Charles. He did everything so well—her favourite table—her favourite kind of flower. She looked round the crowded restaurant, whose decoration always pleased her with its slightly faded splendour, listened to the hum of conversation and the distant rumble of Piccadilly traffic, the one broken here and there by laughter and the other by the notes of motor-horns; let her eyes rest on glass and flowers and silver, bare arms loaded with jewels resting on the white cloths, bright dresses, and the rich reds and yellows of wine, and thought to herself there is really nothing so nice as London in the season. She turned to the Professor at her side.

"D'you remember bringing me here on my birthday, one summer holidays? We sat in the corner over there—and you told me who all the people were who came in. It was only when we came to Mr. Gladstone and the Queen of Sheba that I began to get a bit suspicious!"

"My dear, I remember you looked like a little princess, and that it was all very expensive." He smiled at the recollection of the early days of his guardianship of Julia, and stretched out his hand absent-mindedly to the cocktail in front of him.

"Edward!" Agatha's voice admonished him. "Your tablets."

"Of course, of course—very remiss of me—unusual excitement—" He fumbled in his waistcoat pocket and was about to place a pill in his mouth when a hand descended on his shoulder.

"Still doping, Professor? Sorry I'm late, Charles—had a hell of a day. Agatha, how are you? Julia, you look like a snowflake—can I come and sit next to you? Whew!" Running a hand through his already unruly hair Benvenuto Brown dropped into a chair beside her, dipped his rather long nose towards his cocktail glass and drank the company's health.

"Good man—I thought you'd forgotten us. How's painting—and how's crime?" said Kulligrew.

He looked round the table before answering, his good-humoured, lined face with its long upper lip creased into a smile. Somehow with his coming the party had become a party, and even Agatha, rather primly holding her glass, seemed to wear her scarves at a more jaunty angle.

"Deep depression in both," he said. "Country's too well fed and too well policed—no one buying pictures or committing crimes. Going to have a shot at murder myself in a day or two—I'm painting a woman who wants high lights on every pearl. What's this play you're taking me to see to-night? I don't know Martin Pitt—seem to remember seeing a play by him at some Sunday Society show."

Kulligrew nodded. "He's a most brilliant man and has never been properly appreciated. He was up at Oxford with me, and I got to know him pretty well, though he was fresh from school and I was just demobilized. Most interesting mind. The Professor knows him too—he'll be admittedly a great man one day; don't you think so, sir?"

The Professor looked up vaguely from his caviare.

"Yes, yes, a prophet in his own country—the mind of the masses is slow—think of some of our Australian poets—" He sighed and returned to his food.

"I owe a lot to Pitt," went on Kulligrew thoughtfully. "I can never disassociate him in my mind from Blake, Shelley, Pope—even Aristophanes—I suppose I'd read them all before I met him, but he seemed to make them his own, light them up from the inside and give them to you all alive. The first time I met him he was striding up and down Port Meadow outside Oxford, in the rain, holding his hat over a volume of poetry which he was reading aloud to himself. An extraordinary-looking creature, very pale and lightly made, with limp yellow hair and curiously vivid dark eyes which used to blaze with excitement when he read aloud anything that particularly stirred him. I went up and spoke to him that day. I said, 'I used to sit in a trench in the rain and try to think how that went on—I wish you'd read it to me.' He gave me a quick look and started at the beginning—'The daughters of the Seraphim led down their sunny flocks.' Evidently he considered my remark a sensible one, or he'd have turned on his heel and left me—his manners are non-existent. After that I seem to remember talking with him and reading with him for about four years—he's got a more intense appreciation of literature than anyone I've ever met."

"What's he like as a man?" asked Julia. "I've only met him once, and that was at a polite tea-party. He was introduced to me, but wouldn't speak a word and left shortly after. I thought him beautiful to look at, like some kind of a faun—but I couldn't make him out."

Kulligrew laughed. "He's very like a child in some ways. If you'd talked about something he considered a suitable subject of conversation for a woman, like onion soup or the best kind of shoe leather, he'd probably have responded and been perfectly charming—but he's got the most Eastern ideas of women's mentality, or professes to have. I think actually he's extremely shy of women—and of men too for that matter—and hypersensitive as to his effect on other people, so that he invariably seeks out highly abstract or excessively concrete subjects of conversation in an attempt to avoid the personal. This, of course, unfits him both for tea-parties and for intimate friendships. He's got a rooted objection to discussing for one moment anything which doesn't appeal to him as interesting."

"Bad trait for an author," put in Benvenuto.

"I don't know," Kulligrew considered. "It gives him great singleness of purpose and forbids other people inflicting their moods on him. I admit"—he smiled reminiscently—"it is rather irritating at times when he entirely disregards what one has been saying, and then proceeds to open up a train of thought far more interesting than one's own. I think he needs success to humanize him. He'd never admit it, but I believe that the fact that neither of his previous plays caused anything of a stir hit him pretty hard. I only hope to-night will be a success."

"The town is alive with rumours about it," said Benvenuto. "I suppose that's due to our friend Rourke—who's not only a man with extremely good judgment but one of these damned Irishmen who infect other people with their enthusiasms. You know Rourke, don't you?"

Kulligrew's expression was slightly troubled, and he looked round, almost uneasily, Julia thought, before he answered:

"Known him all my life; we went through the war together. He ought to be here somewhere—Pitt told me he was dining with him. Isn't that their table at the other end of the room?"

Following the direction of his glance Julia saw the yellow head of Martin Pitt, bent in conversation with a lady, the back of whose low-cut pink frock was towards her. Facing the pink lady sat a man who towered head and shoulders above the other two, and even across the distance which separated them, he conveyed a vivid impression of force and vigour to Julia. A mass of iron-grey hair was swept back from a surprisingly young face, and for a moment, across the babble of talk, she thought she heard his laugh, deep and rich. So that was Terence Rourke, the man who, although unheard-of two years before, had created a reputation as London's greatest play-producer. She looked at him with interest, but while she did so found time to wonder why Charles hadn't mentioned who was dining with Rourke and Pitt that night; in reply to a question of Benvenuto's he was explaining that the owner of the pink dress was Louise Lafontaine, Rourke's leading lady, playing the name part in *The Lily Flower*.

"Charming creature," said Benvenuto. "I saw her once. Specializes in vamp parts, doesn't she?"

Kulligrew frowned. "She's a woman who's been damned by her own success. She's created a reputation for undressing on the stage almost as great as Tallulah's own, but actually she's an extremely good actress, and Rourke has had the sense to realize it. You'll see her in an entirely different kind of part to-night."

"She doesn't appear to have changed her habits," remarked Agatha acidly, surveying the bare and unconscious back of Louise. Julia gave a small explosion of laughter that seemed in keeping with the freckles on her nose, and became quickly conscious that Charles was silent. She picked up her glass and drank her wine. She was being ridiculous; why, she was not even sure that Charles had ever known Louise well. In any case, Charles was thirty-eight—presumably she herself was not the only woman he had ever met. For a moment she tried to imagine Charles in Pitt's place, his head bent towards the dark curls above the pink dress, and felt at once, painfully, that the intangible veil of half-shy, half-friendly diffidence that she knew so well would not hang between Charles and that pink dress. It was her own fault, she told herself fiercely— she would break through it. She raised her eyes to Charles, but he was talking to Benvenuto.

"The play is called *The Lily Flower*," he was saying.

"'Thou low-born Lily Flower?'" quoted Benvenuto.

"Exactly," Kulligrew looked at him appreciatively. "It concerns a suburban family, and more especially the daughter Lily, one of those entrancingly lovely creatures that are the miracle of London's suburbs. Have you ever stood outside a big store at about six in the evening and watched them emerge from their ribbon counters and their typewriters—a conquering army with slim bodies and faces like angels, going out to do battle for seats in a Putney bus or an Ealing train?"

"Indeed I have," returned Benvenuto, his fork suspended in mid-air. "They're the most dazzling beauties in the world; and apart from the few who break away and advertise a shampoo powder or get in the Follies, they're entirely unhonoured and unsung. This sounds interesting—tell us more about it, if you can spare time from this engaging soufflé."

"Have some more. Professor, your glass. I won't tell you the plot, it will spoil the show, and it is in any case merely an excuse—an emotional explosive which alights in the midst of this commonplace family and illumines each member of it for your benefit. It is psychologically that the play is interesting— the various reactions of Lily and her family to this event. You might call it a Study of the Effect of Suburban Life on the Soul. But you'll see for yourselves." He smiled at them.

Benvenuto looked at Kulligrew thoughtfully. "I shan't be happy till I've met Martin Pitt," he said. "You've described a most contradictory—But look—look—our friends must be rehearsing."

Round them people were standing up and gazing at Terence Rourke, who, looking magnificently like some cavalry leader at the head of a charge, a long incongruous sword in his hand, was making cuts and thrusts at a frightened waiter. Pitt and the leading lady hung desperately to his coat-tails, but, dragging them behind him, he advanced menacingly, his grey hair waving, the sword-blade glittering in the electric light. "A superb composition," Benvenuto murmured to Julia. "That's his famous sword-stick. I'd better calm him down or we'll have the gendarmes in." So saying, he left her, and walking swiftly across the restaurant put his hand on his friend's arm.

Rourke's fury seemed to leave him as quickly as it had begun, and after saying in a loud voice, "Napoleon brandy! Holy Powers!" he allowed himself to be led up to Julia and introduced, kissing her hand and apologizing in the grand manner for his behaviour.

"I hope you didn't wound the waiter," said Julia, rather at a loss as to how to treat this melodramatic giant. "You seemed careless of his feelings," she added.

"Sure, I'd be wounded myself if you thought so," he replied. "The blighter thought I wouldn't know his damned poteen from Napoleon brandy."

He appeared rather ashamed of himself, and slipping his sword into its stick and tossing back his mane of hair, he seemed to draw himself into the likeness of an ordinary diner, and bowed very formally and gallantly to Agatha as Benvenuto introduced him. She gave him a bird-like smile.

"I consider you were perfectly right, Mr. Rourke," she assured him. "Far too many people nowadays allow inferior articles to be fobbed off on them."

Kulligrew had turned to greet Rourke's fellow-diners who were approaching, and the next moment Julia saw the owner of the pink dress smiling at him.

"Charles," she said, and gave him a small and beautifully shaped hand.

"Won't you all join us for a moment?" he asked. "I want you to meet my fiancée. Julia, this is Miss Lafontaine—Miss Dallas."

Julia saw a smiling mouth and unsmiling dark eyes, heard a clear and very controlled voice say, "I congratulate you both," and then, "I didn't know you were going to be married, Charles," as a smooth shoulder was turned towards her.

Julia talked to Pitt while Kulligrew introduced Louise Lafontaine to Agatha and the Professor, and while she contented herself with conventional remarks about the coming play, felt she would have liked to pat him soothingly on the shoulder. He was obviously nervous and gave her his attention with an effort, his curious and beautiful face very white, his eyes very dark under his yellow hair. She was glad when Rourke summoned them both away to the theatre. She liked Rourke, she decided, if like was a word one could apply to so spectacular a creature, and as she watched him say good-bye to the others, wondered why his manner to Kulligrew should be almost exaggeratedly frigid.

CHAPTER II
"THE LILY FLOWER"

KULLIGREW'S PACKARD crept slowly into place in front of the theatre, and Julia sighed with relief as she stepped down on to the strip of red carpet.

"Thank Heaven we're not late—I can't bear to miss a moment of a first night," she murmured to Benvenuto, walking with him through an avenue of peering faces. "It's even more exciting than the Zoo."

"I agree," he said; "the charm lying, of course, in the fact that one is never quite sure on which side of the cage one is."

He piloted her to a seat in the foyer and went off with Charles and the Professor to put their hats in the cloak-room. Agatha was greeting a friend from the country, and Julia sat back and looked for familiar faces and unfamiliar frocks in the slowly-moving crowd. She sensed an atmosphere of subdued and polite excitement, noticed many writers and theatrical people, and nodded to a dozen acquaintances. The broad back of a famous judge was quickly eclipsed by a movie star, whose face was known so intimately to her that Julia felt inclined to bow.

A rustle in the doorway, and there arrived a group of angular, diamond-trimmed ladies who surrounded, someone whispered, a Royal Princess; and over there, like some exotic flower in a cloud of milky pink, went Tallulah.

Certainly Martin Pitt's play was an occasion.

Julia wondered what he thought about it—just how much he cared for the verdict of this crowd; thought of him, suddenly, walking in Port Meadow in the rain reading a poem— the poem from which he had taken a phrase which had called so much beauty and distinction away from its dinner tonight. *The Lily Flower*—what were they going to do to it—water it with their praise or trample it under their heels? The lynx-eyed woman in green with the gold turban—what would she say of *The Lily Flower*—or that extraordinary old man talking to the German Ambassador? Julia became so interested in him that she forgot the play, and found herself shuddering a little as she watched his thin bent body and the bones of his face showing behind the dry skin. She had just completed an exact mental picture of him as a skeleton when she found Charles bending over her.

"Benvenuto's gone down to watch the first act from the stalls with Rourke. He wants us to meet him for a drink in the interval. Shall we go along? The Professor's bringing Agatha—apparently there's quite a concourse of people from Oxford to see Pitt's play, and they're all worked up about meeting each other."

Julia laughed. "I think that's so natural, Charles. People you only nod to on your native heath become so exciting when you meet them unexpectedly at a bull-fight."

Making their way up the stairs and through the slowly moving crowd, they reached Charles's box, which was next to the stage and on a level with it.

"I hope you'll be able to see," he said. "It was the only box I could get—and we've got to keep these two seats behind for any members of the management or the caste who want to drop in and see the play from the front."

"But that will be lovely—and I can see perfectly," said Julia, wondering swiftly if she would have to entertain Louise. "My dear, what a crowd! Look—there's Eddie Marsh—and Marcus Macgill—and the Vanbrughs—and James Agate—" She stopped to grimace at Benvenuto, sitting in the third row of the stalls, an empty seat beside him.

"And it looks to me," said Kulligrew, leaning over the edge of the box, "as if a bomb dropped on the theatre would extinguish England's literary future. Martin's got a critical audience."

"He'll like that, won't he?"

"He may—" Kulligrew laughed shortly.

Julia looked at him, puzzled. "Is he really so frightfully sensitive?"

"My dear Julia, can you imagine a more terrible experience than to see all those people watching something which is identified so intimately with oneself? Personally, I'd rather undress in public!"

"I believe you would," she laughed at him. "But you're such an inherently modest creature you forget that most people adore publicity. His ordeal is beginning," she finished, dropping her voice to a whisper.

With the last notes of the orchestra the lights were lowered, late-comers hurried into their seats, and, as though some invisible conductor had lowered his baton, the buzz of conversation in the theatre faltered and died as the curtain slowly rose.

· · · · ·

Everyone now knows *The Lily Flower*, almost by heart. But to Julia, and to the hundreds of shadowed people round her, it was new; and from the moment the curtain rose they were conscious of its quality.

The first scene was a suburban house-front, a small garden with gravel path and iron railings in front of it, and then the road crossing the stage, the edge of it coming right up to the footlights. It was the dusk of a spring evening, still light enough for faces to be clearly seen, though in the house, lights showed in the two lower windows. The scene was realistic, with a kind of formal and significant realism as though a Stanley Spencer had turned his attention to the suburbs. Against the iron railings was leaning a motor-cycle, and beside it stood a young man with an oil-can in his hand, whistling spasmodically a few bars of *Ramona*. He bent down to his machine and the tune was drowned in the deafening roar of the engine, while he stood back, gazing at it in admiration.

"Rather an unexpected hors d'œuvre for the highbrows," murmured Julia to Kulligrew; but he, bending forward with his arms on the box, kept his attention fixed on the stage where a girl had just appeared, leaning out of one of the lower windows. A burst of applause from the audience greeted her; during it she leant over the window-ledge quite still, her arms folded, and a hair-brush in her hand, looking at the young man. The beauty of her small pale face was framed by the sculptured folds of a white towel twisted turban-wise over her head; her shoulders above a white bodice were bare, and she had evidently been washing her hair. Her appearance, framed by the window against the soft glow of the lighted room, gave the same impression as the scenery, a significant and selected realism, and the conversation which followed between her and the young man, her brother, was in the same mood.

"Here is a new world—what is going to happen in it?" thought Julia, but to Kulligrew she said, "People in the suburbs don't talk like that."

"Perhaps they think like it," he answered, his eyes on the stage.

Very little happens in the first act beyond a gradual revealing of the different characters in the family—Lily, the Brother, the Mother, the younger Sister, Lily's Fiancé; yet Julia, as she saw unfold the suburban tragedy, formal and inevitable like a Greek play and alive and rich with personal emotion, forgot herself and Charles, forgot that the "Lily Flower" was Louise, and became an instrument on which the drama played notes of comedy and pain. Lily's fears, Lily's feelings, Lily's face, these were reality; and when at the end of the act the first definite shadow of tragedy is cast by the solitary figure of the father, whose coming the family have awaited, crossing the empty stage to the darkened house and trying by the light of a street lamp to wipe the blood from his hands and clothes, it was of Lily that Julia thought as she watched him enter the house and saw the curtain fall.

• • • • •

"The *only* distinction nowadays is to live at Purley—"

"My dear, Louise is *charming*, and so innocent!"

"Myself, I prefer the younger sister—a perfect example of one of Nature's Pillion Riders."

Julia, pushing her way towards the foyer, felt a moment of annoyance as she overheard the remarks. Then, "An English Pirandello," she heard someone say. That was better. She turned to Kulligrew with a sigh of relief as she disentangled herself from the crowd.

"Isn't it wonderful, Charles? Better than I'd dared to hope. I've not got a critical faculty left. I'm just a tremulous mass of admiration. Look—there's Martin Pitt—do let's go and congratulate him."

"Do you like it?" Kulligrew roused himself from the abstraction in which he had been plunged since the beginning of the act, and took her arm as they walked over towards Pitt.

"I was surprised myself by that first act," he went on. "I didn't realize—from reading it—how well it would act. Louise was marvellous, wasn't she? Actually the first act is the dullest of the three—it gets much more interesting later on. But they do seem to be eating it, don't they?"

By this time they had reached the outer circle of a miniature court that had gathered round Pitt, in the midst of which he, in a condition of strained excitement, was receiving congratulations. As Julia and Kulligrew paused to wait their turn at this, the latest shrine, a pompous and bespectacled dramatic critic with a hearty manner brought his hand down on Pitt's shoulder.

"What have you been playing at all this time, young feller-me-lad, hiding your light under a bushel? We can't afford to have people like you skulking in corners, you know. Why, I've been spilling rivers of ink for years asking for a play like this—a play by an Englishman, about English life, for English people—"

"Come on," murmured Kulligrew in Julia's ear. "I can't stand that fellow—and Martin seems pretty well engaged with the adulation of the mob."

But Julia, catching for a moment Pitt's eye as Kulligrew led her away, wasn't able to decide from his expression whether it was kinder to leave him or not. They wandered through the crowd, continuously overhearing favourable verdicts on the play; when suddenly Julia, with something of a shock, encountered the gaze of the old man she had seen downstairs, her imagined skeleton, fixed with a strange intentness on herself and Charles. She was about to attract Charles's attention to him when she felt Agatha's hand on her arm, and looked round to see her with the Professor, who by this time had a comfortable covering of cigar ash over his evening-clothes, but who looked, Julia thought, a little confused and worried.

"Here you are, my dear. And are you enjoying this strange play?" inquired Agatha.

"Indeed I am—and what do you think of it, Uncle Edward?"

He brought his mild eyes to rest on her face.

"Remarkably brilliant, my dear. These young minds are a perpetual revelation to me—so surprisingly humorous—so unexpectedly tender—" he plucked at his beard and frowned. "But is it a Comedy or a Tragedy—one can't tell—one can't tell. How little we understand one another."

The bell interrupted his musing, and there was a general movement to the stairs, the Professor, now quite lost in a dream, being piloted purposefully by Agatha. Benvenuto appeared for a moment on the way to his seat.

"Hullo—sorry I missed you in the rabble. Meet me at the bar during the next interval and tell me the opinion of the cits."

"We will," promised Julia, and followed Kulligrew into the box.

CHAPTER III
CRIES OF "AUTHOR!"

SITTING IN THE box, waiting for the curtain to rise, Julia watched Charles's face bent over his programme, and hardly listened as he told her the time and place of the next scene. She liked the way the light rested on his cheekbones, on his finely-shaped nose and the high, thoughtful forehead from which the hair was beginning to retreat a little. His mouth, she decided, was very expressive and humorous, and gave an attractive warmth and humanity to what was definitely an intellectual head. A cold feeling of loneliness and failure settled on Julia. If only, she thought, we could be commonplace and natural and delightful, and hold hands for a minute while the lights are going down—and her loneliness was increased by the swift, friendly smile he threw her before he turned to the stage as the curtain rose.

The beginning of the second act of *The Lily Flower* did nothing to dispel Julia's mood. Lily, singing to herself while she moved about the living-room, getting ready Sunday morning's breakfast; Lily, seeming to exude a warm and triumphant happiness; Lily, talking to her sister before the rest of the family arrive, when, unable to keep her happiness to herself, she tells the younger girl of the hours spent with her lover in the spring darkness the night before; confides her philosophy of love and her unquestioning belief in what life holds for her; every word, with its confidence and bare simplicity, increased for Julia the knowledge of all that she and Charles helplessly were missing.

Yet gradually the onward movement of the play carried her with it, so that she lost herself in the shadow of calamity which crept over the stage. The mother and the brother joining the two girls over the commonplace business of Sunday breakfast; the arrival of the newspapers with their glaring headlines of murder committed on the common near their home the night before; the gradual realization by the mother of the significance of things she has not understood, and her speech to her children of her suspicions which gradually in all their minds become certainties, that the father is the murderer; the long scene in which they talk without restraint, alternately making plans for his escape and discussing their own reactions, giving themselves away, exposing their secret characters in this moment of crisis; the gradual silence and stillness of Lily as the growing horror envelops her, the realization of the change this must make in her life; and, at the end, the father, silent and enigmatic, coming down to his breakfast as the curtain falls. Julia became for the time merely the vehicle for this strange conflict of emotions, and as the lights flickered up over the theatre and the storm of applause sounded in her ears, she became conscious of herself, sitting in a box in her white dress beside Charles, with something of a shock.

As the applause died down she tried to attract his attention, but he, still turned to the stage with his back half towards her, stared down broodingly at the footlights and answered her abstractedly. Tired by her emotions Julia felt suddenly bitter and offended, and signing to Benvenuto below her in the stalls, she slipped out of her seat and made her way along to the buffet.

He had reached there before her and stood leaning against the bar and stroking his long upper lip, waiting for her. Julia felt reassured as she caught sight of him—if anyone could offer her wisdom Benvenuto could.

"I feel like an orphan of the storm," he announced; "but those parts of me which are still conscious clamour for a drink. What are you going to have?"

"Oh, Ben, it is a lovely play. I feel so highly emotional, I don't know what to drink—what do you advise?"

"Well"—he considered her gravely—"I suggest gin for emotion or brandy for logic—which shall it be?"

"Brandy, please—with soda for thirst." She laughed at him, feeling better; and by the time she had finished her drink wanted to escape from the crowd that surged round the bar, and talk to him.

"I'm getting claustrophobia here, Ben—where can we go and talk?"

"By the look of things the stalls ought to be a positive desert. Come down and sit in our seats until the curtain goes up. It's going to be a long interval."

"Some time," said Julia, when they were seated side by side in the almost empty theatre, "I want to have a long talk with you, Ben."

"Sure," he replied, "on any subject you like; as to why the sea is boiling hot, or whether pigs have wings."

"Yes, that's it, *exactly*. I am the pig and my wings haven't begun to sprout even."

She glanced up at her box, where Kulligrew was still sitting by himself.

"You know, Charles is difficult; he's so much more profound, somehow, than I am. My inferiority complex makes me want to scream when I'm with him. Ben, do you think we're going to make a success of it? Just now and again," she lowered her voice, "I almost *hate* him."

Benvenuto scrutinized her.

"I've felt that way myself. We must face facts and admit that he's moody, sometimes. Why, I can't imagine—he's got everything in the world, you included."

"Not yet!" Julia turned round to him. "He's bored with having everything, Ben; and sometimes I think he's afraid that he'll get bored with having me. That's something I could spare him, at least," she ended bitterly.

"Don't you think you're being a trifle unfair?"

"No, Ben, I don't. You see, before we got engaged we used to get on frightfully well, like normal human beings; and now—oh, it's all perfectly fantastic. We go on like a couple of puppets as soon as we come face to face, smiling and bowing and miming at each other through a sheet of glass. It's acutely painful for me to be left alone with him for a moment—and I believe it is for him too. I've told myself over and over again that it's my own fault, that I'm simply being hysterical and imaginative, and that next time we meet it will be all right, instead of which, next time it's—just the same. Why in Heaven's name did he ask me to marry him, Ben? Oh, please—I'm not being arch!"

"I know you're not being arch, woman. Ten thousand devils! If I hadn't known you in bibs, Julia, and hadn't qualified years ago as your elder brother, I'd—I'd make love to you myself and show the poor boob how it should be done."

"Really, Ben!" Julia shook with laughter. "You do charm me at times. And now—thanking you kindly for listening to my woes—I'd better go before the lights go out. Charles is still in the box, and—" She stopped suddenly, her eyes fixed on the box adjoining Charles's, and sank back in her seat. "Ben—*who is* that old man?" she asked quietly. "It's the second time this evening I've caught him looking at Charles in that spectre-like manner. I think he's too sinister for words, like a skeleton in evening dress."

Benvenuto looked up and chuckled. "My God, what an exhibit! Looks like a Spirit of Evil invented by Dürer. Give me your programme, quick." He took a pencil from his pocket, and with swift glances up at the old man, who was leaning over the edge of his box looking round at Charles, commenced a drawing.

"You'll probably find," he murmured absently, "that it's Charles's long-lost uncle home from Australia. I wish he'd keep still."

Julia shuddered and laughed. "He couldn't possibly be anybody's uncle. Here comes Mr. Rourke—perhaps he can enlighten us."

Benvenuto looked up. "Hullo, Rourke—tell me, who is yonder bird of prey?"

Terence Rourke, looking more than ever like a conquering hero, thought Julia, towered over them. "It is the play that should interest you, and not the audience," he said reproachfully, and for a moment his charming Irish voice seemed to envelop her like a warm stream as she smiled into his laughing blue eyes. "Isn't this night a triumph, Miss Dallas?" He half turned to follow the direction of Benvenuto's glance, then suddenly she saw his whole figure stiffen, and with an involuntary start he stepped back upon her toe. The next moment he was bending over her, full of contrition.

"The clumsy brute that I am—I must have lamed you for life. A thousand pardons, Miss Dallas—forgive me—I must go." And casting another quick look up at the box, all the laughter swept from his face, he hurried away.

Julia looked thoughtfully after him, rubbing her foot.

"What an extraordinary thing," she said; "he was quite upset."

"I was mistaken," said Benvenuto, "evidently he is *Rourke's* uncle."

People were filing into their seats, so saying good-bye to Benvenuto who was putting the finishing touches to his sketch, Julia left him and started towards the exit. Looking up to the box above her she saw Professor Milk bending over Charles, but before she could attract his attention the lights were lowered, and she continued her way in darkness, murmuring apologies to the incoming stall-holders. She went slowly up the staircase thinking about the curious incident of a few moments before—Rourke had certainly been disturbed at sight of the old man; and making up her mind to draw Charles's attention to this mysterious figure before the evening was over she dismissed the matter from her mind as she saw the tall figure of the Professor coming towards her along the corridor from the box She was about to ask him to come back and sit with them, when to her surprise he bent down and took both her hands in his own.

"My dear," he said nervously, "if any kind of—er—trouble—should overtake you, you must be brave."

"Why, Uncle Edward, whatever do you mean?"

"Nothing—nothing, my dear." He dropped her hands as suddenly as he had taken them, and avoiding her eye continued on his way down the corridor. "I must be joining Agatha," she heard him say.

"What can be the matter with the poor darling," thought Julia, staring after his retreating figure half in amusement, half in dismay. He disappeared down the staircase, and suddenly making up her mind she picked up her white skirts and ran after him, only to see him push open the door to the stalls and go through into the darkness beyond.

She walked thoughtfully back towards the box, wondering what the Professor could possibly have been discussing with Charles to have put him into a state of such unusual excitement; it was sufficiently rare for him to emerge from his ordinary condition of vague abstraction for that to be disconcerting in itself, apart from the apparent warning conveyed by his words. She smiled to herself, deciding that the cocktails and the wine and the extraordinarily moving play had been too much for him, and then her thoughts were interrupted by Martin Pitt, hurrying along towards her.

"Oh—have you seen the Professor by any chance? I saw him up in your box from the other side of the house, but by the time I'd got round he had gone."

"You've just missed him—he was here a moment ago, but he's gone down to the stalls."

"I shall have to catch him after the show. I wanted to ask him to come to supper afterwards—we're all going to Bellani's. I do hope you and Charles will both come—you *will*, won't you?"

"Of course we'd simply love to—and thank you very much. I must go—I can't bear to miss any more. I shall come again to-morrow night. I can't tell you how much—" But with a quick wave of the hand he had gone, and Julia decided that Charles was right—Pitt hated being congratulated. She hurried on to the box and quietly pushed open the door. Charles was bending forward engrossed in the play, and she slipped quietly into her seat and allowed herself to become once more absorbed in the tragedy of *The Lily Flower*.

There is a growing sense of darkness and horror about the last act, where the mother, emerging from the first shock of realization that her husband is a murderer, begins to taste the excitement of this violent eruption in her monotonous existence, and gradually, morbidly, dramatizes herself in her own

eyes. On that first night Louise Lafontaine created her reputation as a great actress, when she, as the "Lily Flower," found
her mother before the mirror, a black veil draped over her
face, rehearsing an imaginative farewell to her husband. No
one who saw the play that night will ever forget Lily, a torrent
of words pouring from her lips, whipping the miserable woman with her fury and her scorn, until she crept from the stage;
Lily alone, with her anguish and her despair, knowing that she
has lost everything she valued—her father, her mother and her
lover—for she cannot let him marry a murderer's daughter;
Lily a lovely and desolate figure, walking slowly away out of
the room, out of her home where she has found nothing but
ugliness and cruelty and falsehood.

Julia, sitting tense and dry-eyed in her box, wished that
she might escape from the cycle of this relentless play that
moved slowly forward to its inevitable end; and it was almost
with relief that she heard a voice call her softly from the door.
She turned quickly as Rourke entered the box. Professor
Milk, he told her, had to leave early—could she go down for a
moment and say good-bye to him and his sister? They were
waiting in the foyer. She nodded and slipped away, leaving
him in her seat.

Downstairs she found the Professor and Agatha, fluttering
and apologetic.

"It is most thoughtless of us to drag you away, my dear,"
said Agatha, pecking her cheek. "We are obliged to catch the
last train back, and Edward insisted we must see you and
make you promise to come down to us for next weekend. Now
please do—we've asked Charles too, and a little country air will
do you both good. That's right; now run along. Edward, the
cab is here. Good-bye—good-bye—convey our hearty thanks
to Charles—"

With a last flutter of her scarves she scurried out of the door;
the Professor, a melancholy and drooping figure, behind her.

Julia felt tired and vaguely depressed as she made her way upstairs again. "Can I bear any more of the play," she thought—and her spirits were in no wise heightened to find that Terence Rourke had gone, and in his place was the cloaked figure of Louise, standing behind Charles and watching the stage. In the dim light she thought she saw a fleeting bitter-sweet smile on the face of Louise, who the next moment had gathered her cloak round her and was gone.

"Sorry to be so restless—I had to go and say good-bye to Uncle Edward and Agatha," whispered Julia to Charles, and settled down in her place to watch the end of the play.

The climax of *The Lily Flower*, now so familiar to everyone, where the innocence of the father is clearly proven, came with the first shock of its satiric surprise to the watching audience that night, a cruel prelude to the final appearance of Lily—Lily carried in from the river with the water dripping from her white, dead face. As the curtain fell there was a moment's utter silence before waves of applause broke over the theatre, and Julia, her fatigue forgotten, gave herself up to the excitement of the audience in hailing London's new playwright. It seemed as though they would never let Louise go, and she stood loaded with bouquets, tired but smiling, taking call after call. At last the final curtain, and with it, all over the theatre, shouts of "Author—Author," until at last Martin Pitt appeared on the stage. Julia bent forward to see him the better. "I believe you're wrong, Charles," she laughed, her eyes on the stage. "He's terribly excited—loving it—"

And it certainly looked as though Pitt, his great dark eyes ablaze and his yellow hair tumbled over his forehead, was taking his hour of triumph with both hands. As the cries of "Speech" died down he stepped to the footlights, his slim body taut and upright, his head thrown back, his hands clasped in front of him.

"Ladies and gentlemen," he began—and Julia liked him for the tiny crack of nervousness in his voice—"I want to thank you very much indeed on behalf of Mr. Rourke and the whole of this marvellous company who have played to you to-night—and more deeply still on my own behalf—for the wonderful reception—the wonderful reception—wonderful reception—"

What was happening? Blindly Julia got to her feet. Pitt was coming towards her—stumbling along the stage, choking out a word. "*Look—look at it!* LOOK!" He was coming near-er—he was pointing at her. Oh, God!—no—he was pointing at Charles. Julia put out her hands to Charles, but before she could touch him she saw it—the handle of a weapon sticking out between his shoulder-blades. The box rocked and swung—blurred rows of faces rushed before her eyes—a line of lights—and Pitt, tipping forward, crashing on to his face.

She was slipping—slipping away into darkness with voices following her—voices crying, "He's dead—he's dead!"

CHAPTER IV
"APRÈS LA GUERRE FINIE"

THE ROYAL HOSPITAL Gardens in Chelsea looked extraordi-narily peaceful in the sunlight of a June afternoon. The hard, clear green of early summer foliage on the trees cut bright patterns out of a pale blue sky where small clouds hung, mo-tionless—like the trees and sky of a Baxter print, thought Ju-lia, lingering by the railings on her way down to the river. She turned to look at the placid elegance of Wren's building, the mellowing purple of its walls a perpetual background for the scarlet-coated pensioners, now sunning themselves on the benches with their hands folded on the handles of their sticks, staring dreamily over the gardens. The scene had for Julia a vividness, a feeling of painted unreality as of familiar objects seen through the eyes of a convalescent, and she walked on, deliberately sinking herself in her surroundings, feeling her way gradually back to a normal world. For a week she had lain in a darkened room, fussed over anxiously by Agatha, who had somehow, by force of will and insistence on the paramount importance of everyday things, led her out of a cloud of tragedy and death. She had seen no one but two importunate officials from Scotland Yard who had defied even Agatha's dragon-like defence, but at last with many admonishments as to an early return, she was allowed out to take tea with Benvenuto.

She walked along the Embankment, the slow stream of the Thames on one side, the swift stream of traffic on the other, and by the time she pushed open the green wicket which led through to the court-yard where Benvenuto had his studio, she felt more normal than had seemed possible a few days before. The door was open, and mounting the stairs she found Benvenuto at work in the big room, which was a comfortable confusion of easels, canvases, and big divans pushed against the wall. He came towards her, brush in hand.

"I'm glad to see you, my dear. Come and sit over here—cigarettes in this box, matches beside you. Do you mind if I go on with my 'ballon captif'? I talk better while I'm working."

Her cigarette alight, she leant back among the cushions and watched him putting in the background of a portrait of a fat lady in pearls.

"Your telephone messages, Ben, have been my daily solace, though they've been a great strain on Agatha. I don't think she will ever really *like* a telephone."

Benvenuto rubbed his ear. "I believe you. My hearing is permanently impaired owing to her conviction that space is something to be shouted across. By the way," he went on, after a pause, "during the battle which raged on the 'phone this morning I thought I was able to distinguish something to the effect that you wanted to see me urgently."

"Ben, you did; and I do." She sat forward and went on earnestly. "I want to ask you to do something for me, something that will mean a tremendous lot to me if you agree. I feel nervous about it because I know you're painting hard just now, and—"

"What is it, Julia?"

"Ben, will you take up the investigation of Charles's murder? I know that if anyone can solve it you can; and—and—oh, I can't rest, I can't think about anything at all until this mystery is cleared up. It is almost incredible even now that anyone can exist who could have wanted to kill Charles—Charles, who was liked by everyone who knew him, who was clever and kind and brave—" After a moment she went on. "You can't think what it's like, Ben, to remember how awful I was to him those last few weeks—cold and stupid and introspective. There's only one thing I can do, and that is to help find the mad coward who—who did it. I'm so horribly rich now, since I've inherited Charles's money, which ought to make it easier. So will you take it up for my sake—and for his?"

He swung round from his painting and faced her.

"Of course I will, Julia. In fact, I took it up from the moment I rushed up to the box and saw poor Charles's body. I haven't been exactly idle since, but things haven't got very far. The inquest was a purely formal affair and didn't get us anywhere."

"Ben, remember I've been in bed for a week; I haven't seen a paper or anything, and my mind is a blank. But tell me—have you any idea who did it?"

He looked at her for a moment before answering. Then:

"Yes, I have," he said. "But I may be wrong, and naturally I can't tell you, or anyone else, whom I suspect. The police meanwhile are utterly confused because Terence Rourke has disappeared, and they can't find a trace of him."

"Terence Rourke?"

"Yes. Perhaps you don't know that it was with Rourke's sword-stick that Charles was murdered."

Julia sat speechless, very white. It was too horrible to contemplate—Terence Rourke a murderer, the man with whom she had talked, laughed, a few nights before.

"The first thing to do," went on Benvenuto in a matter-of-fact tone, "is to find Rourke, and to-morrow I'm going to start out to do it."

"But how?"

"I think I know where he is."

"Ben, you are clever. How did you find out?"

"From this, which I found on the floor of the box. It is a message written that night in the theatre by Rourke to Kulligrew, and it says: 'Remember there is a score to settle. The vulture hovers.—T.G.R.' This has both confounded Scotland Yard and given me a clue. They think it is a threat sent by Rourke to Kulligrew before he killed him—as if anyone would do that! No, Rourke was warning Charles against someone."

"I know—I know who it was! The old man you drew!" cried Julia.

"Perhaps. But listen. I am going to tell you a story. Just after the war—you wouldn't remember—there was a man in France, a motor-bandit, a kind of Don Quixote, who held up the cars of war-profiteers and robbed them, and handed the money, or most of it, to the Mutilés de la Guerre. He seemed to know always whom to rob. I remember he held up old Mosenberg's car on the Route des Alpes one night and took half a million francs off him that the old brute was going to build a new casino with at Nice. Next day half a million francs was paid over—anonymously—to the war victims' fund. Old Mose tried to get it back with a lawsuit, but of course didn't succeed; incidentally, he'd made it all out of supplying the troops with tinned meat, not over good. Well, this Don Quixote went on doing this for about two years; it was said that the peasants knew who he was, but they never gave him away; indeed, he was very popular, and the police never caught him. Perhaps even their methods were a bit half-hearted. Then, at the end of two years, the whole thing stopped and became a legend."

"Well, that's interesting," said Julia, "but what's it got to do with poor Charles's murderer?"

"The name the bandit gave himself was 'Le Tigre.'"

"The Tiger?"

"'Tiger, Tiger, burning bright in the forests of the night,'" murmured Benvenuto. "Well, my dear, to continue. The Tiger has reappeared. Read that." He handed her the *Daily Mail* of three days before, and Julia read:

BANKER'S CAR ROBBED BY FRENCH BANDITS

Sir Henry Brooks, who was on his way to the Riviera by car with his family, was held up yesterday evening on a lonely stretch of road between Annécy and Aix-les-Bains, and robbed of a considerable sum by French bandits. On arriving at Aix the words "Le Tigre" were found chalked on the back of the car.

Julia let the paper fall in her lap. "Well?"

"What is Rourke's middle name?" Benvenuto asked her.

"According to you it begins with a G—but I still don't see—"

"It is Gale," he interrupted her. "It was his mother's name. Terence Gale Rourke. T.G.R. Tiger, Tiger!"

"Ben," said Julia, "you're pulling my leg. You're telling me fairy-tales to try and cheer me up."

"On the contrary, I'm perfectly serious. Now listen to me. The day after the murder Rourke's rooms were searched by the police. I was there—the inspector in charge of the case is a friend of mine, one Leech. Well, what do you think we found? Not much, it's true, but some letters addressed to Rourke when he was at college in Dublin over twenty years ago: letters from a girl, love letters, tied up in ribbon inside a dancing slipper. They began: 'Dear Tiger—Darling Tiger.' It was this that gave me the idea. Rourke is rather a figure of romance, you know. I didn't say anything to Leech but he may see the connexion later. Slow but sure."

"I don't see how you can be sure that Rourke is the Tiger," said Julia frowning.

"I can't prove it, of course. But—I know. Everything I know about the man fits. I know, for instance, that he lived in France about that time. Then, he's been a bootlegger in America, and has led a revolution in Mexico—done everything that had a touch of the romantic about it. He's an Elizabethan really, in spirit, and would have made Drake a good lieutenant."

"Drake didn't murder people in the dark with a sword-stick."

"My dear Julia!"—Benvenuto looked at her in a pained way—"neither did Rourke so far as you or I know. But the threads of this affair lead through him, and I'm going to find 'the Tiger' in his lair down in that little south-east corner of France."

"Then I'm coming too. Oh, Ben, I wish I could, but you know I'm not sure your Inspector Leech will let me leave England—he asked me if I intended going away, and I had to promise him I'd be on hand to give evidence whenever necessary."

He looked at her thoughtfully. "I expect I could fix things with Leech so that you could come with me. I'd like it. And you've got some sense; what's more, you look as if you need a holiday—you'll only get morbid waiting about here. All right then—done! My Bugatti's over in Calais and—"

A peal on the front-door bell interrupted him, and the next moment he brought in Agatha, who advanced towards Julia, a large bottle in her hand.

"I might have known it," she announced. "I might have *known* you would forget your Nervine. Young people have no notion of looking after themselves—gadding about here, there and everywhere. How many times must I remind you, my dear—every two hours a teaspoonful in a—"

"Never mind about the Nervine, darling." Julia seized the bottle from her hands and pushed her into the sofa. "Listen. Ben has taken up the case, and he and I are starting for France to-morrow to follow up clues in his car."

"Julia!" Agatha folded her arms and drew her breath in sharply through her nose. "Things have come to a Pretty Pass!" she announced, addressing no one in particular. "Young girls rushing about with strange men in new-fangled vehicles hunting for criminals—"

"But, Agatha," protested Julia, "Ben isn't a strange man—and it's not a new-fangled vehicle, it's a very old Bugatti—"

"Silence, miss!" She fanned herself with her handkerchief and then sat up abruptly. "I have always been considered a broad-minded woman, Julia, but all I can say in the present instance is—if you go, *I* go, though up till now, thank God, I have never left the shores of Albion. And of course I shall bring Archie."

"Archie?" queried Benvenuto in a faint voice.

"My parrot; a most intelligent bird. He pines dreadfully when I so much as leave him for morning service. Fortunately I shall not have Edward on my conscience, as he starts on an expedition to Switzerland to-morrow. And when do *we* start?"

"To-morrow evening," said Benvenuto hopefully, but Agatha nodded her assent.

"That will enable me to purchase a few necessaries from the Stores in the morning. And now, suppose I make some tea."

"My God! I forgot tea." Benvenuto, released as if from a spell which had held him, leapt to his feet, and hurried toward the kitchen.

"Allow me, Benvenuto. No man has ever been able to make a good cup of tea. You have a nice chat with Julia, and *I* will prepare tea."

The door closed behind her, and Benvenuto returned to the divan and sank down beside Julia, mopping his brow.

"Ben," she said in a strangled voice, "I take it all back—I won't come; I mean *we* won't come."

"I beg your pardon," he said firmly, "we're all going. You and I and Archie, and Agatha and Uncle Tom Cobley and all. If Archie can stand it I hope I can. Why, my dear girl, it's the chance of a lifetime—with Agatha beside us we shall see France from an entirely new angle. But tell me—what was that she said about the Professor going to Switzerland?"

"It's his annual holiday, you know. He goes off to Montreux every year, only this year he's starting a bit earlier than usual. He hunts for Alpine plants and encounters undismayed the most frightful perils in tracking down a rare specimen. I'm told he's the wonder and despair of the guides."

"I see. I suppose it's all right. I'd better explain to Leech about it though."

"*Leech?* What on earth has it got to do with him? Why, Ben, you can't possibly mean that Uncle Edward is suspected—" Her voice tailed off into silence.

Benvenuto looked at her for a moment without speaking, then got up and went across to open the door for Agatha, who entered with a tray of tea-things.

Behind the teapot she dispensed cups of delicate China tea, buttered toast and tiny sandwiches, and talked to Benvenuto in the highest spirits; but Julia sat in silence, incident after incident of that night in the theatre chasing each other through her mind, each one of them suddenly, terrifyingly, significant. Terence Rourke, Uncle Edward—it was all too horrible. Her thoughts were interrupted by Benvenuto, who pushed his cup away and turned to her.

"If I'm going to get anywhere near the bottom of this affair, Julia, I've got to get some facts from you; after that we'll make a list of suspects and examine the possibilities."

"A most sensible course," put in Agatha. "Could you wait one moment while I get out my crochet?"

After a pause he went on. "I've really been held up for lack of information from one person—yourself."

Julia nodded, watching him gravely. "Go ahead. I'll answer to the best of my ability."

"What is the last moment during that evening that you can be sure Charles was alive?"

"I've been thinking and thinking," she said slowly. "And it's frightfully difficult for me to say. My feeling is that he was alive at least until I left the box in the middle of the third act to go down to say good-bye to Agatha and Uncle Edward."

"Why do you think that?"

"Because I seem to remember making various remarks to him before that, and he grunted, or so I thought, in reply."

"Well, he was certainly alive until the lights went out at the beginning of that act, because I saw him turn round to greet the Professor as he entered the box."

"Listen, Ben. There's something I ought to tell you." She stared in front of her, miserably. "I met Uncle Edward coming away from the box, and he gave me a—a kind of warning—"

"I know all about that. The Professor has an explanation."

Agatha looked up quickly from her crochet. "Edward has a *perfect* explanation. The police have had the hardihood to browbeat and cross-examine him about it; it's true he contradicted himself once or twice, but he does the same thing if anyone asks him his name without warning, and he *never* knows if it's to-day or yesterday. If Detective Leech is a friend of yours, Benvenuto, I'm sorry for you. The man's nothing but a fool. Edward has the highest reputation for integrity at Oxford, as you ought to know, and no one has been able to cast a stone at him since he received his first good conduct prize as a schoolboy."

"Yes, yes. Exactly. Quite," put in Benvenuto hurriedly. "And now, Julia, tell me who entered the box at the beginning of the third act after you got back, and the times, as well as you can remember."

"Quite a lot of people opened the door, looked at the play for a few moments and left again, but as I didn't look round I don't know who they were. The first person I can actually remember is Mr. Rourke, who gave me the message from Agatha to go down and say good-bye."

"Now, Agatha, did you give Rourke a message to that effect?"

"Certainly, Benvenuto. That is to say, he was sitting just in front of us when I remarked to Edward that it was high time we saw you, Julia, if we were going to catch the train. Some underbred people near us had the effrontery to say 'Hush!' and Mr Rourke turned round and very politely whispered that he would go up and ask Julia to meet us in the foyer. Very courteous and considerate of him, as I said to Edward at the time."

"What time?"

"I beg your pardon? Ah, yes, of course. It was exactly eleven o'clock. Our train goes at the half hour from Paddington, and we were a little delayed as Edward became involved with his gloves, which were under the seat, and someone trod on his hand as he was looking for them. Quite a bruise. Even your Mr. Leech had the courtesy to inquire how he had come by it."

"I see. Thank you, Agatha. So that you left Rourke in the box when you went down, Julia?"

"Yes, he sat down in my place as I went out of the door."

"What was Charles's attitude at that moment?"

"The same as it was all the evening—leaning forward with his arms on the edge of the box, his chin resting on them."

"Now tell me, Julia—think. Do you believe he was alive then?"

"Ye-es. Oh, Ben, I don't know. I was annoyed with him, I must confess it, and was conscious of him without actually looking at him, if you see what I mean. His face was turned towards the stage, away from me. And the box was very dark."

"How long were you away?"

"Not more than ten minutes. Not less than seven."

"And when you came back—?"

"When I came back Mr. Rourke had gone, and Louise Lafontaine was standing just behind the chair he had been sitting in. When I opened the door I didn't know who it was because she was all wrapped up in a cloak—and then she turned round and gave me a sort of malicious smile and went out.

Oh, Ben, surely if Charles had been dead then she—she would have seen—"

"Not necessarily. You didn't see what had happened yourself until Pitt's speech, when the lights were up. And that's easy enough to understand because when we had a reconstruction of the affair, at the theatre, it was evident that Charles's back was in complete darkness during the play. You could see the expression on Louise's face because the lights from the stage reflected on to it. Now, did anyone else come in during that last act?"

"Yes—the door was opened once or twice after that, but I was awfully interested in the play and didn't turn round to see who it was. I know no one came near Charles or myself—they stood at the back."

"So you don't think that anyone could have stabbed Charles whilst you were with him?"

"No, Ben, it's impossible. I just feel it's impossible."

"I agree with you. It narrows down the time considerably. Now, to go back to the beginning of the last act, after you left me in the stalls—"

"I went up the stairs, and in the corridor I met Uncle Edward, who gave me the mysterious warning about trouble coming to me. Ben, what did he—?"

"Go on."

"What did I do then?" She put her hand to her head. "I know—I thought I ought not to have let Uncle Edward go in such a strange condition, so I ran after him, but he went into the stalls before I could reach him. I went upstairs again and then I met Mr. Pitt."

"Pitt?"

"Yes, he was looking for Uncle Edward to ask us all to supper with the company. He'd seen him up in our box just as we did, but when he got there and looked in at the door Uncle Edward had gone."

"Did you tell Leech this?"

"No, I don't think so."

Benvenuto got to his feet and went over to the telephone. "I'm going to ask Pitt to come round here," he said.

There was silence in the studio except for the rustle of pages as Benvenuto looked for Pitt's name in the telephone book, and "One! two! three!" from Agatha, as with her head bent over her crochet she counted under her breath.

One—two—three, echoed in Julia's mind. Terence Rourke—Uncle Edward—Martin Pitt. She clenched her hands until they hurt, and went across the room and stared out of the window. She wanted to scream aloud and wake from this awful nightmare where the ordinary human beings of her world, people she knew and liked, danced before her with murderers' masks over their faces.

"That would be very good of you, Pitt," Benvenuto was saying. "Yes, the green wicket. Push open the door and come right up. Good-bye."

He hung up the receiver and came back to his seat. "He'll be round in ten minutes. Meanwhile, I'm nearly through, Julia, but there are one or two more things. Just how long do you think elapsed between your leaving me and your entering the box?"

She turned and walked slowly back to him.

"Again about ten minutes, I should think. I was awfully late and apologized to Charles, but he didn't say anything. Oh! my God—" She covered her face with her hands and sank into a chair.

"When you were talking to Pitt or Uncle Edward, could you see the entrance to your box?" went on Benvenuto, and his level voice steadied her.

"No, I couldn't. The corridor curves. Oh—and Ben—I don't know if you noticed, but I remember now—just past our box was a door, which I suppose led into the wings."

"Right—there is. Well, now I'll give you a few facts in return. The sword-stick handle had no finger-prints on it. The case was found leaning up beside the door you've just mentioned. By the way, Agatha, do you remember if Mr. Rourke had a black stick in his hand when he went up with your message?"

"I'm sure he had not."

"I don't think he had either," said Julia.

"That seems to be the general opinion of people who saw him during the last act. Naturally everyone possible has been questioned. In the confusion after poor Charles was found dead and you had fainted Rourke left the theatre. Nothing has been seen or heard of him since. The old man, the skeleton, whose name by the way is Herr Goetz, has also disappeared—in fact, he had already gone when I rushed up to your box, because I looked."

Julia looked up with a gleam of hope in her eyes. "He did it, Ben—I'm sure he did it. Oh, don't you see—none of the other people could possibly have done it. And—I'll tell you something else. Whoever did it was an enemy of Terence Rourke's—that's why he used the sword-stick."

"Not necessarily," returned Benvenuto. "You must remember that there isn't a large choice of death-dealing weapons in an average theatre. In fact, presuming the crime was not premeditated, the chances are that if Rourke had left his sword-stick at home that night poor Kulligrew would still be alive. However, I'm trying to find out the connexion, if any, which exists between Goetz, Rourke and Kulligrew.

"Now about Uncle Edward, before Pitt arrives. According to him he was sitting in the foyer during the last interval when a page-boy came up to him and said, 'A letter from Miss Lafontaine, sir, for Professor Milk.' I've got a copy of that letter here."

He took a typewritten sheet of paper from the desk at his side and gave it to Julia.

DEAR PROFESSOR MILK, [she read]

As I understand you are the guardian of Miss Julia Dallas, I am writing to tell you of certain facts which, as you will see, make it quite impossible for the proposed marriage between Miss Dallas and Lord Charles Kulli-grew to take place.

I lived with Lord Charles in Monte Carlo for six months last year, and I consider myself his wife in all but name. I hold letters from him containing repeated prom-ises to marry me, and unless the engagement between him and Miss Dallas is broken off I shall not hesitate to claim my rights.

We parted as the result of a misunderstanding, but I have never for one moment doubted that we would come together again in the end. Lord Charles loves me and I love him, and I shall go to any length to prevent this ab-surd marriage.

Can I rely on you to help an unhappy woman?

LOUISE LAFONTAINE.

Benvenuto took no notice of the bewildered eyes which Julia raised to his face as she finished reading, and went on, giving her no time to speak.

"Well, that gave the poor Professor a bit of a turn, as you can imagine. He went straight up to Charles, naturally, and gave him the letter and asked him to read it and to come down to Oxford for the week-end, as the matter was serious. Charles said he would like to come, and put the letter in his pocket, and then the Professor left the box just as the curtain went up, and after the lights were down, met you in the corridor, uttered his awful warning, and went down and joined Agatha in the stalls. That's his story. The letter was found in Charles's breast pocket when his body was searched by the police. Now, if his story is correct and Charles was alive when he left him—"

"Benvenuto!"—Agatha's voice was shrill with indigna-tion—"I *will not* sit here and hear aspersions cast at my poor brother when he isn't present to defend himself. To hear you talk anyone would think that poor Edward was a—a gangster. First that Detective Leech with his innuendos, turning and twisting dear Edward's words until he got what practically amounted to a confession out of him, and now you, a blood relation—"

"Agatha, *please*," implored Benvenuto. "You know that no one could have a greater liking or respect for the Professor than I have, and—"

"A fine reason for placing gyves upon his wrists!" She glared at him, and was about to continue when the front-door bell mercifully interrupted her. Benvenuto hurried from the room, and when he came back a few moments later with Martin Pitt, Julia had succeeded, at least partially, in appeasing her.

CHAPTER V
BLACK LIST

"HAVE YOU had tea, Mr. Pitt?" inquired Agatha.

Martin Pitt, sitting on the sofa beside Julia, looked up vaguely. "Tea? No, I don't think so—is it tea-time?"

"I don't believe you've had any lunch, either." She looked at him accusingly, and he smiled faintly.

"I've been trying to work, you see, and I'd no idea it was so late. But please don't bother—I don't want anything."

"You must have a boiled egg," she said firmly, getting up. "Benvenuto, have you an egg?"

"What's that, Agatha?" He turned round from some papers he was sorting on his desk and came towards her.

"I inquired whether you have an egg."

"Good Lord, yes, I expect so—I'll go and see." They went into the kitchen together, followed by protests from Pitt.

"I wish they wouldn't bother," he said to Julia. "I don't want anything to eat."

"You'll be doing a great kindness to us all if you allow Agatha to feed you," she said, smiling. "She's most frightfully upset by the Professor getting involved in all these inquiries, and it will put her in a good humour at once if she's allowed to fuss over somebody."

"The Professor?" He looked at her, startled, no vagueness in his voice now. "How perfectly monstrous! What on earth could he have to do with it?"

"Absolutely nothing of course, but until the murderer is found the most horrible suspicions surround everyone."

"I say, I'd no idea things were as bad as that." He jumped to his feet and paced up and down in front of her, his yellow head bent; then suddenly he turned and faced her. "Miss Dallas, I've been a brute. I've never told you how sorry I am for the bad time you must have been having; in fact, I've been simply trying to bury myself in work and forget the whole thing. I told Leech, the Scotland Yard man, everything I could the morning after it happened, and since then I—well, I've been trying not to think about it, without much success. I can't work—I can't do anything, except keep on remembering—"

Julia, looking up at him, noticed how drawn and white he was, and felt suddenly desperately sorry for him, realizing all at once the capacity for feeling that lay in the impersonal faun-like face.

"It must have been a ghastly shock for you," she said gently.

"It was ghastly for everyone," he said. "I shall never be able to forget it all my life. You see, I was excessively worked up and excited—and then—seeing it like that—it seems to be photographed on my brain."

Julia was silent, wondering what she could do to take his mind away from the thing which was haunting him. At last: "How does it feel to have such a terrific success—to have the whole of London applauding you?" she asked.

He came and sat down beside her again and lit a cigarette.

"What ought I to say? I suppose I ought to say that it was nothing at all—that it was entirely due to the production—that the public will forget as soon as they find somebody new to applaud. All of which wouldn't answer your question. Actually, the winning of mass-admiration is the most powerful intoxicant in the world; it's the inspiration behind all heroic deeds, though nobody will admit it. Apply the idea as an acid test to the heroes of history, and the martyrs of religion, and you'll see very few of them will survive. Never believe anyone who tells you he or she doesn't like admiration—there's no one who wouldn't die for it in some form or another."

Julia watched him doubtfully as he talked. How much of it was true—how much of it did he believe to be true? It was an uncomfortable doctrine, but in expounding it he had at least forgotten everything but his own argument, which was what she had wanted. The next moment he was complimenting Agatha on the food which she put before him, discussing earnestly the relative merits of different ways of cooking eggs, while she, all her vexation forgotten, watched him approvingly as he ate a large tea. Julia smiled to herself. Martin Pitt, she decided, was a young man who would cheerfully argue that black was white if he thought it would make the conversation interesting—probably he had thought her very poor company for making no attempt to dispute his statements. Of course, she said to herself, the low opinion of humanity which he had just proposed to her was denied out of his own mouth in *The Lily Flower* by his creation of Lily herself.

Benvenuto had returned from the kitchen and was busy at his desk, from which he presently came towards her, pen and paper in his hand.

"What I propose, Julia, is to make out a dossier of each suspected person, putting down as clearly as we can anything incriminating or possibly incriminating, that we know against him, or her, together with motive and opportunity for committing the crime. Will you act as secretary while I dictate, and any of you interrupt with anything you think is important which I leave out?"

"Yes, of course, Ben. Carry on," answered Julia, her pen ready.

"Use a separate sheet for each person. First of all we'll take Rourke—Terence Gale Rourke."

Martin Pitt, listening from the tea-table, seemed about to protest, but sat back in silence as Benvenuto went on.

"*Possibly Incriminating Facts.*

"1.Disappearance immediately after crime.

"2.Rourke's sword-stick was the weapon used.

"3.Note to Kulligrew in Rourke's handwriting found in the box, wording of which can be construed either as a threat or as a warning.

"4.Rourke makes an opportunity of being alone in box with Kulligrew by offering to take a message to Julia calling her down to the foyer in third act.

"5.Is known to have been a close friend of Kulligrew in the past, but relations between them noticeably strained when they met in the restaurant before the play.

"Is there anything else? We'll take the defence afterwards," he added, as Agatha and Pitt were about to speak. "No? Very well, then.

"*Motive.*

"The only one I can offer at the moment is the wording of the note 'Remember there is a score to settle . . .' together with our knowledge of the likelihood of some quarrel having taken place with Kulligrew.

"*Opportunity.*

"1.Is known to have been alone with Kulligrew in the box during third act.

"2.The fact that Rourke was the producer would make his movements during the performance seem perfectly natural, and would enable him to make use of the door leading through to the wings.

"Now for the defence." Benvenuto looked expectantly at the three people watching him.

Martin Pitt was the first to speak.

"If Rourke had committed the crime," he said, "I don't believe he'd have been fool enough to leave behind him such incriminating evidence as his own sword-stick, and a threatening letter to Kulligrew."

"I entirely agree with you, Mr. Pitt," said Agatha decidedly. "Now, Benvenuto, may I be allowed to speak? I have no patience with the way you sit there and blackguard that nice Mr. Rourke, attributing the most base and cunning motives to a simple act of courtesy which he offered to me. Heaven knows it is rare enough nowadays to find anyone who'll so much as offer one a seat in a bus, what with railway porters in Parliament and mixed bathing in the Park, and here you go idling about weaving ridiculous theories round a gentleman of the old school, while I've no doubt an organized gang of Socialists is already searching for their next victim. *I* shall probably be the next to go—nothing would surprise me after seeing the foolhardy way that Detective Leech went on with poor Edward, and I think it more than likely he's a member of the gang himself. However, nothing that I can say will stop you, so I shall go home and commence packing. Julia, my dear, remember that dinner is at seven-thirty, and don't excite yourself if you find Benvenuto putting *my* name down on the list. Good-bye, Mr. Pitt, and don't forget the importance of taking regular meals. You must come and visit us again at the Brambles some time— Edward would be delighted. *Good*-bye."

CHAPTER VI
BLACK LIST—*CONTINUED*

WHEN BENVENUTO came back from seeing Agatha out, he sat down wearily and turned to Julia.

"Under 'Defence of Rourke,'" he said, "put down 'Agatha believes him innocent.'"

"Well, Ben," replied Julia laughing, "I must say I agree with her. He certainly didn't strike me as being a criminal type. What do you think, Mr. Pitt?"

"I don't believe he did it," Pitt answered firmly. "Of course he's a passionate sort of chap and used to get in terrific rages during the rehearsals, but I can't see him as a murderer."

"Let's take the next suspect," said Benvenuto. "Professor Edward Milk.

"*Suspicious Evidence.*
> "1. His state of agitation on meeting Julia in the corridor and his warning to her.
> "2. His early departure from the theatre.
> "3. His decision to leave England immediately.

"*Opportunity.*
> "He is known to have been alone with Kulligrew after the lights were lowered.

"*Possible Motive.*
> "His affection for Julia and the shock he received from Louise Lafontaine's note.

"By the way, Pitt, you won't have heard about that." He quickly ran through the facts regarding the letter and then went on. "It's almost unnecessary to put down evidence in favour of the Professor because we all know him so well. It makes it a thousand times more difficult in investigating a case like this to know the characters intimately, because I am convinced the majority of murders are not committed by what Julia just now called the 'criminal type.' If they were, Scotland Yard would have an easy job. Yet even if one believes that we are each one of us potential murderers, one's theory begins to wobble directly one tests it on a personal friend.

However, we have one definitely sinister figure we can put down on our list—the mysterious old man whom Julia called 'The Skeleton,' and who occupied the box next to Kulligrew's. His name, I have discovered, is:

"*Adolf Goetz*, and the evidence against him is of the flimsiest.

"*Suspicious Facts.*

"1.He was seen by Julia to look very intently at Charles during the first interval, and was seen by us both to be leaning over the edge of his box watching Charles just before the third act.

"2.When Rourke's attention was called to him he obviously recognized him with something of a shock, and immediately made an excuse and left us. It is at least possible that Rourke may then have gone off to write that note to Kulligrew.

"*Opportunity.*

"Seems fairly obvious, as Kulligrew was presumably alone in the box between the time the Professor left him and the time Julia entered.

"*Motive.*

"We're unable to suggest.

"Next we have Louise Lafontaine, and here both opportunity and motive are clear—Opportunity because she was found by Julia alone in the box with Kulligrew, and wearing a long cloak in which she might easily have concealed the swordstick; and Motive is of course, suggested in the letter she wrote to the Professor. I wonder—" He got up and went across to the window and stood there with his back to them, while all three were silent. At last he went on:

"The next name on the list is—Julia Dallas."

Julia's pen made a meaningless scrawl on the paper and fell to the ground. The outline of Benvenuto's figure against the window became blurred, and a black mist seemed to be creeping round her. For a moment she thought she was slipping away again into that unknown darkness—the unknown darkness where voices followed her—voices crying—With a tremendous effort of will she pulled herself back and opened her eyes wide on to the room where a voice had just said, "The next name on the list is Julia Dallas."

For a moment, she wondered who had spoken when she heard her own voice say, "What do you mean?" It sounded so funny, dropping into the silence.

The next moment Pitt had risen and was advancing towards Benvenuto.

"Is this a joke?" he said. "Because if so I think it's a bad one. Good God! what motive could Miss Dallas possibly have for killing Kulligrew?"

Benvenuto swung round from the window.

"Twenty thousand pounds is a pretty substantial motive from a police point of view," he answered, then crossed the room to where Julia was sitting, and put his hand on hers. "Julia, my dear, come with me over to the window—I want to show you something."

She stumbled to her feet and followed him, and stood staring out. There was nothing there—nothing but the little Chelsea street, the old houses with their painted shutters and small gardens, some children going home with their nurse, a cat sunning itself on a doorstep—and, farther down, a man leaning against some railings reading a newspaper. She looked at Benvenuto and shook her head. "I don't understand."

"No? Well, look carefully at that gentleman over there who's so immersed in the daily press, and when you get home presently look out of the window and the chances are you'll see him again. You won't see him to-morrow, because I'm going to get hold of Leech to-night, and have him taken off duty."

"You mean—I'm being followed?"

"Got it in one. Now, look here, you two. Don't either of you go running away with the idea that I think Julia killed Charles—I don't. But there's been a brutal cowardly crime committed, and it seems to be my job to get to the bottom of it. I'm commissioned not only by you, Julia—I've promised to help Leech too, for I've been able to give him a hand before in one or two cases. And until I've succeeded, or he's succeeded, you won't be cleared, Rourke won't be cleared, the Professor won't be cleared, and a lot of other people besides. So you must let me go to work my own way. Remember, we're not the only people who are interested in suspicious facts, and possible motives—there's another person who's even more interested, and that's the murderer. Every doubt that exists in our minds is a weapon which, if he can succeed in sharpening it, might be used to cut his noose. So sit down and help us make out a case against you, Julia."

She managed to smile at him, went back to the sofa and picked up her pen again.

"Julia Dallas," she wrote. "*Suspicious Facts*, Ben? Wait a minute, I'll do this myself. Was considering breaking off her engagement." Her voice shook a little but she went on: "Was alone with Professor Milk after he had received the letter from Louise Lafontaine, and may have learnt the contents of it from him. He naturally would not admit this for fear of implicating her. *Opportunity*: Was alone for a considerable time with Charles in the box. *Motive*: There are two possible motives, aren't there, Ben? 1. Jealousy. 2. The fact that she is Charles's heiress. There—that's quite a strong case, isn't it? What a fool I've been not to realize that suspicion must rest on me."

"Suspicion rests on everyone who went into that box," replied Benvenuto.

"Then you must put me down too," said Martin Pitt. "I went into the box, though it's true I wasn't alone with Charles. It seems to me, though, that in the dark the crime might possibly have been committed when someone else was present."

Benvenuto shook his head. "Julia doesn't think so—and Scotland Yard doesn't think so. The risk was obviously too great unless the crime was committed by a lunatic. When did you go into the box?"

"At the beginning of the third act. I was trying to find the Professor, to ask him and Agatha to come to supper afterwards, and I'd seen him up in Charles's box from the other side of the house. When I got round I stuck my head in at the door, but the Professor had gone—Charles was in the seat nearest the stage, bending forward with his arms on the edge of the box, and Rourke was standing up by the other seat. I don't think either of them even saw me. I could see they were engrossed in the play and I slipped away. Then I met Miss Dallas—don't you remember I asked you if you'd seen the Professor?"

"Yes," she nodded, "and I told you he'd gone down to the stalls. We talked for a minute or two and then I went back to the box."

"Rourke had gone when you got back, hadn't he?" asked Benvenuto.

"Yes. Oh, Ben, I expect that was the time when he gave Charles the note—it was just before that that he'd seen the old man and gone off in such a hurry."

Benvenuto nodded. "I expect it was. Curse the fellow! If he didn't commit the crime himself, he's done something nearly as bad in disappearing at the critical moment. Let's hope our trip won't turn out to be a wild-goose chase."

"Trip?"

"Yes." Benvenuto turned to Pitt. "Julia and I, to say nothing of Agatha and a parrot, are off to France to-morrow to try and follow up a very faint clue which may lead us to Rourke."

"I wish to God I could come and help you. But I'm chained to the theatre until Rourke reappears, or until we get someone to take his place—there are a terrific lot of things to be seen to in his absence."

"You can help me a damn sight more by staying here— that's to say, if you agree."

"But of course—what can I do?"

"Keep an eye on Louise Lafontaine, for one thing. I've reason for supposing that she may decide to leave London before long, and if she does I want you to follow her and let me know immediately where she goes."

Pitt stared at him. "But—she can't go away. She's under contract with us till the end of the run, and—"

Benvenuto laughed. "I don't imagine Louise would find it too difficult to produce a doctor's certificate if it served her purpose."

Martin Pitt blushed. "Of course—what a fool I am. I'll undertake that, absolutely, and anything else you say."

Julia felt secretly amused at the idea of this Shelley-like person in the character of a detective, and rose to go.

"Good-bye, Ben—I'll leave you to confer with your lieutenant. Will you 'phone in the morning and tell me what time the train goes?"

CHAPTER VII
OUT OF ENGLAND INTO FRANCE

IN BURGUNDY the sun shone, and small clouds, wind-driven, cast moving patches of shadow on the round hills and rich valleys. Benvenuto at the wheel of his Bugatti drove swiftly over the white roads and sang Provençal songs, rich and southern, and very much in keeping with the sunshine. The sun was almost as hot as in the South, thought Julia sitting beside him, only here the landscape was green and watered, and the road led through woods and over streams, and past the endless vineyards of the famous wine-growing country. Small villages lay at the foot of the hills, villages of whitewashed cottages covered with a dark cloak of thatch, while at a little distance from them, aloof and reserved within its high stone walls, stood the inevitable chateau bearing some name familiar to the connoisseur of wine. Julia looked curiously at these great houses with their round pointed towers, and their roofs, shiny and patterned like linoleum, and wondered what the people were like who passed in and out of the high wrought-iron gates and lived behind mysterious shutters, closed against the sun. France is exciting, she thought, exciting and elusive; somehow more foreign and less comprehensible in the North, where only a small strip of water separates it from home, than in Provence, the land of harsh beauty and charming dark-skinned people, which was brought back to her so vividly by Benvenuto's songs. Where would their search lead them, she wondered; what adventures lay in wait for them along the road?

An underlying feeling of excitement filled her, a new-found courage and energy. From the mere fact of crossing the Channel she seemed to have arrived at a new angle of vision, to have left the mists of tragedy and horror which had enveloped her, behind a barrier of blue water and salt spray. Actually, nothing was changed—the tragedy and horror were no less real, the mystery no more comprehensible, but from the soil of France she felt she could face it sanely, courageously. They were all infected by the change of scene and the swift passage through the fresh morning air, she thought, looking sideways at Benvenuto, whose beret was pushed rakishly on the back of his head, and whose check shirt was open at the throat. Even Agatha, wrapped in shawls in the back of the car, seemed in the best of spirits, and attempted to join in the chorus of Benvenuto's songs.

"Very pretty," she shouted as he finished "*Les Fraises et les Framboises*," "quite an old-world air!"

The car climbed a hill, and below in the valley Julia could see the roofs of a small town.

"That's Chagny," said Benvenuto. "What about a drink? I'm dry, and I expect you are; and besides, I want to get the papers to see if there's any more news of that hold-up."

The day before, the French newspapers had been lively with indignation about a hold-up which had taken place between Orléans and Nevers. A peasant on his way to work in the early morning had come upon a large open touring car, its bonnet half in a ditch, and on going to investigate had found the body of the driver propped up by the steering-wheel, bullet wounds in his head and an empty dispatch-case beside him. He had been dead for some hours, and beyond faint tyre tracks in the road the police had no clue to the identity of his assailant. The motive for the crime had obviously been robbery, and though the familiar white chalk signature of the Tiger was missing from the back of the car, the papers believed it to be his work, and were loud in their denunciation of the police for allowing this terror of the motorist to escape them.

If it had indeed been the work of the Tiger—and if the Tiger were Rourke—Julia shuddered as she thought of it, and felt a growing conviction that they were on the track of Charles Kulligrew's murderer. Benvenuto had been noncommittal about it, only saying that the papers were in the mood to attribute every crime in France to the Tiger, from pocket-picking to arson, but all the same it was obvious he was worried. As they drove into the village Julia felt, for some reason, half in dread of the news they would find there.

Benvenuto drew up in front of a café in a cobbled square, and, climbing down, helped Agatha from the back of the car.

"Drinks first, detection afterwards," he said, and led the way to a table under a coloured awning. "What are we going to have? Pernod lays the dust; how about a Pernod, Agatha?"

She beamed at him and Julia, as she untied the scarf which anchored her hat to her head.

"Certainly I will try a Pernod, since you tell me it is innocuous and *not* a cocktail," she said. "Really, this is most agreeable, Benvenuto—everything looks so *French*. Dear Edward has often told me that foreign travel broadens one's outlook, and I begin to believe it. The *only* fly in my ointment, if I may so express myself, is the absence of Archie. Had you not discovered, providentially of course, that sea-sickness is fatal to parrots, it would have been delightful to have had him with us. The dear bird is most intelligent and notices everything."

There was silence for a few minutes while the three travellers relaxed and watched the townspeople walking about the cobbled square. It was market day, and under canvas awnings there were stalls holding great piles of cheeses, fruit and vegetables.

Agatha's contentment increased as she finished the last of the pale cloudy-yellow liquid in her glass.

"A delicious herbal beverage," she said. "My dears, this sun is making me feel quite girlish. May I have another piano? I find they do me good, and see, Benvenuto, Julia has quite regained her colour. Really, I cannot understand how these nice French people, so polite, ever countenanced that man Buonaparte. Of course I find it a little difficult to accustom myself to the policemen not wearing helmets, and the sanitary arrangements are deplorably socialistic; but still as I sit here and see people imbibing all round me, I can *quite* understand dear King Edward's love of Cans."

"*Cans*, Auntie?"

"Yes, my dear, a town on the south coast."

"Well," said Benvenuto, "it's grand to be back in France, and I feel quite like King Edward myself. I think we'll lunch here and push on to Lyon to-night. There our holiday may be over—there'll be letters waiting for us, and I've a feeling things will begin to hum. That reminds me, I must get a paper. *Chasseur!*" He sent a boy in search of the *Journal* and turned to Julia. "You'll find the journalists will still be full of the idea that it was the Tiger who did in that unfortunate chap yesterday, in spite of the fact that he's never been known to use violence over a robbery. The whole thing is absurd—why, ten years ago they were practically making a popular hero of him."

Julia watched him doubtfully, and as the boy came back and handed him the paper, saw a change come over his face. She bent over his shoulder, and saw a big headline,

LE TIGRE, CHEF DES GANGSTERS.

Slowly Benvenuto read the article aloud, translating as he went along, an account of a night attack on a mail van near

Montélimar, letters and 40,000 francs being stolen and the drivers kicked and beaten and left trussed up on the roadside. The attackers were two men in a powerful Renault, which made off at great speed, and in doing so knocked over and killed an old peasant woman, Marie Thérèse Prunier. Chalked on the mail van were found the words "Le Tigre."

Half-way through the usual tirade against the police he stopped reading and dropped the paper on his knee, staring in front of him.

"We seem to be near the field of battle," he said slowly.

"Oh, Ben, it's horrible. You must admit *now* that if you are right, and Rourke *is* the Tiger, a man who is capable of that kind of hold-up is capable of having killed Charles."

Agatha patted Julia's hand. "There, there, my dear. If you'd only pay attention to me, you'd realize that that nice Mr. Rourke would never go masquerading about committing these dreadful things. *Tiger*, indeed! Fiddlesticks!"

But even her eloquence failed her, and she and Julia watched Benvenuto silently as he took out a map and laid it on the café table. Presently he looked up. "I rather think the Tiger will be moving south—this district up here must be getting a bit hot for him. My idea is to go to Lyon to-night, get our letters, park you both in an hotel and go off for a day or two in the car. If I decide to go farther south I'll either pick you up or you can follow me by train. I don't like the look of things at all; before this happened I was convinced of the identity of the Tiger—and, for a good many reasons, I still am. But if I'm right it looks as though Rourke has lost his reason. Come on—let's go to lunch."

They found a pleasant little restaurant with a garden where they sat at a green table beneath the trees, but it was a silent meal, Benvenuto being lost in his own thoughts, Agatha looking a little drowsy in the midday heat, and Julia engaged in unhappy speculations about Terence Rourke. If, as Benvenuto had suggested, Rourke had become insane, it would explain everything. She thought of his splendid muscular body—as tall as Charles had been—and his handsome head and waving mass of grey hair. He had reminded her of some magnificent animal—he was more like a lion than a tiger, she thought—and he would be a terribly dangerous person to deal with if it were true, and madness lay behind his fierce bright eyes. She determined she would not let Benvenuto go after him alone— somehow she would arrange to leave Agatha in the hotel and go with him. After all, she thought a little complacently, re-membering stories she had heard of Terence Rourke as the hero of romantic adventures, probably I would be able to deal with him much more effectively than Ben could.

It was with a feeling almost of excitement that she got back into the car after lunch, and watched the streets of the little town slip away. Secretly, though she would have admitted it to no one, she longed to do something dangerous and hero-ic, something both clever and courageous which would bring Charles's murderer to justice; and though she told herself it was for Charles's sake, she knew somewhere in the back of her thoughts that it was her own peace of mind she wanted to ensure. Everyone had been so good to her—given her so much sympathy—Agatha, the Professor, Benvenuto, Martin Pitt, all her friends—and all the time she felt conscience-strick-en, guilty. It was true that Charles's death had hurt her, hurt her horribly, and that even now when her mind went back to that awful moment of discovery, she felt faint and sick; it was true that she had liked and admired, and even in a way loved Charles, she told herself, and that she would miss him terribly. But she could not pretend that her life was broken up, that she had lost everything she valued; could not pre-tend that every now and again a demon inside her did not lift its head and say, "You're free—you're free." She told herself that she was some kind of monster, cold and heartless. While Charles had been alive she hadn't given him anything—any-thing real; now that he was dead, couldn't she even feel a grief that was sincere? She frowned at the sunny landscape, not seeing it, and hated herself.

Benvenuto's voice interrupted her. "There's some infernal great car trying to pass me," he said. "Wave him on, will you? There's just room here."

Julia obediently waved him on, looking anxiously at the narrow road, and then the deep throaty note of a klaxon sounded in her ears, the roar of a powerful engine accelerating, and an enormous pale grey car with the longest body she had ever seen swept past them, two men in livery sitting in front and all the blinds down over the windows.

"Hog!" muttered Benvenuto, and suddenly Julia clutched his arm, nearly sending the Bugatti in the ditch. "Ben—look! Quickly—the Skeleton!"

For an instant the blind over the back window of the car in front was raised, and peering out was the unmistakable face of Adolf Goetz, stranger than ever under what appeared to be a cotton nightcap. Then the blind was lowered and the car swept on, clouding the road with dust. Benvenuto trod on the accelerator.

"Good God!—what amazing luck. We'll catch him up and stop him, or die in the attempt. Hold tight!"

Julia did so, and thought his second alternative more than likely. For the Bugatti developed a surprising speed, rocking and swaying over bad surfaces and round corners until the distance between the two cars was appreciably diminished. In five minutes Julia could see clearly the number-plate with the letter D beside it, two minutes more and they were up to it. The blind was still down over the back window; Benvenuto sounded his horn and, with a final burst of speed, passed the big car.

"Stick your hand out and give them the signal to stop," he shouted to Julia, and slowed down a little, keeping well in the middle of the road. But to her horror the klaxon shrieked in her ear, the great engine roared and the car raced past them, two wheels up a bank, while the angry face of the second man in livery glared out at them, and she heard a volley of oaths in some unknown tongue that sounded like German.

"Damn!" said Benvenuto, and recommenced the chase. This time luck was against them and with their prey, for at every moment something held them up. First a dog ran across the road, then a farm-cart lumbered out of a turning and precious moments were wasted until it got into the side. The car ahead was gaining ground rapidly, and then, as a final blow, the great red arms of a railway crossing descended over the road just after the grey car had swept through. Benvenuto crammed on the brakes and the Bugatti came to a standstill.

"How provoking," came Agatha's voice from the back. "I don't know who your friends were, but I fear we have lost them now."

And it was true—the grey car was disappearing over a hill-top.

CHAPTER VIII
HOLD-UP

IT WAS DARK before they reached Lyon. A repair to the Bugatti and dinner at a small roadside restaurant saw disappear the last of the twilight, and as Julia followed Agatha and Benvenuto out of the brightly lit terrace where they had dined, she looked back regretfully at the three empty chairs under the vine, and the comfortable figure of Madame in her apron clearing away dishes from the white cloth. With raised hands Madame had talked through dinner of the terror of the Tiger, described the extra bolts her husband had fixed to the doors, and warned them volubly against stopping their car on the roadside for any reason at all—"C'est un monstre, ça, et tout le monde a peur."

Along the dark road lined by darker trees Julia sat tense at Benvenuto's side, and watched the bright leafy cavern of light made by the head-lamps. It was absurd perhaps, yet somewhere, close to them in the silent woods, she seemed to feel the presence of the Tiger, watchful and menacing. Each time the lamps of a car approached them her heart raced, and each time she laughed at herself shamefacedly as some harmless traveller sped by on the road to Paris. Where was her courage now, her longing for danger? Certainly danger, she thought, seemed less and less attractive at the end of a long day's run, and found herself longing for coffee and liqueurs, and then a hot bath and a bed in some civilized hotel. She hoped that when at last they encountered the Tiger, as she had no doubt they would, it would be in daylight, and the lines of Blake's poem ran through her head:

"Tiger, Tiger, burning bright
In the forests of the night—"

No, it would be at night, and he would leap at them suddenly out of some dark wood like the one they were passing through now—and when the time came she would be frightfully brave and save the situation. Only she hoped it wouldn't be to-night. . . .

The car raced on and on, through silent villages, along endless stretches of flat road, over low hills—and at last from a hill-top she saw a thousand lights like a jewelled mantle flung over the countryside.

"Lyon," announced Benvenuto. "Thank the Lord! Ten minutes more and we'll be ordering drinks." And he put on speed.

Buildings were more frequent now, then factories, street-lamps, tram-lines, a gendarme at a cross-road and gradually all the smells and bustle of a great city. It seemed enormous, endless, as big as London, thought Julia, and felt very secure and rather foolish now that the lonely road was behind her.

The car stopped before the doors of the Hotel Louis Philippe, and uniformed *chasseurs* ran down to carry the luggage.

"Expensive but comfortable," said Benvenuto. "I feel good beds are what we need. Five hundred kilometres since breakfast—not bad."

In a moment a gentleman in almost faultless evening-dress was describing the beauties of the rooms in almost faultless English, and Agatha and Julia left Benvenuto at the desk filling up forms, promising to join him for coffee in ten minutes, and were borne upwards by a gleaming lift. They alighted on soft carpets under soft lights in the almost religious hush that pervades an expensive hotel, and Julia sighed with relief as her bedroom door closed discreetly behind her. A pink brocaded bed and a gleaming tiled bathroom were the height of human felicity, she decided, and pulling off her hat she lit a cigarette, opened the window and leant out, watching the lights of the city, until her luggage arrived. Soon her room was untidy and familiar with her creams and scents and slippers, her nightgown limp across the bed, a skirt over a chair; by the time she was, washed and combed and powdered and immaculate in a slim black frock it was nearly ten o'clock—her ten minutes had stretched to twenty. She hurried out and rang for the lift, and in another minute had joined Benvenuto downstairs. He dropped a paper he was reading and eyed her cheerfully.

"My dear, you look what is usually described as 'a treat.' As for me, I feel swell and opulent enough to be the Tiger's next victim. Let's go and moan at the bar. Agatha has decided on a nice cup of tea in her room, and says you're to go to bed early. Young gairls, she believes, should not keep late hours."

Julia laughed and took Benvenuto's arm as they strolled across towards a door marked "American Bar." "This young girl has no intention of going to bed until she's had several drinks, and her companion has outlined a plan of campaign." She paused at the door and turned to see Benvenuto

staring at a commotion which was disturbing the dignity of
the main entrance.

"What on earth—?"

Through the doorway came several attendants supporting
a stout lady in an hysterical condition; behind them, a motor-rug wrapped round her, followed a bewildered-looking
girl in spectacles, clutching at the rug with a desperation sug-
gesting that it was her only covering, while at the rear came an
elderly little man in plus-fours, his head in a bandage.

"My God, it's Lady Hopkins!" exclaimed Benvenuto. "The
woman I painted with the pearls."

The next moment he had hurried across to the distracted
group of people and was bending solicitously over the fat lady,
who immediately gripped his coat with her podgy hands and
brought the procession to a standstill.

"Oh, Mr. Brown!" Julia heard her say as she came up.
"We've been attacked—by that Tiger! He's taken all me jewels including them lovely pearls you painted, swiped Fred one
over the head and took off Gladys's clothes, and God knows
what would 'ave 'appened to the poor girl if the huge brute,
more a hanimal than a man, 'adn't seen a car coming. Gladys,
go and put on my pink georgette, you'll find it in the big trunk.
Well, as I was saying 'e'd put down tar all over the road, and
Ponsonby, that's the shofer, he 'ad to slow down, and the next
thing was a man put his 'ead in the window with a black thing
over it saying 'All yer money and jewels now, quick about it,'
and my Fred says 'Hi! 'oo are you,' and the brute 'it 'im on
the 'ead with the end of a gun, I swear 'e did, bundled us all
out of the Rolls and put his 'and down my bosom looking for
diamonds, 'e said"—she paused to gulp at the recollection and
swept on—"nothing would do but Gladys 'as to take off all 'er
clothes even 'er undies, poor dear, lucky it was a warm night
because he said she was concealing something, and on to the
tar they went and Ponsonby was 'eroic but he fell over in the
tar and another of the brutes two of them there was sat on 'is

'ead and then a car's lights coming over the 'ill and off they went with my jewel case and Fred's watch presented to 'im by the brewers in a twinkling."

"Which direction?" asked Benvenuto, hurriedly taking advantage of a pause.

"This direction," moaned Lady Hopkins.

Julia suddenly catching sight of the disconsolate figure in the motor-rug, crossed over to her, whispering in Benvenuto's ear:

"I am removing Gladys to my room."

"Right—see you later," he said and addressed himself soothingly to Lady Hopkins.

Gladys followed Julia passively to the lift, murmuring, "It's ever so kind of you, I'm sure," and once in Julia's bedroom sat down on the bed, still clutching the rug, and looked admiringly round her. "What a beautiful room. Oh, no, I couldn't wear that lovely dressing-gown—really I couldn't—well, it's ever so kind of you, Miss—er—"

"Dallas—Julia Dallas is my name. You must have had a terrible time. Wouldn't you like a hot bath and then let me send some supper up to you?"

"Well, I could do with a wash after that person pawing me about."

"Was he—a big man?" asked Julia.

Gladys nodded enthusiastically. "*Ever* so big—we never saw his face because he had a black cloth over it. It wasn't so bad reely, but I do wish Mum wouldn't take on so—I don't know what you must think, Miss Dallas." She giggled suddenly. "Mum didn't half look funny when that chap put his hand down her front—it was almost worth losing my lingery. Now, that's what I call style, that is," she went on, picking up Julia's nightgown from the bed. "I always told Mum we didn't ought to have ordered that coffee-coloured lace on that bright pink. Do you mind if I copy this for my next set, Miss Dallas? It's *ever* so pretty."

"Not a bit," replied Julia cheerfully. "Now I'm going to turn on a hot bath, or you'll catch a cold. Use anything of mine you want. I'll send you up something to eat, and by the time you've had it I expect your own room will be ready. Here are some slippers—now run along."

Gladys reluctantly tore herself from a study of Julia's possessions and disappeared into the bathroom, while Julia exhaustedly powdered her nose at the mirror. Behind the pure comedy of the characters lay the story of a brutal outrage on the unfortunate Hopkins family, and she felt that her fears along the dark road had been more than justified. Half an hour later and it might well have been their own car that was attacked—or perhaps the Tiger had watched them pass and let them go as being unworthy of notice. There were two robbers, Lady Hopkins had said—who could be the confederate? Julia laughed and shuddered, remembering the shrill, voluble description of the Tiger—"a black thing over his 'ead—more a hanimal than a man—" The whole thing had an element of the insane, she thought—the absurd daring of a hold-up at ten o'clock at night on a main road a few miles from Lyon, and the brutal stripping of the wretched Gladys. What would Ben do, she wondered—would she find herself in a few minutes out again in the darkness hunting for this wild thing? She jumped up from her mirror, determined she would not let him go alone, and hurried out of the room while Gladys splashed happily in her scented bath.

She heard the lift doors closing on a floor above and rang the bell, tapping her foot impatiently. Suppose Benvenuto had already gone? Smoothly the lift came down, and the descending passenger opened the door for her.

"Merci, m'sieur," she said automatically, stepping in, and opposite her in the mirror which covered the back of the lift she saw the doors close, while a very tall, well-dressed man fumbled with the mechanism. An Englishman she thought idly, judging by the cut of his clothes—and what an immense height he seemed in the tiny enclosed space. The lift-boy must be off duty—she hoped they weren't going to get stuck. Even now Benvenuto might be starting up the Bugatti.

"Can I help you?" she said, and found herself looking into the face of Terence Rourke.

CHAPTER IX
TIGER, TIGER—

SHE MUST DRAG her eyes away from those fierce bright eyes above her—she must. What had someone once told her—as long as you stare into the eyes of an animal it will not attack you. This was absurd—what could he do to her here in the middle of a huge hotel? But she was locked in a cage with him—a cage—the Man in the Zoo—incoherently her thoughts raced. The eyes were blue, brilliant like the sea—she would drown in them if she didn't look away—little creases were surrounding them—they were laughing—and a great laugh, deep and vibrating, filled the cage.

"By all the powers it's Miss Dallas! I seem fated to harm ye—last time I saw ye I crushed your little foot—and now I've got ye trapped in this infernal lift. And how do you come to be here?"

"We've just arrived." Somehow she was smiling, her body tense and rigid, her hand clasped in his own.

"I've just arrived meself—this very minute. I've been up to see me room. Now if I can get ye out of here we'll go and have a drink together, if you can forgive my clumsiness."

Of course he'd just arrived. She could have told him that. Did he know his victims were within a few yards of him—would they recognize him? In a flash she caught herself terrified that they would. He was *her* prey—hers and Benvenuto's. No one else should capture him. She must keep cool—think, think carefully. If he knew Benvenuto was downstairs he would guess they were after him, and escape. So she mustn't tell him; she must talk, keep him amused till she could lead him to Benvenuto. She bent forward, laughing.

"I'm losing faith in this conveyance. Don't you think the prisoners might escape and walk down the stairs? It's only two floors."

Prisoners—dear me, she ought not to have said that. But he was laughing now.

"What kind of a fool am I not to have thought of that me-self? There, Miss Dallas, come and taste the joys of liberty."

He handed her out so gallantly that she felt like a lady alighting from a sedan chair, his deep Irish voice rumbling above her head like rich music in the bass. Her five feet five felt extraordinarily insignificant walking down the stairs beside him; puny she felt, lost in the amazing vitality of his presence. It was like walking with an emperor, she thought, as a pale waiter carrying a tray backed out of their path; no, it wasn't that, it was like walking with a lion, and she and the waiters were small helpless creatures of the jungle. They were down in the foyer now, and she looked sideways up at him as they paused for a moment, saw his great head thrown back and his eyes roving round the room, resting speculatively for a moment on a group of gendarmes that were talking with the manager.

"The bar is through there," she said hurriedly, longing to get him out of their sight.

"Splendid!" the great voice boomed as he strode beside her. "I've been on the road all day and I'm as dry as the desert."

What could those puny gendarmes do to this Colossus?

Over there was Benvenuto, perched on a high stool talking to the barman—he hadn't seen them. In an instant Rourke had left her and was beside him.

"Benvenuto Brown! Merciful heavens, aren't I in luck this night?" said he, bringing his hand down on Benvenuto's shoulders.

"Mind my drink, you mad Irishman! How did you get here?"

They were shaking hands warmly, and Julia's triumph in her capture trembled and died.

"I got here in me car—but the reason why is too long to tell you in this place. Let's go somewhere where we can talk. Miss Dallas—of course you know—"

Julia laughed. "Ben is my cousin, and I'm here with him and my aunt."

"To think of it—and you never told me. Now, what are you both going to drink?"

"The drinks are on me," interposed Benvenuto. "Suppose we all go up to my room and have them there in peace?"

"Sure we will—good idea. Irish whisky for me."

· · · · ·

Julia sat on the end of Benvenuto's bed and smiled at the two men as they drank to her.

It seemed a remarkably tame climax to their journey—the three of them in an hotel bedroom, glasses in hand, Benvenuto with his feet in the fireplace, Rourke balanced on an inadequate gilt chair that creaked under his weight. There was silence for a moment, and then: "Where are you two off to?" asked Rourke.

"We're not off to anywhere—we've arrived," said Benvenuto. He jumped to his feet and went across to the tray of drinks. "Listen here, Terence. I'd better explain at once that the reason Julia and I are here is because we've been looking for—you. I will also explain"—he paused while he measured some whisky into a glass—"that you are suspected of being both Kulligrew's murderer and—the Tiger."

Crash went the little gilt chair and bounced pitifully over the floor, while with one spring Rourke was across the room, towering over Benvenuto. Somehow Julia found herself beside the Tiger, clinging to his raised arm. She could feel his body shaken by his panting breath, the muscles of his arms like wood under her fingers. Benvenuto was looking at him calmly, then down at the glass in his hand into which he carefully squirted some soda.

"Take a deep breath, Terence, and count ten. You can knock me down when I've finished if you still want to. Meanwhile shall we sit?"

At last Rourke spoke, glaring at Benvenuto, his words fighting their way out of his throat, taking no notice of Julia as her fingers slid from his arm.

"*You think—I—killed—Charles—*Charles, who was more than me brother—then may you be damned for a—"

Benvenuto shook his head, just in time to arrest another charge which Rourke made at him.

"No, I don't, you madman! And what's more I shall never find out who did if you go on behaving like a rogue elephant. I want help from you, man—not warfare."

Terence Rourke ran both his hands through his mane of hair and collapsed suddenly into a chair. Julia, watching the two men breathlessly, knew that her presence was forgotten. Rourke's head was bowed, and when he raised it and looked across at Benvenuto all the fury was wiped from his face and was replaced by a kind of wistful apology.

"I'm sorry—you sent me crazy," he said, his voice quiet and almost humble. "I think I've been half crazy ever since I saw Charles dead with my sword in his back. The brute had gone before I could catch him—but catch him I will, the black-hearted villain."

"Catch whom?" inquired Benvenuto gently.

But Rourke shook his head. "You wouldn't know anything about him—I'm the only man alive that knows who killed poor Charles, and why. Miss Dallas"—he turned to Julia remorsefully—"all this must be inexpressibly painful to ye. Will you believe me when I say that there's no one living, except maybe yourself, who can know what Charles's death means to me—

and so no one who can sympathize with you as I can? I can never forgive myself for quarrelling with him. He'd always been my friend, he always will be—but this foul divil went and killed him before I could tell him so."

He took Julia's hand and kissed it, and she found herself unable to speak or even to meet his gaze. He sat back in his chair, sighed and lit a cigarette, and then in a more matter-of-fact tone he began his story.

"Listen to me, Ben, and I'll tell you about this business right from the beginning. It started during the war, towards the end of it. Charles and I were in the Intelligence. There was a man, a German agent who called himself a Swiss journalist, whom we had our eye on. We finally—it doesn't matter how—trailed him down to a place called Villers-Bretonneux in March '18. The Americans were in possession of the village. This man was then disguised as a British officer, but we knew him. We trapped him in the parlour of a little house, an incongruous enough place with its stuffy furniture and gilt mirrors; he sat on a chair by the window, and we sat on the table and had it out with him. He was tall, thin and malignant. We offered him bribes, his life, his freedom, to give away his agents, and particularly the agent to whom he had just handed his report on the American positions. We knew he'd made the report, and it wasn't on him. We tried for three hours, but he was as silent as an oyster. Fighting was going on in the village, and a whizzbang came through the window of the room above. The Boche was advancing and time was short—at last I couldn't stand it any longer, and I got up and started to knock the chap about a bit to make him speak. I wasn't armed and neither was he—the guns were on the table. The next thing I knew was some foul chemical he'd flung in my face, and the most terrific pain in my eyes. I couldn't see a thing—I staggered back and fell over a piece of furniture and must have knocked myself out as I fell. When I came round I was lying on the floor with a splitting pain in my head, and all the divils of hell tearing at me eyeballs. I was blind in one eye, but I could see a bit out of the other—and there on the floor was the Boche writhing about in agony, and Charles standing over him with a smoking gun, looking like hell. 'Have you made him talk?' I said, and Charles said 'Yes,' and came over to where I was and pulled me up. While he was helping me towards the door the creature on the floor yelled after us, 'I know you, Kulligrew—I'll get you for this one day,' and I shall never forget his face, seen through a kind of bloody mist that was over my eyes—all twisted up with pain and hate it was, as he shrieked after Charles. If ever a son of a Hun meant what he said that one did. Well, we had to leave him there squealing on the floor because the Germans were almost in the village, and we only just got away in time. Charles had a pretty useful report to send in, and I had to spend a spell in hospital. For a bit they thought the sportsman had blinded me—but not he." The blue eyes twinkled across at Julia, and he reached out his hand for his glass. "Here's to his confusion. And now we get on to Chapter Two. The next time I met Adolf Goetz was after the war, and it was then that he discovered I was the Tiger."

Rourke paused again, this time for dramatic effect, and looked proudly at the other two. Julia gave a little gasp and felt her heart sink.

"So—it's true," she said, her voice very low.

"Sure I was the Tiger!" The rich, deep laugh filled the room, and he bent forward eagerly to go on with his story. His irrepressible spirits had come back, and with them his Irish brogue.

"I had some pretty times! I couldn't stand doing nothing after the war, so the great idea struck me of adjusting some of the wealth that was made by the damned *embusqués*—shark-fish the Italians call them. It was easy enough—and I've got a little farm-house near Castellane where I used to retire and write poetry when things got hot. All went merry as a marriage bell, and I ranged the roads like Dick Turpin, bless his soul!

This God-damned bustard has stole all me tricks, including the tar."

"Tar?" queried Benvenuto.

Rourke's smile was that of a delighted child explaining a game.

"You see, I'd put tar down on the road when I saw me victim coming, being warned by me trusty friend—he's dead now, poor chap—who acted as a herald on a motor-bike. Then I'd step out on the road dressed in a false beard and a red lantern, and hold up me hand; me profiteer would stop his car and I'd warn him about the tar. While he was being properly grateful me friend and I closed in and took the money, which I sent on to the poor divils of wounded soldiers, less a small commission I'd keep for ourselves. They always paid up, although sometimes, glory to Heaven, we'd have a bit of a fight. I never had me gun loaded, and no one was any the worse except in their fat pockets. I enjoyed meself like mad. Now this damn Goetz is ruinin' me first-class reputation as a Tiger; he's nothing but a ferret, shooting unarmed men and murthering peasants. He's doing it to smirch me honour. But there—it makes me so mad to think of him and his dirty tricks that I'm telling me story upside down.

"Well, this went on for a couple of years and then came the last hold-up. I'd been warned by me spy that a big car, a Mercedes, was due down the Route des Alpes with a fat financier on board. It was a winter's night, and I stopped the car in a mountain pass not far from me little farm. Me friend got a good hold of the chauffeur, and I flashed me lamp inside to frighten the financier. My God, if it wasn't Goetz, he all wrapped in rugs, and out of them sticking his thin neck and his face like a damned skull. We recognized each other at the same moment, and just then the chauffeur, who was a brawny Boche, got me friend one in the wind and started up the car. I dropped off. But Goetz knew who I was. Next day I was back in England, and away in America in a week, running a nice little line of good Irish whisky from Canada through the Adirondacks.

"I was fed up with highwaying anyhow, and I made sure Goetz would blow the gaff. But he didn't, the damned rascal; he thought of a better revenge—to make the name of the Tiger stink in everyone's nose and *then* denounce me. He's bided his time and now he thinks he's got us both. He's murdered poor Charles, and, God forgive him, it was me own sword that he did it with."

"The Tiger's" head was sunk in his hands, and the room was utterly still. Benvenuto, leaning back in his chair with a dead pipe in his hand, showed by no sign that he listened except for the two bright points of light between his half-closed eyelids, bright points that were fixed unceasingly on Rourke. At last:

"Tell me what happened that night in the theatre, Terence," he said.

Rourke's head came up. "I smelled mischief as soon as you called me attention to the old divil up in the box, and I rushed off and wrote a note to Charles warning him. We hadn't spoken to each other for months after a damn fool quarrel we had over a woman, but I didn't think of that when I saw Goetz. I sent the note up to Charles by a messenger, but even then I couldn't get the business out of me head, and at last I put me pride in me pocket and went up to speak to him. I made an excuse of offering to send Miss Dallas down to the Professor; and then when I was alone with Charles I asked him if he'd got the note, and he—he wouldn't speak to me. I got up in a rage and went out of the box, and I've wondered since, Ben—d'you think he was dead, then, when I spoke to him?"

"The police haven't been able to find out what time he was killed."

"God, I wish I could be sure about it. After that I wandered about the theatre in a hell of a temper—couldn't pay any attention to the play—and then, right at the end, I happened to be near Charles's box when poor young Pitt saw what had happened from the stage, and I was the first to get to the box. When I saw my sword in Charles's back I knew at once what divil had done it, and I rushed into the next box, but of course Goetz had gone. I dashed out of the theatre with the one idea in me head, that I mustn't let him go, and, as luck would have it, I saw him drive away in his car. Into a taxi I got and chased him, and as long as we were in London I managed to keep him in sight. He took the Brighton road, and then of course me miserable taxi soon lost sight of him, though the driver did his best. I turned things over in me mind and realized there was a boat from Newhaven soon after midnight, so we drove straight to the docks. Of course it had gone, and Goetz on it, as I found out by posing as a detective and inquiring among the porters. I was in a bit of a quandary then, because I didn't want to be arrested meself before I could get hold of the swine, and I realized that the ports would probably be closed against me.

"I wandered along the shore and came up with two fishermen, an old man and his son, who were just starting off trawling. They looked a nasty sort of pair, but I couldn't pick and choose, so I talked to them for a bit and finally struck a bargain by which they took me with them, and dropped me on the shore of France. 'Twas a fine boat with a good strong little engine, and we must have been a fine sight setting out to sea, me in evening-dress perched in the bows, if there'd been anyone to see us, which fortunately there wasn't.

"Everything was going well, I thought, and we were out in mid-Channel, when I noticed father and son conferring in low tones. Dirty work, says I, and sure enough along comes son and says they've decided they ought to take me back to England, and will do so unless I double my price. There was only one thing to do and I did it. Gave son a straight left to the jaw which quieted him, and told father I'd do the same for him if he didn't behave. I took the boat on myself, and more by luck than judgment ran her safely into the sand-hills somewhere south of Calais, in a nice thick morning mist. I made a speech to father and son promising them a present of fifty pounds if they kept their mouths shut for two months, and I rather think they believed me—anyway they agreed, and they also sold me at a fancy figure an old oilskin coat and cap they had on board. Armed with these I made a grand fisherman, and was able to get through Calais successfully, at the same time providing myself with clothes to get to Paris in. I should never have done it except that fortunately I not only speak French but know a good number of the local patois. In Paris by the aid of discreet inquiries I got track of Goetz, and found I'd just missed him. So I bought a car and started south."

"How," inquired Benvenuto idly, "do you come to be wearing your own clothes?"

Rourke chuckled. "Hark at the detective. I told you I had a place of me own near Castellane, dear boy, and I got them there."

"Yes, of course. And money—how are you off for money?"

"Oh, money—" Rourke waved his hand airily. "I have good friends in Paris who keep me supplied with all I want till this business is over and done with. Now, where was I? Oh, yes—I bought me car and hurried after the old divil to Dijon, where I missed him again—so then I made straight for the coast where I'd found out he'd got a villa near Monte Carlo. I found the place, but it was all locked up—for the summer, the neighbours said; and the next thing was I read in the papers about the return of the Tiger. In a flash I understood. It was all part of a plan to bring me down as well as Charles, and a damned dirty ingenious plan too. I went off to Castellane to fit meself out with some clothes, and then to Aix-les-Bains, where the first robbery had taken place. And there sure enough, in the visitors' book at the Hotel des Lindens, was his name as large as life—Herr Adolf Goetz. Of course he was away by the time I got there, and not another trace of him have I found, though the news in the papers of his goings on has sent me nearly wild. All he's doing is to wait till the Tiger is a name that spells murder and robbery all over Europe, and then he'll go to the police with his little story—or maybe he's waiting to see if I'm arrested for the murder of Charles before he weighs in with his evidence. By God! I've got to find him—"

Rourke had sprung to his feet and was gazing wildly in front of him. He seemed about to make for the door, when Benvenuto spoke:

"Gently, Terence. The best thing you can do is to join forces with us. I can get information from the police where you can't, for one thing. And for another, I've got two bits of news for you. One is that we saw your friend Goetz on the road to-day—in fact, I tried to stop him, but he wasn't having any. The second is that there's been another hold-up to-night, just outside Lyon. He's travelling in a car which is so big it looks as if it's been rigged up to sleep in, which is probably why you've found no trace of him lately. I can give the police a pretty full description of that car, so it ought not to be very hard to trace it."

Rourke's face was wreathed in smiles. "To think of the luck of it! May I *really* work with ye? Then between us we'll catch him. Don't go to the police, Ben, darlin'—between us we can do it, what with your brains and my fist—and it's a bird I want to bring down meself. He's done *me* enough harm, God knows. Merciful powers, you've made a new man of me this night."

"Well, don't go flinging your weight about too much till to-morrow," said Benvenuto, "and then we'll work out a plan of action. There are a dozen questions I want to ask you about different people and different times, but they'll keep till breakfast. Meanwhile, my eyes feel as if they're popping out of my head, so I suggest we all get a bit of sleep. Good night you two."

"Good night, Ben, and good night—Tiger!"

Rourke beamed at her. "Let me take you along to your room, Miss Dallas."

Out in the corridor he took both her hands and looked at her searchingly.

"So—when you found me in the lift to-night you thought you were alone with a murthering highway robber, did you—and never a sign did you give."

The blue eyes held her own, held them until she lost herself in their brightness. Then, very gently he bent his head and kissed, first her right hand, then her left.

"Good night."

• • • • •

For a moment Julia stirred as the morning light came in at her windows, while an echo crept through her mind. "Dear Tiger—darling Tiger."

Then she smiled, and slept.

CHAPTER X
GONE AWAY

"WAKE UP, Julia—the Tiger's gone."

"Oh, Ben, I was so fast asleep. Hullo, Agatha, darling—good morning. What did you say?"

Julia yawned and smiled and pushed her waves of hair away from her face. She sat up in bed, blinking at them, and pulled the creamy lace of her nightgown into place on her white shoulders.

"I said the Tiger's gone—hopped it—vanished, and there's never a note on his pin-cushion."

"*Gone!* But—but, Ben—he can't have gone. He said—"

Benvenuto laughed shortly. "I know what he said, my child, but when I went along to his room this morning I found the bird had flown—'his little bed unslept in,' etc., as Tennyson has it. How d'you account for that? He must have made tracks as soon as he'd left us last night."

"Benvenuto has told me the whole story," interposed Agatha, "and I am convinced there is some mistake. That nice Mr. Rourke would never have gone off in such ungentlemanly haste had it not been a case of sickness or an urgent message from some relative. Plenty of people have foreign connexions—my own grandmother was Irish. It is true I was somewhat shocked to learn of his activities as a Tiger after the war, but so far as I can judge from Benvenuto's extraordinary account his victims were all people without breeding who had made money out of the poor dear soldiers, in which case I have no sympathy for them. Mark my words, Mr. Rourke will appear after breakfast with a perfect explanation, and very foolish you will look with your suspicions."

Benvenuto shook his head. "I've already inquired whether any message arrived for him last night, and the hotel people say there was none. All the same I hope you're right, Agatha, and that it's a case of a dead grandmother. I'm going off now to find out what I can about his car—it wasn't garaged at the hotel, so I suggest you dress yourself, young woman, and I'll report progress over breakfast."

The door shut behind him, and Julia sat very still in the middle of her bed, staring down at her hands as they lay on the sheet—first her right hand, then her left. Slowly the colour crept into her face, stained her cheeks and her forehead and throat, and suddenly she leapt from her bed and seized the startled Agatha by the shoulders.

"Listen to me, Agatha. Never, never again, let me hear you say 'that nice Mr. Rourke.' He isn't nice—he's a fiend and a devil, and I hate him—hate him—*hate him*! And I'm never going to rest until he's in prison. Now go quickly—I'm going to have my bath."

She half pushed the amazed Agatha into the corridor and banged the door, and the next minute had stepped into a bath that was far too hot for her, and was trying to pretend, as she angrily soaped herself, that the drops on her face were entirely bath water.

It was a pale and very determined-looking Julia who, half an hour later, joined Benvenuto at the breakfast-table.

"Well?" she demanded.

"It appears to be a case of exit through gap in hedge again," replied Benvenuto, carefully buttering a roll. "I found out from the chasseur the address of the nearest big garage, and when I got round there it was easy; Terence, not being the kind of person one would overlook, was recognized at once from my description. When five francs had changed hands the garagiste explained that the m'sieur had arrived in a Renault about half-past nine last night, saying he'd want a garage for one night, or possibly more, and went off to look for an hotel, leaving his luggage in the car. Then, to the chap's surprise, he turned up again about half-past twelve (that's just after he left us) and ordered the tank to be filled with petrol, also the reserve tank, jumped in the car, chucked out a hundred-franc note and dashed off without waiting for change. Meanwhile the manager of this hotel is highly indignant, as he says the m'sieur took the room for the night saying he'd send round for his luggage, and has not only gone off without paying but has taken the key of his room with him, leaving nothing behind in his bedroom but his hat. I said he'd left me a note saying he'd been called away suddenly, because I didn't want the police fussing round; and then as a final touch of irony the manager suggested I might like to pay his bill. Funny his leaving his hat behind—it looks as if he may have had some sudden reason for going off."

"Nonsense!" Benvenuto looked up in surprise at the bitterness in Julia's voice. "That's precisely what he wanted you to think when you went into his room—that he'd gone out and was coming back. Reason indeed—I should think he had a reason. Having quieted all our suspicions and told us a pack of ingenious lies the whole evening, he had the best of reasons for getting away as quickly as possible while we were innocently sleeping. He's made fools of us both, Ben—don't let him do it again. Why—don't you see"—she leant across the table, her eyes flashing in a way that promised no good to the absent Rourke—"he told us absolutely nothing last night that we can prove: even the man who was with him during the dramatic meeting with Goetz on the mountain pass is dead now, according to him. *Very* convenient. Then his mysterious 'friends' in Paris from whom he gets enough money to buy a Renault and stay in the best hotels—he didn't tell us their names, you notice. Of course they're simply the unfortunate victims of his hold-ups, Lady Hopkins included. The little farm-house near Castellane—rather funny he didn't tell us the address, don't you think? Even the story about poor Charles and Goetz during the war—I don't believe a word of it. Charles never told *me* anything about it. Oh, Ben, don't you see—he made us believe him, and he got away, and now he's laughing—laughing at us *both*."

She watched Benvenuto irritably as he frowned into his coffee in silence.

"Surely," she burst out—"surely you think he's clever enough to have invented the whole thing?"

"Good Lord, yes—he's clever enough. I've heard him tell better tales than that." To her intense annoyance he looked up at her and laughed. "You know, he let drop one thing I wanted to know pretty badly, and I don't believe you noticed it."

Her question was arrested by Agatha, who came hurrying towards them, her cheeks pink with excitement and her eyes positively snapping.

"Benvenuto! My garnets!"

"Your garnets, Agatha?"

"I repeat, my garnets. The gift of my dear father to my dear mother on their betrothal—sixty-four perfectly matched stones falling on the chest in the shape of a Welsh harp. Julia, my love, they were to have come to you on my death!"

"*Were* to have? Do you mean you've lost them, Agatha?"

"Lost them! *Lost* them indeed! I am not in the habit of losing things, apart from the occasion when I lost my spectacles, and even then dear Edward found them in the chicken-run—unbroken, thank God!"

"What's the trouble then, Agatha?"

She sighed. "Evidently I have not made myself clear. Now will you please pay attention, both of you?" She sat down at the table and used a coffee cup to emphasize her words. "When I retired to my room last night I sat at my dressing-table, and placed my garnets there—no, *there*. I remember the position exactly because one of my hair-pins became entangled in the clasp. Do you follow me? Very well, then. When I rose this morning I said to myself, 'I shall wear my Liberty blue'—which I did. However, after being shall I say ejected from Julia's bedroom, I happened to notice a nasty spot right on the front and thought it must be that Pernod—so, providentially as it turns out, I changed my blue for my claret poplin. *That* was how I found out."

"But—found *what* out, darling?"

"Really, Julia, you surprise me. Have you never remarked the perfect harmony between my claret poplin and my garnets? But for that I might not have discovered the theft."

"I say, Agatha, I'm awfully sorry about this. If you're sure they've gone I'll go and see the manager at once."

"And *why*, Benvenuto? May I ask *why*? I fail to understand how you can sit there and call yourself a detective and suggest accusing some unfortunate domestic when you've already admitted that you sat up till all hours drinking with a Robber."

Benvenuto hurriedly bent down under the table-cloth to retrieve Agatha's hand-bag which, in her excitement, had slipped from her lap. The contents had scattered over the carpet, and when he emerged he held in his hand some tram tickets, a bottle of aspirin and a very fair likeness to a Welsh harp in garnets. Agatha received her treasures with a good deal of composure.

"There you are," she said triumphantly. "The last place *I* should ever have considered putting them. Evidently he was disturbed in his rascally attempt and fled."

"No doubt that was it," murmured Benvenuto; "and now, if we've finished breakfast, how about going along to the post office—I'm waiting for letters, and I expect you are."

"Yes, indeed," said Agatha. "There will be quite a budget from dear Edward describing his adventures in Montreux. I am always nervous whilst he is in the neighbourhood of those treacherous glaciers. Come, my dear."

• • • • •

"Nonsense, my good man. Regardez encore," said Agatha kindly but firmly as she peered through the *guichet* of the poste restante. "Il y a une lettre de mon frère. Oui. Le nom c'est Milk—M-I-L-K. Lait; ce qui se trouve dans le café. Really, Benvenuto, the foolishness of this person passes belief— he appears to be ignorant of his own language. Would you mind *insisting* that he gives me my letter?"

"Rien pour Miss Milk," repeated the man imperturbably.

"I'm sorry, Agatha, but there really don't seem to be any letters for you. I only got a coal bill myself."

"Benvenuto, I refuse to be trifled with in this way. Dear Edward may be absent-minded, but he is always *most* punctilious in writing to me. This man is nothing but a fool and I insist on seeing the Postmaster-General."

Benvenuto smothered a groan. "It's not the slightest use, Agatha; believe me, the poste restante service is absolutely efficient. Look at the number of people collecting their mail at this moment."

Suddenly and distressingly Agatha's face puckered.

"I always *knew* how it would end," she whispered, groping for her handkerchief. "It simply means he's slipped over one of those nasty glaciers. I must go to him at once—please take me to the station."

Julia took Agatha's arm and led her out of the post office, doing her best to reassure her, while Benvenuto followed more slowly, a frown on his face.

"Look here, Agatha," he said suddenly. "Montreux is only a day's run from here, and I suggest we all go in the car. I'm certain the Professor is all right, but I want to ask him about something myself, so we might as well run over and see him. I'll leave a note for Rourke in case he turns up again, and we can get back here by to-morrow night."

"My dear Benvenuto, you are a true friend," said Agatha, wiping her eyes. "You must allow me to pay for the petrol, and now pray let us take a cab to the hotel."

In half an hour they were on the road again, the Bugatti pointing towards Switzerland.

CHAPTER XI
SWISS MILK

BENVENUTO SLOWED down the Bugatti and looked at Julia, his eyes twinkling, then back at Lake Geneva, hard, blue, and flat in the midday sun.

"I don't hear those exclamations of distinguished enthusiasm that are customary on first viewing a Swiss lake," he said reprovingly.

Julia's face crumpled with laughter for the first time that day.

"Ben, isn't it too shaming? Nature copying, not Art, but a picture post card—it makes me feel positively embarrassed. The only humorous note is that absurd cloud on a mountain-top—just like a cotton-wool poultice on a troublesome tooth."

He laughed. "Got it in one, particularly as the mountain is called the Dents du Midi. The whole thing is a bit self-conscious, I agree, but believe me Switzerland is a remarkable country. The natives have brought plumbing and cuckoo clocks to a degree of excellence elsewhere unknown, besides which they do a fine trade in sport, scenery and milk chocolate." He looked over his shoulder at Agatha, who had put on her spectacles and was gazing earnestly about her. "Bad painters are sent here," he said, "and are fed on chocolate until they die."

She smiled brightly and nodded, not having heard him. "Now, Benvenuto, if you could only paint this," she shouted, "I believe you would have quite a success at the Royal Academy."

"Blue paint far too dear," he replied gloomily, avoiding by inches a charabanc labelled "Seeing Europe."

"Two kilometres to Montreux," announced Julia laughing, "and lunch with Uncle Edward."

Benvenuto looked round quickly at her and grunted, "Optimist."

What on earth did he mean?

At the Hotel du Beau Lac the Bugatti came to a standstill, and at once the heat enveloped them like a warm bath.

"Le Professeur Milk?" inquired Benvenuto of the clerk who hurried down the white steps.

A curious expression flickered across the man's face and he hesitated. Then, "Un moment, m'sieur, s'il vous plait," he said. "Je vais chercher le patron," and was gone.

Agatha, who was fumbling with the door handle, looked up with a smile. "Patron, indeed! That comes of dear Edward's recklessness in tipping, but it is a great relief to know he is sound in wind and limb."

"I'm afraid—" began Benvenuto, but was interrupted by the approach of the manager, tripping fatly down the steps.

"You also seek the Herr Professor, m'sieur—dames? I repeat—I know nothing, *nothing*," he exclaimed excitedly, flinging out his white ringed hands, palms uppermost. "He came—he eat and sleep two days—he pay his bill—he go, and now my hotel it is a Gendarmerie! Each day come the police, march in and out, search the room of the Herr Professor, question me until almost I lose my head. Never, never before does this 'appen to me."

Benvenuto jumped down from the car and went into the hotel with the angry and voluble little man. Julia, following with Agatha, heard Benvenuto ask if he had any knowledge of the direction taken by the Professor, and heard also the emphatic negative of the manager's reply. She persuaded Agatha to sit down while the two men disappeared into the office, and looked at her nervously. Agatha was trembling and, unexpectedly, quite silent.

In a moment Benvenuto emerged, holding a key in his hand.

"The manager is allowing us to see the Professor's room," he said. "I doubt its being littered with clues, but we may as well look round."

And indeed the little bedroom, neat and impersonal with its clean linen and shining taps, looked singularly unpromising. Benvenuto threw back the shutters from a window which overlooked the lake and wandered about. All at once he was on his knees beside the wash-basin, and Julia, watching him curiously, saw that as he rose he held in the palm of his hand some tufts of white hair. Agatha bent to look at the find, and an expression of real alarm came into her face.

"Benvenuto," she almost moaned, "my poor brother must have gone out of his mind, to have started cutting his own hair."

He made for the door abruptly. "Come on—I'm going to see the police and then we'll push off."

Down in the hall he stopped in front of a big map which hung on the wall.

"If you wanted to get out of Switzerland in a hurry, Julia," he said in a low voice, glancing at Agatha who was talking excitedly to the manager, "which way would you go? Look here— this is the nearest road into France, but impassable in winter and very steep. It leads under the brow of Mont Blanc."

"But why should Uncle Edward want to leave Switzerland?"

He smiled. "There you have me. I fancy it is one of those things that only Uncle Edward can explain. I'll just find out from this chap where the Gendarmerie is, and we'll stop there before leaving the town. By the way, you might keep Agatha in the car while I talk to the police—I don't want to cause too much of a stir."

As they climbed into the car, Benvenuto left them for a moment and disappeared into an oculist's shop next door to the hotel. He came back without comment, and, starting up the Bugatti, drove off once more, coming to a standstill in front of a large building with the Swiss flag over the door. Julia and Agatha sat still, not speaking, while Benvenuto went off to see the gendarmes.

Why should the Professor suddenly begin to behave so unnaturally, thought Julia. She sighed, thinking of him, kind and vague and forgetful, yet somehow comforting and reliable, always there when she had wanted him. What had happened to him now?

A midday hush had descended on Montreux, the sacred hour of *dejeuner*. The little square in which they sat was deserted, the air hot and humid. An inspiration sent her across to a restaurant to buy some fruit and cakes, which Agatha, however, declined. Julia sat in the car and ate them herself, lit a cigarette and felt slightly better.

After what seemed an interminable wait, Benvenuto came out of the Gendarmerie and climbed up beside her, but made no attempt to start the car. Absent-mindedly he took a banana from her lap and peeled it.

"Well?" said Julia.

"It isn't well," replied Benvenuto. "Your illustrious ex-guardian has disappeared. Nor has he fallen over a precipice. He's just—well—escaped."

"Escaped!" echoed Agatha, indignantly. "Am I to understand that these policemen, not even British, dared to arrest my brother, the most harmless and law-abiding of men?"

"The Professor was allowed by Scotland Yard to come to Switzerland after the inquest on condition that he reported daily to the local police," said Benvenuto, tilting his hat over his eyes and lighting a cigarette. "They were to keep an eye on him on behalf of the C.I.D. Kind of international courtesy."

Agatha snorted. "International fiddlesticks!"

"Three days ago he vanished," he went on, "and the Chief of Police here, who is quite a lad though he lunches exclusively off garlic, says he is not in Switzerland. He's had a lot of trouble trying to trace him. Well, the Professor has gone, and of his own accord apparently."

"How do you know he hasn't had an accident with an Alp?" quavered Agatha.

"I think not; he made preparations for going away, getting money from Cook's, and—er—other things," said Benvenuto vaguely. "He's either in France, Italy or Germany. No taxi has been found that took him anywhere. Now, the nearest frontier is French—in fact that is France across the lake. He may either have taken a boat across, though one hasn't been traced, or walked over the mountains in the direction of Chamonix. I favour the latter idea—he's a great walker, and knows the country. I vote we try Chamonix and make inquiries from there." He glanced at both of them and added, "I'm sorry about this; but don't worry—we'll find him."

He turned the car and they slipped out of the town towards the high Alps. Before them rose what looked to Julia an impassable wall of mountains; pines, then bare rock, and higher still the everlasting snow. Soon they were off the main road and rising, twisting, turning, the Bugatti roaring on low gear. Higher and higher they climbed, swinging round hairpin corners, until all Switzerland seemed to lie below them; up and up towards the snow, out of the heat, into an air thin and stimulating as wine. Once Benvenuto stopped the car to let the engine cool, and sitting in the shade of a tree they could hear the melancholy notes of goat-bells from far up a steep green slope. The animals were not in sight; and the thin falling notes of the bells seemed to increase the strange, enormous loneliness of the landscape. Julia's eye wandered over the grand inhuman architecture of the mountains, the small tenacious pines, and the great drop on her left to a valley so distant that no habitation could be seen, and she felt lost and depressed. She was glad when the engine started, and carried them onwards. Once they passed an *estaminet*, where a shepherd sat on a bench drinking a glass of wine, and then, a few miles farther on, they could see from a bend in the road a small white building hanging perilously on the edge of a precipice, and on its wall written in blue letters, "Auberge du Drapeau Rouge."

"Voilà!" cried Benvenuto. "Food and Drink!"

A short, twisted climb and the car drew up at the door, where in a moment appeared a tall dark-eyed peasant woman with a small dark-eyed boy peeping round her skirts.

"Bonjour, madame. Ce n'est pas trop tard pour déjeuner?" demanded Benvenuto.

"Bonjour, m'sieur, dames. Mais, non—entrez."

Her voice was low and a little harsh, rather as if she did not use it very often, Julia thought, and her manner shy yet dignified. The little boy watched from a safe distance with the beautiful scared eyes of a young animal, and apart from him and his mother the little house appeared deserted, as the three travellers walked through a bare whitewashed passage with a scrubbed wooden floor.

On either side were doors opening on to square white rooms, empty except for benches and tables of bleached wood, and, at the end of the passage, a balcony with tables and chairs ranged along it. The *patronne* spread a coarse check cloth, as immaculately clean as everything else in the house, and inquired if they could eat "une bonne soupe, une omelette et un rôti de veau." They both could and would, they assured her, and ordering three vermouths they went and leant over the rail of the balcony. A green meadow fell from the house so steeply that Julia clung to a pillar for support, her head spinning; then below it were the tops of trees, and through them occasional glimpses of the twisting snake of the road. The whole earth seemed tipping, straining to right itself, yet frozen into immobility in the midst of a monstrous landslide; two distant mountains stood like sentinels between the arrested motion of the land and a blue infinity beyond.

"This is the most terrifying place I've ever been in," announced Julia. "For goodness' sake give me a drink before I slip into the void. I feel like a depressed and unsubstantial wraith."

"Altitude," said Benvenuto, handing her a glass, and tipping his vermouth down his throat. "That's better—and here's the soup. It's an inner void that's troubling me."

A vegetable soup fragrant with cheese, crisp chunks of bread and dry red wine, had a magical effect after the clear mountain air; by the time Madame appeared with her grave silent dignity and an omelette, even Agatha seemed cheerful.

"Has a tall old gentleman with a white beard been here during the past day or two?" asked Julia in French, but Madame shook her head.

"Non, madame—et nous n'avons pas beaucoup de monde en ce moment, vous savez."

As she turned away Benvenuto looked up from the omelette he was serving.

"Has a clean-shaven old gentleman with dark spectacles visited you, madame?" he inquired.

An unexpected and amused smile flashed across Madame's face.

"Oui, m'sieur," she answered decorously. "Il est venue hier pour déjeuner."

"Yesterday for lunch," repeated Benvenuto thoughtfully. "I see. Did you notice anything peculiar about him? You may be frank—this lady is his sister, and we are looking for him."

Madame looked at him doubtfully, and then making up her mind she proceeded to describe the Professor's visit.

She had been alone in the house with the child when the gentleman arrived, and had been surprised and, to begin with, rather frightened by his behaviour. He had insisted on looking into every room in the house before he would consent to sit down, and having done this he decided to have lunch in the sitting-room, having first pulled the blinds across each window. After laying the table she had gone off to fetch his lunch, leaving him reading the visitors' book in the half darkness of the curtained room; but when she came back with the soup he appeared to have gone. However, a slight noise led her to look under the table, and there, to her alarm, was the gentleman on all fours. He seemed, she thought, relieved when he saw who she was, and proceeded to get up after making a remark in some language she did not understand. When questioned by Benvenuto she said it had sounded like Peep-bo. All went well, and the gentleman ate his lunch peacefully, until a party of people in a car arrived for drinks; but when she went into the sitting-room with cheese for the Professor, he had indeed disappeared. It was not until her other guests had departed that she caught sight of the *pauvre m'sieur* looking nervously round the door of a little hut among the cabbages. She persuaded him to come out and finish his lunch, and before he left he was very *gentil* and gave her little boy some chocolates and five francs. Then he had departed on foot in the direction of Chamonix—"et je crois que la pauvre viellard etait un peu piqué," she finished.

Benvenuto thanked her and turned to Julia and Agatha, who looked at him speechless.

"All just as it should be," he remarked.

"Are you *mad*, Benvenuto? Just as it should be indeed—" exploded Agatha. Then, despairingly, "Can't you realize that something terrible has happened to poor Edward? I guessed he must have gone out of his mind when we discovered he'd been trying to cut his own hair—now I am sure of it. If you are under the impression that my dear brother is in the habit of getting under tables, all I can say is, God help you," she finished acidly.

"But, my dear Agatha, the very fact that he *did* get under the table proves that he is as sane as—as ever he was. If he had climbed *on to* the table, now, I should have been inclined to agree with you. As things are, every action of the Professor's is perfectly straightforward and logical once we realize the fact that he is nervous of somebody or something, and is trying to make a get-away. The sooner we can get hold of him the better, so if you've finished lunch I propose we push on to Chamonix."

Agatha shook her head dubiously, but nevertheless followed him out to the car without further argument. They said good-bye to Madame, standing aloof but friendly at the door of her lonely dwelling, and Julia turned to wave to the small boy, still sheltering himself behind his mother's skirts.

Soon the road wound tortuously downwards, and half an hour's run brought them to a flat valley from which rose the cloud-shrouded mystery of Mont Blanc. For the rest of the journey Julia forgot her own personality and the complications and mysteries surrounding her, lost them in the overwhelming drama of the great Alps. They seemed to forbid human admiration or human comment, their strange icebound peaks rising with unearthly dignity above the clouds and spearing the highest heavens. The road twined darkly under the brow of Mont Blanc, twisted its way through a leafy gorge overhung with clouds, and passed the boundary between Switzerland and France where they were held up for a few minutes at the two customs stations. Julia, sitting overawed and silent in the car, felt relieved when they came to a small village, and by way of reaction began to giggle as she saw the curious human types sitting at café tables clad in various styles of climbing regalia.

"They all look like vegetarians or art workers," she whispered to Benvenuto. "Can't we slow down?"

"Wait till you get to Chamonix, my dear, if you want to study the human zoo," he replied. "It invariably contains superb specimens."

Another few kilometres, with confused impressions of ice-green glaciers and turbulent streams, tweed-clad figures with meat-red faces, and, as a background, immaculate stretches of snow, and they drew into Chamonix, to be greeted by strains of music as the car stopped in front of the principal outdoor café. "Your Mouth is Made for Kissing," announced the orchestra feverishly, while hob-nailed climbers beat time with their alpenstocks, waiters rushed to and fro with loaded trays, enormous limousines crawled through the crowd of pedestrians and added to the general noise with their urgent hooting, professional guides lounged a little self-consciously at street corners, and at the end of every street the great mountains towered, grim, menacing, and cloud-capped, throwing a curious twilit gloom over the little town.

Julia sank into a painted chair between Agatha and Benvenuto, and gasped. "There are moments," she said, "when I am overcome by the triumphant impudence of the human race."

"And when I'm introduced to one—,
I wish I thought, what jolly fun,"

added Benvenuto, and ordered drinks for Julia and himself, and a nice fresh pot of tea for Agatha.

Julia sat watching the crowd, in which beer-drinking German tourists seemed to preponderate, and then her eyes came back to Benvenuto. He looked tired after the day's drive, and his pleasant face, just a little like a humorous camel's, she decided, bore an expression of deep thought. After a moment he relaxed and raised his glass.

Does he really *know*, she thought; is he really going to solve all these mysteries which envelop us like a London fog? She sat up. Benvenuto's glass was still raised to his lips, but was arrested there, and his expression had changed to one of intense interest. Then the glass was put down slowly, untasted, and he continued to stare with a puzzled frown at something behind her. She turned, and saw a man's back clad in rather loud, badly-fitting tweeds, and above the tweeds the shaven bristly head of the typical bourgeois German. Benvenuto put his hand on her arm.

"Digestive tablets," he murmured.

The German was certainly raising to his lips a kind of lozenge he had taken from a small box at his side. As he did so he glanced round, peered at them through dark glasses, rose to his feet, and with a curious sliding motion commenced to make his way to the street. He was tall, bent, clean-shaven and—yes—Julia almost screamed, yes, it was Uncle Edward. She started up, but Ben's restraining hand still pressed her arm.

"Leave it to me," he whispered, and rising he hurried after the strange figure, which, disappearing round a corner of the café, knocked a couple of glasses off the end table with its flying coat-tails.

CHAPTER XII
"IF ONLY I COULD REMEMBER—"

IN AN IMMACULATE bedroom of a little hotel four people sat in intense physical and mental discomfort. Professor Milk leant forward with his face in his hands, and beside him sat Agatha, holding a sodden handkerchief.

"Edward, the time has come for you to explain All," she said, and glanced at Benvenuto, who nodded and smiled gently.

"Much the best way, Professor; get it off your chest," he said, looking out of the window at the frozen heights. But the old man shook his head, and put his hand in Agatha's. Julia, watching the scene with anxiety, saw Benvenuto turn towards them and address the bent figure in the chair.

"To the best of my knowledge and belief," he said slowly, emphasizing every word, "what you are imagining is—just—imagination."

Milk looked up quickly, then slowly dropped his head, seeming to shake it slightly in a dejected negative.

"How do you know—" he asked, after a moment's silence—"what I imagine?"

Benvenuto seemed to come to a quick decision; he moved forward and placed his hand on the other's shoulder.

"You think," he murmured, "that you're going to be accused of the murder of Charles Kulligrew."

A frozen silence ensued. Julia's fingers dug into her palms, and the room swayed slightly as if the echo of an earthquake had reached it.

"If only I could remember," muttered the Professor absently, "where I put the sword."

"Edward!" Agatha cried out shrilly, protestingly. "*Nobody* knew about the sword!"

"Come, Professor, let's have the whole story," said Benvenuto, and his voice, crisp, commanding, almost bullying, seemed to pull the old man together like a strong drink.

"I *had* the sword, I know." He was sitting up now. "I found it leaning against my seat in the stalls, and I remember thinking I would take it and give it back to Rourke. That was—yes, yes, at the end of the second act. It was in the stick, of course."

He glanced at Benvenuto, who nodded encouragingly.

"Yes—you took the sword-stick with you when you went into the foyer at the end of the second act?"

"That was it. I remember distinctly doing that. Then a page-boy gave me a letter from the actress. It distressed me very much. I felt very angry, and distressed. Angry with Charles. Because of Julia, of course."

Julia felt tears come into her eyes, but she did not interrupt the old man's rambling story.

"I thought to myself," he went on, "I must go and see Charles at once. So I went to his box."

"Still carrying the sword-stick?" asked Benvenuto.

"Yes, for I remember I inadvertently tripped up a lady with it as I was going upstairs. She was annoyed. *Quite* justly, of course. Very, very clumsy of me." He sighed, and his fingers wandered to where his beard should have hung.

"And then?" prompted Benvenuto.

"Then, of course, I apologized," said the Professor rather sharply.

"And after you had left the lady?"

"After that, you know, I find great difficulty in recalling *what* happened. I have gone over and over it in my mind. Many times. I was very—er—excited I know—and I seem to remember giving the letter to Charles, and getting, most irrationally, of course, almost—er—furious when he wouldn't read it at once. The lights were going down, and then—" he stopped and pressed his hands against his temples. The three people round him almost ceased to breathe.

"The next thing I can recall," he spoke so low that they bent forward to hear him better, and Julia shuddered involuntarily at his next words—"was—washing my hands in the cloakroom. Suppose"—he whispered—"suppose, Benvenuto, it was to clean them of—*blood*?"

Benvenuto looked at him calmly and shook his head. "Not a chance of it, Professor. If you'd had blood on your hands, Julia would have noticed it."

"Julia?" The old man's eyes wandered to her in perplexity. "But—Julia wasn't there."

"Of course, Uncle Edward—don't you remember? You met me in the corridor as you were coming away from the box, and you took my hands and—and—warned me—"

A great light shone in the Professor's face.

"It all comes back to me! I remember seeing you in your white dress—yes—yes—and what did I say to you, Julia?"

"You said"—her words came with difficulty—"you said—that if trouble came to me, I must be brave."

The Professor seemed to droop again, and he looked at them despondently, and shuddered.

"Blacker and blacker," he muttered. "It must have been my guilt that made me say that."

"Stuff and nonsense, Edward," said Agatha briskly. "I have no doubt at all that you were referring to the letter you had received from that barebacked hussy. What is more, I don't believe you went near the cloak-room—I remember distinctly your sitting down in the stalls and telling me you had that moment left Julia."

Julia leant forward eagerly. "Agatha is right, Uncle Edward—because I ran after you to speak to you, and I saw you disappearing into the stalls."

He rocked from side to side, holding his head.

"My poor head—my poor head," he murmured. "I can remember washing my hands—I know I can, and being very, very worried and upset about something. It is all mixed up with the soap, which was brown Windsor, such as we had when I was a boy. I was very, very distressed."

"About the soap?" queried Benvenuto.

"No, no, about the—of course! That was it—the mystery of *The Lily Flower*."

Benvenuto looked at him sharply. "What mystery?" he asked. But the old man drew himself up and a look of obstinacy came into his face.

"I refuse to answer," he said. "I feel it would be dishonourable. When I have no proof. And who can tell—who can tell! Ars longa, vita brevis—" His voice had become vague and dreamy, and there seemed little hope of getting anything definite out of him. Benvenuto studied him for a moment in silence, and then spoke again.

"Was it after the first act that you washed your hands, Professor?"

"Perhaps, perhaps," murmured the old man; "who can tell?"

"*I* can tell," cut in Agatha firmly. "Certainly it was after the first act, Edward. Don't you recall meeting the dear archdeacon's wife in the first interval, and how she kindly offered us chocolates? They had become somewhat moist from resting in her lap, and not only that, when I took one I discovered that it contained alcoholic liquor. I remember being extremely surprised at the time, as she is the last woman I should have suspected of drinking. In chocolates too. Almost *fast*, I thought it. When I got home I found a nasty stain on my bodice, and I have no doubt dear Edward got some on his hand," she finished triumphantly, looking at Benvenuto.

The Professor roused himself from his abstraction and looked at them timidly.

"I hesitate to ask you, Benvenuto," he said, "but do you sincerely feel there is a reasonable chance I may not have done this terrible thing?"

"I do, Professor—a most reasonable chance. But we must try and get things straightened out and discover what really happened after you gave Charles the letter."

The old man shook his head again, dejectedly. "If only I could remember—about the sword," he said.

CHAPTER XIII
BAL MASQUÉ

"THEY WILL take off their masks at midnight," said Benvenuto, detaching a red paper streamer from Agatha's front hair, "and I shall then discover whether the blonde in black is really the most beautiful woman in Annécy."

"My Italian count says that I am," retorted Julia. "*He* is too beautiful for words, dressed as Casanova, and so romantically mysterious—not to mention the fact that he wants to buy me an emerald necklace to go with my red hair. I am his Bella Rossa. He informed me during the last tango."

"Fear the Greeks when they bring gifts," murmured the Professor, getting up and hurriedly removing a coloured paper crown as he caught sight of himself in a mirror. "I think we should get to bed now, Agatha. Good night, Benvenuto; I have thoroughly enjoyed our little jollification, my dear boy—it has taken my mind off many things."

"Good night," said Agatha, giving Julia a kiss. "Do not burn the candle at both ends, and above all, my dear, *do* not gamble. This casino is quite delightful, Benvenuto, and not at all what I had been led to expect. I have been much amused."

As the Milks walked towards the door, Benvenuto drew his chair next to Julia's and, taking a cigar from the table, gestured towards the crowded dance floor where masked couples, locked together, swayed to a languorous Blues.

"They will unmask at midnight," he repeated. "I wish I could say the same of Kulligrew's murderer."

Julia, glancing at him, saw that he was in a serious mood, and as if he read her thoughts he went on:

"Champagne, dance music, and coloured streamers invariably have the effect of turning my naturally bright and sunny disposition into a state of morbid introspection." He smiled. "Look at those streamers, Julia; here is one of a bloody red. It ascends in an inverted parabola to that modernistic chandelier in the middle of the room. There it is inextricably entangled with a thousand others, green, red and blue. Where does it finally lead? Isn't it like this murder case? One of the coloured ribbons, followed through the tangle, will lead us to the murderer. But watch; I pull on it too hard—and it breaks; the clue, the thin red line leading to the murderer, is gone. We must go gently, Julia."

She stared at him. "*Gently*, Ben? Why, we don't appear to me to be moving at all. What have we done since leaving England? Absolutely nothing, so far as I can see, except let one suspect make fools of us, after which we proceeded to make fools of ourselves by chasing after poor Uncle Edward, who's no more capable of having committed a murder than a baby is. Why, he wouldn't hurt a fly, whatever he may suspect about himself, poor darling."

"My dear girl, not so fast. We have made immense strides, got farther than I had dared to hope in so short a time, since both Rourke and the Professor have provided us with extremely valuable information. And you're wrong in thinking a gentle and loving disposition forbids murder—on the contrary, it may be a great incentive towards it, as in the case of Luela da Costa." He looked at her, half mockingly. "Remember, Julia, the Professor regards you with the deepest affection."

"Oh, Ben, don't, don't go on. You make me feel like the. criminal myself. You can't *really* believe Uncle Edward killed Charles?"

"My dear, I confess I can't see a shred of evidence that incriminates him. All his peculiar actions are explained by the fact that he *thinks* he may have done it, and there's no doubt the police put that idea into his head when they questioned him. Had he committed the crime and remained unsuspected, he'd never have suspected himself, provided he's suffering from a genuine lapse of memory, as I certainly believe. By the way, what a magnificent actress is Agatha. You realize that she's known all the time that the Professor visited Charles's box with the sword in his hand, and although she's been questioned both by the police and by me she kept the guilty secret locked in her bosom until Edward blurted it out yesterday."

Julia nodded. "I noticed that. Poor Agatha—she'd sacrifice her immortal soul to save the Professor from any kind of harm."

"Yes," agreed Benvenuto. "The Professor—or you. You're the two fixed stars in her firmament. And talking of stars—I had an interesting account of one this morning from Martin Pitt. Read that."

Her heart suddenly beating with excitement, Julia took the closely written sheets from Benvenuto's hand.

500 Ebury St., S.W.1

DEAR BROWN,

London is a dusty slut and I am heartily sick of her—longing to get away to the sea and the mountains, anywhere away from this stale sunlight, this roar of traffic, footsteps, voices. I suppose I should rejoice in the fact that each night the traffic accumulates into a snarling immobile monster outside the theatre, the footsteps lead towards The Lily Flower, *the voices are still raised in applause and the box-office waxes fat—but I'd give anything to escape from it all and join you in your Big Game hunt across France.*

Have you found Rourke yet? As a matter of fact I shall see you before you have time to answer this letter, and here I must offer my congratulations to you as a Minor Prophet. I'll explain. I have, as you suggested, been keeping watch on the movements of Louise Lafontaine since you left England, and I must say emphatically that she has neither said nor done anything in the least suspicious, at least to my inexperienced eye. I have hesitated to write to you before because I felt that knowing her so little my opinion would be valueless. Now, however, I do feel that I have begun to know her rather well. We have lunched or dined together almost every day, and I have to thank you for what has been, and is, a charming experience. She is an enchanting creature of an intelligence and subtlety rare enough in a woman—and above all she retains, always, a sense of mystery and reserve which is perpetually alluring. If I am not careful I shall break into a sonnet. Enough!

She has been, up to a point, confidential with me; and, though in ordinary circumstances I would not betray her confidences, in a matter of this gravity I hardly feel under the seal of confession. After this rather portentous prologue, you will expect something startling; whereas really all I have discovered is that she was very much in love with Kulligrew—and feels bitterly about poor Julia Dallas. Further, against all the evidence she continues to believe in the innocence of Rourke. I said suddenly to her the other day, "Who do you think murdered Charles?" in order to watch her reaction. But she merely smiled sadly and shook her head. You are well aware of her merits as an actress.

She is still magnificent as the Lily Flower in spite of the fact that she is obviously in a state of nervous exhaustion, and nearing the end of her tether. The tragedy on the first night of the play was, of course, a terrible emotional experience for her, and she badly needs a rest, which on the advice of her doctor she is about to take. She is going abroad (just as you foresaw) and I feel I must tell you that I am sure her illness is perfectly genuine. In spite of my own conviction about this, I went to see the nerve specialist she consulted, as I felt you would want me to do so. However, he was extremely short with me, and practically showed me the door—so I needn't have troubled.

Louise is going to Monte Carlo, to lie in the sun and recuperate. She starts in about a week's time, and her understudy will fill her part—luckily the play has suffi-

*cient momentum to survive her absence for a fortnight.
I want to get away too—I have found someone to look
after things in Rourke's continued absence, and I shall
accompany Louise when she goes south. I think this is
wise, don't you?*

*Give my best regards to Miss Dallas if she is with you.
I hope to see you both before long—a line to the Hotel
Russie, Monte Carlo, will find me.*

Yours sincerely,
MARTIN PITT.

"What do you think of that?" asked Benvenuto non-committally, as she finished.

"I think—I think it's surprisingly logical, considering it's from a poet."

He laughed. "Believe me, I knew what I was about when I made him my lieutenant. But I was referring to the subject-matter."

Julia stared at the dangling end of the broken red streamer before she answered. Then she looked at Benvenuto with troubled eyes.

"It's awfully hard for me to be fair. You see, Ben, there's no love lost between me and Louise Lafontaine, and, perhaps because of that, I've tried not to consider the possibility of her guilt. I don't trust my judgment where she's concerned—I can't. But—oh, my dear—if you want to know, I think she's horrible—horrible and cruel—and—and it would be easier for me to believe that she was concerned in Charles's death than—anyone else."

"You think so, too," murmured Benvenuto.

"I—*too*? What do you mean, Ben?"

"Well, don't you think Pitt suspects her?"

Julia laughed a little bitterly. "I think he would—if he, too, weren't half in love with her. I think he's fascinated by her, and that he *does* suspect her in spite of himself. Look at his letter. He doesn't realize it—but he exalts her—and condemns her—and defends her—all in the same breath." She paused, then looked up at him sharply. "What about you, Ben? Why did you set a watch on her if you don't suspect her yourself?"

As she looked at him she thought he had not heard her question—either had not heard or did not wish to answer. Then, slowly, he said, "Perhaps—because I don't suspect her enough—"

Julia almost wrung her hands.

"Ben—have mercy on me. How much do you really *know* about all this?"

He shook his head at her reprovingly. "Nothing," he answered.

"Well then—how much do you *suspect*?"

He bent forward and looked at her earnestly. "I will tell you this. I suspect—that this was a crime committed by someone with a clever and subtle mind, a mind inflamed by a passion that is incomprehensible to the forces of law and order that are arrayed against it now. Yet I believe that this passion was the commonest of all motives—jealousy."

"But who—of whom? You mystify me more than ever. Tell me—tell me whom you suspect?"

He shook his head. "I can't. If I told—even *you*, Julia—I might break my red ribbon and lose the game. Your knowledge might be fatal when the crisis comes. Besides—I have no right. I told you—I suspect *imaginatively*."

"Then you mean—it's someone I know?"

"Yes, I believe—it's someone you know."

She sighed. "What do you propose to do now?"

"I propose to carry on as I had meant to all along. To-morrow we'll go to Monte Carlo, where Edward and Agatha can lie on the rubber beach until their shattered nerves are soothed. Meanwhile we can keep a watch on Goetz's villa—I don't feel I know half enough about that gentleman—and we can have a look for Rourke's famous head-quarters at Castellane. Damn that fellow Rourke—we must find him again; he's the key to a problem—but whether it's *the* problem I honestly don't know yet." He jumped to his feet. "Come—I find my blonde is nothing without her mask. She should wear it always. Let's go."

Throwing a last smile to her handsome Casanova, who watched her reproachfully from across the room, Julia walked beside Benvenuto to the door, then stopped with a gasp of astonishment as her eyes fell on the gaming table in the next *salon*. A few people were still standing round the green cloth, throwing their stakes on to the numbers, but sitting beside the croupier, her cheeks flushed and her hair in disorder, sat Agatha, her eyes fixed earnestly on the revolving ivory ball.

"Tiens, tiens," murmured Benvenuto, then strode over to her side. She looked up with a start and blushed guiltily.

"My *dear* Benvenuto," she said in an excited whisper, "*do* let me explain. A most kind old gentleman has shown me an infallible system of winning—and really one has only to stay here long enough to amass quite a fortune. I cannot understand why the poor dear authorities have not discovered it. Why, I myself have acquired seventeen francs. Dear me, where is my reticule?"

"The kind old gentleman has doubtless gone off with it," answered Benvenuto grimly. "What was in it, Agatha?"

"But—but—why, I had twenty francs—two very dirty notes, I remember distinctly—"

"Then you're three francs down, my dear. Cut your losses, and let's go to bed."

CHAPTER XIV
ROUGE ET NOIR

LIFE SEEMED to Julia to hang fire. What was the matter with her, she asked herself irritably, staring out of her bedroom window at the blue sunlit sea? Here she was, in Monte Carlo, for the first time in her life: Monte Carlo, which she had always imagined as an amusingly vulgar place where the last generation but one had spent its money on gambling, champagne, and patchouli-scented chorus-girls in frilly drawers; Monte Carlo, which she had always longed to visit if only in order to taste for herself an atmosphere of late Victorian indiscretion. And now here she was, sitting in an hotel bedroom after lunch, feeling terribly alone and dull. The whole trouble really was, that while lying in bed that morning she had received a note from Benvenuto, saying he had gone off in the Bugatti for a day or two, and that she was to have a good rest. Rest, she felt, was the last thing she wanted; with Benvenuto gone and Rourke still mysteriously vanished, the adventures she had anticipated seemed, more than ever, elusively round the corner. Certainly, she said to herself, she would like an adventure—but it must be in the proper company. Almost she felt like being a Tigress as a relief from the rather melancholy presences of Uncle Edward and Aunt Agatha, with whom she had spent the morning.

Coming to a sudden decision she jumped to her feet, shaking off the afternoon languor and her depression with it; Benvenuto might go off with his mystery story hidden in his brain like a pearl in a very selfish oyster—at least she could go out and find an adventure of her own. She went to her wardrobe.

Black organdie, she decided, and pearls, besides being becoming to her hair and skin, would accord well with Monte Carlo. She would be an adventuress to-day, not a *jeune fille*. She dressed quickly, excitedly, as though she were keeping an appointment, and laughed rather ruefully at the completed picture as she paused at a mirror before leaving her room. "You certainly don't look," she said to herself, "as though you were going to have tea all alone."

Outside, the streets had been freshly watered, and there was a hot smell of geraniums, roses, and damp earth from the florist's at the corner. Julia strolled through the gardens which led to the Casino; under the trees there were patches of shade, and men were spraying the highly artificial-looking grass with hose-pipes. So far, she thought, the setting was perfect for the Monte Carlo of her imagination, for the gardens were like nothing so much as a backcloth of the Folies Bergères. Outside the railings stood a line of fiacres, gaily painted horse-drawn carriages with tasselled awnings; they were charming, she thought, they reminded her of ham sleeves and flower-strewn hats and, for some reason, of the first sewing-machines. She crossed the road to the Café de Paris, sat down at a table facing the Casino, and ordered a drink. Although Monte Carlo had seemed deserted during her walk from the hotel, she was surprised to see a continuous stream of people entering the rococo portals of the building opposite. "A sinister den of vice," Agatha had called it. Well, it certainly didn't look very sinister from the outside; in fact, it was very like a railway station, she decided, watching people hurrying up the steps as if late for their trains. Something must be wrong somewhere, she reflected sadly, for there were no Champagne Charlies, and the people going in and out looked for the most part like commercial travellers, a little shabby.

She finished her drink and looked in her bag. It contained her passport and twelve hundred francs. After all, why not go in and see this notorious gambling-hell? Even though it didn't look very gay it would be more amusing than going back to the hotel to have tea with Agatha. She paid for her drink and left.

Inside the Casino the resemblance to a railway station was even more marked; having shown her passport and bought her ticket, she stood in perplexity in the great hall until an official, like a very withered churchwarden in a frock-coat, offered his advice and help. Walking beside him she suddenly felt a thrill—they were entering the roulette room. This was even vaster than the hall she had just left, and extremely businesslike in appearance except for the buxom (buxom was the word) females, rocketing in paint across the gilded ceiling. On second thoughts it was like a church—or perhaps a cathedral—and all the hushed people who stood at the tables were worshipping, very seriously, their god. Bald and pale men in black, like priests, incanted continuously, raising their rakes and sweeping away the offerings of the pious on the smooth green altars.

The god, it appeared, was round and white and made of ivory. It moved in an inscrutable and mysterious way; spun, trembled, fell, and clicked into a number.

"Zéro," chanted the chief priest, and all the offerings on the table vanished from beneath the eyes of the faithful, from whom came a faint communal sigh.

What a *very* curious game, thought Julia.

A woman, smartly dressed in black with a widow's veil, pushed past her and placed a red plaque on the number four, her fingers trembling slightly. The plaque bore the sign "1,000 francs." Again the white ball span; "Rien ne va plus," cried the priest; the woman turned away and looked at the ceiling. Julia bent forward, hardly breathing, and heard the words, "Quatre, noir, pair et impasse." The woman went very pale and touched her throat; she had won three hundred pounds.

"If Mademoiselle desires to play?" queried her guide.

Julia nodded; her heart was beating a little. At a brass grille in a corner she changed her crisp notes into symbols—hundreds, twenties, and tens of francs. Her guide bowed and left her, and feeling excited and potentially wealthy she walked back to the table she had left, her bag hard and bulky with plaques.

For a few turns of the wheel she stood behind a croupier at the end of the table, threw a few of her ten-franc pieces down "en plein," and watched them as they were raked away. On either side of her were serious-faced men and women, many of them with account-books in which they carefully entered every number as it came up. After a time Julia ceased to wonder why they practised this rite, and, deciding it must be merely a convention of gambling, she turned her attention to a bullet-headed German who was playing systematically on the dozens. Presently he took out his watch, looked at it, and gathering up several neat piles of plaques he put them in his pocket and rose. Julia slipped into the vacant chair. Here is a sensible system, she thought, and at the end of twenty minutes found she was a few hundred francs down. Obeying a hitherto-unsuspected strain of superstition she got up—the seat was no doubt an unlucky one—and hurried to another table, feeling sure she would win. Probably, she told herself, half laughing half in earnest, the ivory god must be propitiated—he revenges himself on the timid player.

She bent over the croupier's shoulder and cast five one hundred franc plaques at random on to the table, holding her breath as she heard the spin of the ball. What were her numbers—sixteen, thirty-two, twenty-seven—click! Before she had time to notice the numbers of the remaining two she saw them all raked into the side, and caught her breath. She had lost—and lost all the money she had with her, excepting one hundred-franc plaque which was gripped tightly in her left hand. She would put it on her birthday number, she decided, and, bending forward once more, she placed it on the twenty-three. This time she would look away—as the woman in black had done—and raising her eyes from the table she found them caught and held by another pair, dark as black olives in a handsome Italian face. She started slightly, her lips parting in a smile. It was Count Carrado, immaculately dressed in the smartest of grey suits, but still recognizable as the Casanova of Annécy. He was quite the best-looking person in Monte Carlo, she thought quickly as he bowed to her; in fact the only person who seemed appropriate, somehow. She looked at him in surprise as suddenly his hand shot across the table and gripped the cotton-gloved wrist of an old woman who was seated in front of her. Whatever was he doing? Then she realized what had happened—her number had come up—she had won, and the withered and painted hag in front of her was taking advantage of her absence of mind to scoop her winnings. Julia felt herself blushing painfully as, after a few murmured words between Carrado and the bank, a croupier pushed her winnings towards her.

She walked away from the table with the Italian at her side, and cashed her plaques at the grille. "Three thousand five hundred francs—and I owe it all to you really!" She laughed up at him. "If you hadn't intervened at the critical moment I should have gone away without even the price of my tea on me—I had lost everything."

"Then I consider myself indeed fortunate to have been at hand. Signorina, won't you let my fortune hold a little longer and honour me by having tea with me?"

"I—I should like to very much."

A few moments later she was seated again on the terrace of the Café de Paris, her romantic escort beside her.

"I'm beginning to enjoy Monte Carlo," she said, "though all day I have been rather dull and solitary."

"That I find hard to understand," he returned gallantly. "But indeed, signorina, you seem, an exception to every rule. Such good fortune at the tables in a woman beautiful as yourself—it is phenomenal—indeed unnatural. You know the proverb—it holds good in all languages—lucky in games of chance, unlucky—"

"Yes, I know it," said Julia, smiling a little bitterly.

"It is too much to ask me to believe it is true of yourself. For you to be unlucky in love—it is unthinkable."

"Unthinkable, perhaps, but nevertheless true. Let us talk of other things," said Julia. "How do you come to be in Monte Carlo—and at so miraculously the right moment?"

"You have not guessed? Then I will tell you. I meant to stay in Annécy, to swim in the lake and to fish and to enjoy the beauties of the old town for a few days. Then, suddenly, all is changed for me. I go to the Casino, to amuse myself—to dance—and I encounter a bright flame which sears my heart.

Like the poor moth I have to follow my flame even though I burn my wings, for I am dazzled, and the world is grey until I see you again. I remember you say you may come here to Monte Carlo, so—I jump in my car and speed after you." He raised his glass. "I drink to the bright flame of your hair and to your beautiful eyes, my Bella Rossa."

Really, thought Julia, smiling at him as for an instant his hand met and covered her own—really this is the most superb comic opera character I have ever met. She found herself responding surprisingly well to his flowered speech, and began to feel excited and pleased with her adventure. Tea had taken the form of champagne cocktails, iced and delicious; the sun shone in a blue sky; and at the next table a pair of lovers murmured to each other, oblivious of the rest of the world. Carrado was really charming, she thought, listening to his conversation, which he had tactfully subdued to a more prosaic level; and if he wasn't especially intelligent at least he had the wit to imply that he thought *she* was. If he were English she would be more critical of him, she decided, but really he was too disarmingly romantic for her to mind trifles like rings— and suede shoes—and too smart clothes. At the first pause in the conversation she wondered frantically what would interest him besides gambling, the tango, and Love.

"Isn't that a lovely car," she said, looking at a gleaming and highly coloured Stutz which was drawn up to the pavement.

"You like it? It is at your service whenever you wish."

"It is yours, Count? You will find yourself a victim of the Tiger if you drive in that at night."

"Ah—Le Tigre!" He paused. Then—"We have already had an encounter, for he attacked me on the Route des Alpes a week ago," he announced dramatically.

"Count!" She bent forward, her eyes sparkling. "Tell me— please tell me about it. You escaped him?"

For an instant the Italian frowned. "But no, he escaped *me*," he answered proudly.

By now she had lost the last of her reserve and questioned him eagerly, her eyes sparkling with excitement as the story unfolded. For once, it seemed, the Tiger had met his match, for after the hold-up Carrado, leaping from his car, had knocked away his assailant's revolver and had engaged in a hand-to-hand combat with him. Although he hesitated modestly, Julia gathered that he had given the Tiger a terrible punishment until the moment when, his foot slipping, he had lost his balance and with it his advantage, and the bandit had made off through the dark woods. Carrado had attempted, unsuccessfully, to catch him, and in the end had returned to his car, and, leaving the Tiger's Renault by the roadside, had driven off to the nearest police station to summon help. All night he and the police had hunted the roads, but the robber had disappeared, apparently into the air, and that was the last of the affair. There had been no mention of it in the papers, and Carrado, not having reported it himself, imagined that the police were hushing the matter up for fear of reproaches at letting the Tiger slip, once more, through their fingers.

Julia heard him to the end, and then, her heart beating uncomfortably, she said:

"Was he—a very big man?"

"Signorina, he was enormous—a veritable giant. His face I cannot describe to you, for the night was dark—but he had the strength of an ox."

"And was he—was he English?"

The Italian shrugged his shoulders. "That I cannot tell you either. If so, his French was surprisingly good, the little I heard of it. We were chiefly concerned with—how you say?—deeds, not words. I think perhaps he was not French. I do not know."

Then Julia remembered—Rourke had said he could pass for a Frenchman, had indeed done so on his journey in disguise from the coast to Paris. That part of his story at least was probably true. But her last lingering doubts as to his being the

Tiger had vanished when she heard the Italian's words, "Signorina, he was enormous—a veritable giant."

She would have something to tell Benvenuto.

"Tell me a thing which rouses my curiosity. All the world interests himself of the Tiger—but for you—has he an especial significance?" Julia hesitated, slowly sipping her third cocktail. The champagne was making her a little dignified. Finally she raised her eyes to those of Carrado and smiled sadly.

"You are very—swift to understand. Yes, it is true, the Tiger interests me, and in a very tragic sense." She hesitated again, and then went on confidentially. "You have to-day done me a service much greater than rescuing my winnings from that old woman at the Casino, though you do not realize it. Your description of the Tiger has done a great deal more than satisfy an idle curiosity—it has finally set the seal of knowledge upon my previous suspicions which amounted, almost, to knowledge. Don't think I am mad when I tell you—it is because of the Tiger that I am here in the South, and I am determined on his capture. I want it—more than anything in the world!"

The Italian sat back and stared in astonishment at the vehement and charming face of Julia. When he spoke his voice, though sympathetic, was faintly tinged with incredulity.

"But you, dear lady, what can you have to do with this bandit?"

"I know you must think me absurd, hysterical. You meet me at a bal masqué and then at the Casino, and I tell you I am here to hunt down the Tiger. Yet it is true, only too tragically true. You see—he killed my lover, murdered him, stabbed him in the back."

She stared in front of her, her hands clenched. She was pale, very beautiful and appealing in her black dress; Carrado's rich southern voice was deep with sympathy as he bent forward and stroked her hand.

"My poor little one—my Bella Rossa. Come, let us go away from here and drive into the mountains, where it will be peaceful. You shall tell me everything, and you must let me help you in your search for this assassin."

A few minutes later the Stutz had left Monte Carlo behind, and was gliding swiftly up the tortuous road under the skilful hands of Carrado. Julia felt relaxed and comforted by his sympathy, and enjoyed the cool air sweeping past her face. Suddenly a thought struck her. He had offered to help her; why not take him at his word and ask him to drive her to Castellane, where they might search for Rourke's farm-house? There was at least a chance they might get news of him. When she proposed it her companion instantly agreed, and soon the car was pointing towards the Route des Alpes, while Julia bit by bit described to him the story of Kulligrew's murder, the disappearance of Terence Rourke, and their subsequent meeting with him in Lyon. Carrado was a good listener, his few questions unfailingly tactful, and, when she had finished, his renewed promises of help made her feel comforted and hopeful. In dealing with Rourke they couldn't have too many recruits, she felt, and Carrado was a particularly valuable one since he not only possessed a powerful car and plenty of leisure, but had a private score of his own to settle. She asked more questions about his meeting with the Tiger, and his every answer confirmed by some little touch the identity of Rourke.

Gradually they fell silent, enjoying the beauty of the late afternoon sunlight on the mountains. It was difficult to keep one's mind in tune with crime and dark mysteries in a classic countryside where white rocks piled up against a blue sky, and the scent of wild lavender hung in the air. For the most part the road was deserted, though sometimes they saw peasants gathering lavender on the hillsides, and once they slowed down to pass a herd of goats under the charge of a small boy. Towards Castellane the country was greener and more fertile, dotted with farm-houses, and seemed, thought Julia, like the Promised Land. As she looked at the isolated farms she wondered whether one of them belonged to Terence Rourke;

some stood proudly on the tops of small hills and reminded Carrado of Italy, he told her, with their massive stone walls and round towers.

At last they reached Castellane, and both exclaimed at the beauty of the small village, built round a dramatic upheaval of rock surmounted by a statue. They drew up in the village square, where local youths were playing a half-hearted game of *boule*, and found the car door opened for them by a decrepit-looking old peasant, whose grey hairs straggled over a dirty and bearded face. Julia got down quickly to escape from an aura of garlic which spread round him, then pulled herself together. If she was to do any useful work she mustn't be squeamish, she told herself; and turning back she proceeded to describe Rourke to the old creature, asking if he had seen a monsieur like that in the village. But he shook his head. He was a stranger, he announced, a *poveretto* who wandered the countryside with no home and many afflictions, he went on, proceeding to unbutton his shirt. Carrado hurriedly stepped between them, and throwing him a tip told the old man to look after the car while they dined. Then he took Julia's arm and led her towards a restaurant with a terrace giving on to the Place.

"The first throw was unlucky," he smiled at her, "but in the end you win, as you did at the tables."

"Thanks to you," she reminded him. "Perhaps it was an omen."

Monsieur and Madame at the little restaurant received them with many bows, and after installing Julia in a chair from which she had a charming view of the village street, Carrado went off with them to attend to the mixing of cocktails himself. Julia sat back and powdered her nose at the little mirror in her bag. Surveying herself critically she realized she was looking better than she had for days—her eyes bright, and her cheeks, perhaps because of the champagne, slightly flushed. For a moment she wished Carrado wouldn't give her so many cocktails; then, half defiantly, thought after all—why not? For weeks, indeed for months, she had lived in an atmosphere of repression, never feeling wholly happy or natural during her engagement to Charles. Then had come tragedy, and after it mystery and uncertainty all round her. For to-day at least, she decided, she would escape from her own life and live an absurd, gay and artificial existence, as though she had, for the time, taken upon herself a new personality. Not only the champagne had gone to her head—everything, meeting Carrado, winning money at the tables, and above all the feeling of being once again in the South; everything conspired to help her reaction of half reckless gaiety. When her host returned, followed by the *patron* with ice-dimmed glasses on a tray, Julia greeted him radiantly. He looked at her across the table.

"For hunting Tigers," he announced, "and for other big games one must eat. Otherwise one has not the courage—and is oneself devoured. So let us dine here, in aria fresca, behind this bay tree whose leaves shall crown our glorious attempts. Imagine, signorina, the hearty cheers of crowds when you, like Diana, and I your Italian servant, your slave, your worshipper, shall lay at the foot of a policeman the corpse of the assassin!"

He rose from the table, and, bending forward, gracefully kissed Julia's hand, retaining it in his own as he sat down again and smiling across at her. His enthusiasm for victory was a little premature, thought Julia, but that was typical of his race. What better adjutant could she have than this tall, athletic, handsome Italian? What fun if they really caught the Tiger, after the cavalier way in which Benvenuto had treated her, going off by himself.

"We will make some inquiries after dinner," she said, "and perhaps come up here to-morrow—if you have not a rendezvous elsewhere."

"Do not be cruel," he murmured. "How can the poor moth make rendezvous—save with the bright flame which draws him?"

It was a little difficult, she decided inconsequently, eating one's dinner with only one hand; but still Carrado's animated conversation, his lively descriptions of Italy interspersed by the most tender gallantries, well made up for any slight inconvenience. Also perhaps it was rather comforting in a way, she thought a little later, to have something to hold on to—in a world which had a tendency to sway and tip. She would not, she decided, bother to eat any more—after all, she wasn't hungry—the evening was too hot. How strangely the late sun illuminated the village, bathing it in a yellow light where things became confused and unreal. Everything seemed strange, even the behaviour of Carrado who, with his free hand, was writing something on a slip of paper, handing it to the *patron*. Surely one did not write notes while entertaining a lady. But then Carrado was an Italian—he was different, everything was different in this vague and sunlit world. She smiled at him forgivingly.

How charming he was—how charming life in general was. She was just thinking that the one thing she wanted to make her happiness complete was a comfortable chair, where she could lie back and slip into the delicious dream world that seemed to summon her, when she found the *patronne* bending over her, a fat and homely presence with a smiling face. How kind she was, thought Julia, following her into the house, and how sympathetic. The little staircase was narrow and dark, but at the top a door opened into a large room, cool and twilit behind its closed curtains. And there was a great bed— smooth and white and welcoming. Delicious!

• • • • •

Her heart beating violently, Julia found herself sitting up in bed in a dark room, with the memory of a crash, heard in her sleep, still ringing in her ears.

Where was she?

There was the noise again, and this time something came flying through the window and landed with a bump on the floor. Hardly knowing what she did she groped for a switch beside her bed, found it, and turned on the light. Then she remembered; she had been dining with Carrado—but it was dark now. She had been asleep. Heavens! Had he waited downstairs for her for hours? Her mind racing, she bent down and picked up the thing which had been thrown in at the window. It was a stone, and round it a piece of notepaper with something scribbled on it. She bent down to the lamp by the bed. "*Echappez vite*" she read, scrawled across the paper in an uneducated hand. Shivering she put her hand to her head and ran to the window. There was no one below; then back across the room to the door.

But it was locked.

CHAPTER XV
FLIGHT IN THE DARK

IT WAS TOO fantastic; Julia laughed, thinking to herself that the adventure she had desired was working out in the good old-fashioned way—quite the Elephant and Castle tradition; if only one had a hatpin one could use it as a weapon of defence. Seriously, she thought to herself, she had better be careful, and going to the door she slid the bolt and wedged a chair underneath the handle. That was better; only unfortunately it had the effect of making her feel more like a prisoner than ever.

She looked round the bedroom again. The window was small, though not impossibly so, and she was about to go and examine it as a means of escape when the door handle turned softly from the outside. Obviously Carrado, she thought calmly; the successful adventurer come to Clasp her in his Arms. She must get away quickly; but where? He would follow her into the village and, possessing the only car, had rather a mean advantage.

"Cara mia! Open thy door!"

Italian, the language of romance, thought Julia, suppressing a nervous desire to laugh. Far from feeling romantic she was cold, and had a slight headache.

What *was* the most sensible thing to do?

Coming to a sudden decision she went quietly across to a huge armoire that stood against the wall, and opening it she looked inside. Evidently it contained the family wardrobe, for she saw a dingy collection of hats and coats, shoes, dresses and trousers. Quickly she selected a long black cape, a wide straw hat such as peasant women wear in the fields, and, as a last thought, an umbrella. In an instant her organdie frock, her pearls, and her bright hair were covered—with the hat tied beneath her chin her face was almost invisible and, the big black umbrella in her hand, she resembled quite surprisingly a local country-woman.

She hurried to the window, to a rising accompaniment of passionate murmured Italian which came from the other side of the door, and looking out into the darkness of a little court-yard she saw to her astonishment a ladder leaning against the wall, provided apparently by Providence. Though the cloak and umbrella were difficult to control she reached the ground in safety, and hurried down a passage-way into the street. Her half-formed resolve of driving off in Carrado's car had to be abandoned, for the Place was given over to revelry and *boule* playing, and there beside the Stutz lounged a *garde champêtre*. It was impossible to face him in her present costume; there was nothing for it but to make her way on foot to the next village, and hire a car back to Monte Carlo. So thinking, she turned up a narrow lane between houses, which looked as though it might lead round again to the main road. It was dark; only the stars gave a faint glimmer of light, and she felt fairly secure; which was fortunate, for her high heels slipped on the rough cobbles, making progress difficult.

Well, it wasn't so bad. She had shaken off her passionate count, and even though she had made no discoveries in Castellane—beyond learning the technique of Italian love-making—the day had not been entirely fruitless, owing to Carrado's account of his meeting with Rourke. She would, she supposed, get home somehow; so what was there to worry about?

Only it was rather lonely in the solitary lane; she had left the houses behind and on either side of the cobbles rose a stone wall. She walked on more quickly, her footsteps echoing loudly. Darker and darker it grew, away from the lights of the town, louder and louder the echo of her steps, curious and uneven. She stopped, her heart in her mouth.

Footsteps were following her, rather heavy footsteps; quickly and menacingly they followed her. Clinging still to the cloak and umbrella as to familiar mascots, she ran forward up the lane which now climbed steeply away from the town and the lights of the main road. Soon she was breathing quickly, so steep was the ascent, and behind her the man was running, catching her up. Gasping, she stopped and turned at bay, the umbrella, her only weapon, held in the "prepare to receive cavalry" position, as a bright light from a torch blinded her.

"You damned little fool!"

Julia gave a hysterical laugh and sat down suddenly in the road.

"Ben!"

He snorted, and sat down beside her.

"Confound you, Julia; next time you want to train for the Ladies' Marathon leave me out. I presume you were under the impression that you were exercising an elegant Italian—let me disillusion you."

He turned the flash lamp on his face, revealing himself—she almost shrieked—as the filthy and ragged tramp from the village.

"Ben! Oh, Ben, you wretch—you were there all the time."

"Fortunately for you, young woman, I was—and a fine mess you've made of everything. I'll explain. I got into Castellane early this morning in my present costume, and was getting along excellently, scraping acquaintance with the people, who are an amiable lot, and doing various little jobs for them like dealing with garbage and chopping wood. This afternoon the grocer took me on, telling me to decant some wine from a barrel into bottles—and while he was having a quiet drink with a friend, I managed to snatch a glance at the shop ledger. I only had a minute, so I looked for one thing—whisky. I found it—Irish whisky too—sent in large quantities to the 'Clos des Oliviers' for Monsieur Orage. What does *orage* mean in English, Julia?"

"Storm, I believe," she answered coldly. He was rather unsympathetic, and seemed to be talking nonsense.

"Exactly. Storm. Gale. Terence Gale Rourke? It's at least possible, you know—combined with the whisky. Anyhow, I managed to find out by stealth where the Clos des Oliviers is, and hear it's a farm-house about three kilometres away in a lonely spot on a hillside—this hillside in fact. Belongs to Monsieur Orage, but there's no one there now. I was hanging about waiting for nightfall when you and Carrado turned up—most romantic, but a little ill-timed so far as I was concerned. However, I wasn't going to worry about you—it was your affair—until the patron at the hotel, who was giving me some food, started to talk about your cavalier. He'd been there before, the old chap said, with an actress; and with many nods and winks he gave me to understand that you were obviously a 'poule de luxe,' one of the expensive English kind. Then I began to think you might have bitten off rather more than you could chew, and when I saw young Casanova mixing cocktails himself I was sure of it. I hung about the place, and when you'd had dinner, I saw your boy friend slip a note into Madame's hand, after which she proceeded to take you upstairs to a bedroom. I realized by then that he'd put something into your drink, but I couldn't do anything without revealing myself as a false tramp, which was the last thing I wanted; Carrado sat on the terrace and drank with the patron, and as soon as he showed signs of moving I sloped off, borrowed a ladder from a neighbouring shed, wrote you that note, chucked it in at the window and retired to await developments. The next thing I knew you were strolling about the square dressed as a witch, and then streaking up this lane as if the Fiend were after you. I followed as soon as I could, and here we are—with the whole evening wasted."

Julia stared at the stars in silence. She didn't feel a very distinguished figure, but she still had one trump to play.

"Ben," she said, "I know you think I'm an awful little fool as well as a damn nuisance, and I'm inclined to agree with you. But at least I've found out something to-day which will interest you. And it's about Rourke."

"What's that?" inquired Benvenuto sharply.

"Well, my romantic escort, the Count Carrado, was held up by the Tiger one night last week, and hopped out of his car and had a hand-to-hand fight with him in the dark. The Tiger escaped into the woods, leaving his Renault by the roadside, and Carrado lost him. He reported about it to the police at the nearest village, but they failed to catch him."

"What's that got to do with Rourke?"

"Everything, silly. I questioned Carrado closely about the Tiger, and from his answers there isn't a shadow of a doubt that Rourke and the Tiger are one and the same. He said he was enormous—a veritable giant with the strength of an ox, and when I asked if he was English, he said he couldn't tell— the few words which he heard the Tiger speak being in perfect French, yet somehow giving the impression that he wasn't a Frenchman. It seems to me conclusive—there aren't many people of Rourke's size in the world."

Benvenuto grunted. "I must meet your boy friend—he sounds interesting. Meanwhile I'm cold, so I suggest we get a move on. What do you say to coming up to the Clos des Oliviers with me? I want to nose round it to-night—and you look sufficiently like a peasant to avert suspicion if we should meet anyone."

In a few moments the curious-looking pair were climbing the hillside towards a lonely farm-house.

CHAPTER XVI
IRISH WHISKY

THE RISEN MOON painted the olive grove a silvery grey and touched to life the black window-panes of the house which rose above the trees.

"Odd," remarked Benvenuto in a low voice. "Looks as if someone went off in a hurry, to have left the windows unshuttered. It seems deserted—let's go round to the back."

It was a typical Provençal farm-house, square and strongly built of stone with a deep over-hanging roof of curly tiles. It looked peaceful and domesticated, the garden and vine-shaded terrace showing signs of careful tending, and was quite unlike the outlaw's retreat that Julia had imagined. In fact it was exactly the kind of house she would like herself, she thought, sniffing the scent of lavender and fragrant herbs as she followed Benvenuto down the garden.

As they turned the corner into the court-yard at the back, both stopped in amazement. Far from the house being deserted, a party appeared to be going on. The back windows were shuttered, but between the shutters came streaks of light and the sound of a deep throaty voice, singing:

"Le Chef de Gare il est cocu!"

As the verse ended there was a roar of laughter, then a crash, followed by more laughter.

Ben and Julia looked at each other in astonishment.

"Too bad we weren't invited," he murmured, then clutched her arm as another voice, also masculine but rather high and tremulous, started to sing in English.

"Why did they dig Ma's grave so deep
Under the clay so dee-eep—?"

came quavering out into the darkness; Benvenuto darted forward, Julia behind him, and pulling the shutters slightly apart, peered into the room.

It was a large, bare, whitewashed kitchen with an open fireplace hung with gleaming copper pots. In the middle of the room was a scrubbed wooden table bearing several lighted candles which illuminated two men who sat at either end, apparently in rather strained and uncomfortable positions, in two heavy wooden armchairs. Before each man was a whisky bottle with a straw sticking out of the top; and the two watchers at the window saw one man, who was large and fat and wearing uniform with his cap tilted over one eye, bend stiffly forward and suck with a good deal of satisfaction at his straw. The other man, who was small and sandy, had his eyes fixed on the ceiling and was engaged, with morbid relish in his voice, in bringing his song to a triumphant conclusion:

"Why did they leave me here to weep?
Why did they dig Ma's grave so deep?"

Benvenuto's face expressed both astonishment and delight as he looked at Julia.

"Of all the—Julia, you see me for the first time completely bouleversé," he whispered. "Do you realize—inside that room a responsible inspector of the C.I.D. and a French agent de police are making whoopee?"

Julia stifled her laughter. "Of course—it's Mr. Leech; I recognize him now. But why are they both holding their hands behind their backs? And drinking through straws?"

Benvenuto chuckled. "A solution occurs to me. The poor boobs are tied in their chairs."

"But how—?"

"My dear Julia, you can depend upon it, it's an Irish joke—like the whisky."

"Ben—you mean—Terence Rourke has been here?"

"And how! But we'll soon know. I think we'll have to rescue the combined police forces of France and England, and hear their story."

Inside the room the fat *agent* was speaking. "Très bien, mon vieux—très bien," he roared. "Tu connais 'Les Fraises et les Framboises'?"

"Non," replied Leech, and looked round with an exclamation as Benvenuto smashed a pane of glass, opened the window and climbed into the room. He walked across to the table, took a knife from his pocket and, without saying a word, cut the cords that bound the two men.

Julia, from outside, saw them staring at him open-mouthed, then stagger to their feet and, supporting themselves against the table, begin to rub their numbed legs and arms. The *agent* addressed Benvenuto in French.

"A thousand thanks, monsieur—we have been overpowered by superior—er—numbers. We represent the *Law*, and the assassin shall not escape us!" He attempted to straighten his cap but the effort was too much, and he fell under the table. Benvenuto assisted him back into his chair and moved across to Leech, who addressed him carefully. "Une verre d'eau, s'il vous plait, monsieur."

"My dear old Leech, you shall have one," responded Benvenuto cheerfully, "and so will I, with a little of that whisky."

"Good gracious me, if it isn't Mr. Brown!" gasped Leech. "Wherever did you spring from, sir?"

Benvenuto set a jug of water on the table and sighed. "If my painstaking and somewhat tedious progress through the night can be described as a spring, the answer is—Castellane. Here is my cousin, Miss Dallas, who sprang with me. Sit down, Julia, and have a drink. Really, you know, Leech, our presence here isn't surprising at all—you knew we were out here, and for what purpose—but *your* present situation really intrigues me. How did you come to occupy it?"

Leech looked embarrassed and gave a slight cough.

"Well, here's your very good health—*and* yours, Miss Dallas. Fancy you turning up like that. Wonders will never cease, as the saying goes."

He put down his glass and then addressed them in firmer tones.

"I've been sent out by the Yard, sir, with a warrant for the arrest of Terence Gale Rourke. I know *your* views on the subject, Mr. Brown, but it wasn't possible to delay the matter any longer—the evidence against him is too strong. We got the address of this little place from a letter from Rourke's caretaker, which arrived at his flat in London, and I arrived here to-day together with—er—Gustave there, who's an *agent* from the Sûreté, and who joined me in Paris. We heard in the village that the accused Rourke, who goes by the name of Orage, meaning Storm in these parts, was away and hadn't been seen for some time. I came up to this place this evening, and finding the back door open I entered and commenced a search for certain papers which we believe to be here. The house was apparently deserted, and I decided the caretaker had left the door ajar, and that Gustave and I had the place to ourselves, and then—well, Mr. Brown, I'm not usually caught napping, but this time I *was*. It won't do me any good at the Yard, and if you and Miss Dallas would preserve a spot of sub rosa about it I'd be very much obliged I'm sure. Anyhow, this is how it happened, sir. I sent Gustave upstairs while I did the ground floor, so to speak. I finished examining that bureau over there, and then I turned my attention to the big chest under the window. I'd just opened the lid when someone got me by the back of the neck, if you follow me, with a grip like iron, took hold of my feet with his other hand, and there I was in the chest on a lot of damp linen—unpleasant it was, I can tell you—with the lid shut down and locked before I could say Mussolini. I shouted to Gustave to look out, and heard him coming down the stairs, and then a bang at the bottom, by which I inferred, and rightly as it turned out, that he'd been tripped up. Before he knew where he was his hands were tied behind his back, so he told me, and he was bound and gagged in that arm-chair. All this time our assailant was laughing as though he thought it was some kind of a Christmas party."

Leech's aggrieved expression at this point was sufficiently comic to make Julia want to smile, but a glance at Benvenuto restrained her. He nodded at Leech encouragingly, and the story went on.

"At last the lid of the chest was unlocked, and a big man who I recognized as the accused Rourke, knelt on my chest and went through my pockets, taking out a pair of handcuffs and the warrant for his arrest. He soon had the bracelets on me, my movements being a bit restricted as you might say, and then he hauls me up and ties me in the arm-chair at the other end of the table from Gustave, roaring with laughter all the time. When he stopped laughing for a minute I said to him, 'I am a police inspector from Scotland Yard. I arrest you, Terence Gale Rourke, on a charge of murdering Lord Charles Kulligrew.' I gave him the usual warning, but this made him laugh more than ever, and considering everything perhaps it wasn't the best moment for arresting him, if you follow me."

"I follow you perfectly, Leech," said Benvenuto sympathetically.

"Well, he lit the candles and read the warrant for his arrest, and then in spite of my protests he took out a fountain pen and wrote something on it. What it was I don't know, for his next action was to take a carving knife and affix the document to that beam."

Julia's eyes followed the direction of Leech's indignant gesture, and saw a long knife which quivered slightly in the candlelight and which served to hold in place a sheet of paper on the timbered ceiling. In an instant Benvenuto had mounted a chair and removed the warrant from its undignified position; Julia, looking over his shoulder as he spread it on the table in front of Leech, saw that the words "Terence Gale Rourke" had been crossed out, and in their place was written in a firm hand "Adolf Goetz."

Leech looked up at Benvenuto with wrinkled brows.

"Adolf Goetz, eh? Now where have I heard that name before?"

"You're going to hear it again before you've finished," said Benvenuto. "I want to have a talk with you about him. Meanwhile, how does the end of the story go, Leech? We hang upon your lips—metaphorically of course."

"Well, there's precious little more to recount, Mr. Brown. The accused having brought in the whisky he placed bottles in front of each of us, with straws in them, took the bracelets off me after making sure I was firmly secured by ropes, pushed our chairs close up to the table—quite thoughtful he was—and then went out—though not before he'd taken some papers out of that very chest I'd been lying in, and burnt them in the grate. After we'd heard his car drive off Gustave and me looks at each other, and takes a sip or two of the whisky. We shouted a bit, but no one came near, and in the end we decided to pass the time away by having a little sing-song. What Gustave was singing just before you came along was his national war song, so he tells me."

"And Rourke?" asked Benvenuto. "Did he say anything before he left?"

Leech shook his head dolefully. "Not a single word the whole time. He just laughed."

"Too late again," sighed Benvenuto. "We were on his track ourselves, hence the fancy dress. We can't do anything here—let's get back to Monte Carlo. And, once there, I want to have a serious talk with you, Leech."

He crossed over to where the *agent* was peacefully sleeping off the effects of unadulterated Irish whisky. "Upsy daisy, Gustave. Allons y," he said.

CHAPTER XVII
GATE-CRASHERS

THE PATH WOUND steeply up through cork and olive trees and the sun burned in a hard blue sky, its heat reflecting from the dry rocks. Far below on the edge of the placid sea lay Monte Carlo, like some charming and innocent toy city with its pink roofs and tiny harbour, while across the blue water the white sails of scattered yachts hung in a painted stillness. On the high mountain path no breath of wind disturbed the air, and the whole earth, the hard rocks, the scented herbs and the grey leaves of the olive trees seemed arrested, lifeless and brittle under the sun. There was no sound but the harsh, monotonous creaking of the cicadas, and the rattle of stones that rolled from beneath the feet of two people who struggled, panting, up the path.

Julia led the way, a big hat pushed back on her head like a straw halo round her bright curls, and a frown of determination showing above her small freckled nose as she scrambled on, holding her cotton skirt high above the stones and bushes. Behind her marched Benvenuto, painting materials strapped to his back and a pipe in his mouth, looking cheerful and cool in spite of the heat in a pair of paint-bespattered trousers and a blue and white striped *tricot*.

"Should the enemy feel disposed to pour boiling oil on our heads," he remarked, pausing and looking upward, "now is his time."

"I feel like a mass of boiling oil as it is," returned Julia gloomily, "and I'm very much afraid, Ben, that the enemy isn't in residence. Have you ever seen anything more lifeless?"

Above their heads a great yellow stone building, more like a fortress than a house with its shuttered windows and two round watch-towers, rose magnificently from the crest of the rock. Formal lines of cypress trees surrounded it, piercing the sky like black swords, and adding somehow to the air of unconquerable strength and dignity that pervaded it. It was difficult to give any date to the architecture, it seeming as though the house had always stood there, the natural conclusion to the uprising strata of rock.

Benvenuto shook his head. "Impossible to say whether it contains the quick or the dead. Anyhow it's worth the climb to see it at close quarters. That must be the main gate round the corner—you can just see the road coming over the top of the hill. Courage—we're nearly at the top."

Another ten minutes' scrambling, and they stood breathless on a dusty road before a great wrought-iron gateway. Within the gates a cypress-lined drive led to a paved courtyard in front of the house. Julia peered through the delicate iron tracery, and saw rows of shuttered windows and a magnificent front door with stone carving above it. Utterly silent the house lay, the court-yard and the yellow stone walls shimmering in the heat, and yet giving an effect of frigidity by their stern aloofness.

"It's rather fine, Ben, isn't it?—and yet rather—sepulchral somehow. Exactly the sort of house the Skeleton ought to have. I can imagine him clanking his chains round those shuttered rooms." Julia instinctively lowered her voice, though she was smiling.

Benvenuto's hand was on the gate. "Locked," he announced. "It looks deserted enough, but I don't feel entirely satisfied." He pondered a moment. Then—"Look here, Julia, I'm going to get into that garden. It ought to be possible to scale the wall somewhere. Suppose you go along to the village and wait for me in a café? You could get a drink, and cool down."

She almost snorted. "My poor Ben, if you think you're going to have all the fun after I've climbed a practically vertical mountain and burnt myself black in the sun, you're *wrong*. You can't shake me off while there's the remotest chance of putting up a suspected Tiger, so forget it. Come on."

She set off quickly along the side of a high wall which enclosed the garden, Benvenuto after her. For about a quarter of a mile they followed a rough track, until Julia began to think the wall enclosed half France and began also to despair of ever finding a possible foothold in the smooth stonework.

Gradually the track was leading them round two sides of a square towards the edge of the precipice, and when they came to a clearing where woodcutters had been at work Benvenuto stopped.

"If you'll give me a hand we'll roll a pile of these logs under the wall. It's our only hope of getting over," he said.

And in a few minutes, perspiring but triumphant, they were astride the top of the wall. Julia looked about her and gasped, while Benvenuto jumped down on to some soft earth below. The great house faced her, half obscured by the tree-grown garden, and from where she sat she could see one of the round watch-towers, and a façade broken by curved iron balconies in front of the windows. The garden was well kept and beautiful, elaborate with fountains and statuary, and on her left she could see the grey and green mountain-side falling sheer down, then flattening into a map-like view of the town and the sea.

"D'you mind coming to earth? You're just a shade conspicuous up there," came Benvenuto's voice from below her, and she jumped into his outstretched arms. They wandered cautiously along shady paths in the direction of the house, and still there was no sound or sign of life. A turn in the path brought them suddenly to an open space where a Roman lady in stone presided over a grove of laurels, and Benvenuto gave an ecstatic exclamation.

"I've got to make a sketch of this, Julia. Here, you sit down and keep an eye on the house. I won't be long."

Julia, seating herself under a tree, realized that she, Adolf Goetz, and the adventure, were forgotten. Benvenuto's hands were busy with tubes of paint and brushes, while with head on one side he studied the scene before him. It didn't seem much good keeping an eye on the house, silent and desolate, a hundred yards away from her. He'd said that just to keep her quiet—like offering a picture-book to a child.

Really men are impossible, she thought, absurdly transparent. Even the very nicest men, like Charles or Martin Pitt or Ben, who listened to one's conversation and one's theories of life, only did it as a kind of convention of gallantry, to humour one, as it were. Perhaps, after all, the Latins were the most honest, men like Carrado who made no pretence of offering one anything more intelligent than a well-turned compliment, and started to pinch one right away. Still, even if the Anglo-Saxon approach *were* only a convention it was a very pleasant one, she decided, and entailed discussions on books and pictures and life, before one's hand was so much as squeezed. *Il faut en profiter*. Of course Ben was different—he was her cousin, and he seemed—he always had—more like her elder brother than anything. He played the Mental Equality game as well as anyone—only sometimes he forgot. She smiled affectionately at the back of his rumpled head and watched the swift strokes of his brush. Dear me, she was forgetting the house—and turning her head she looked at it, still silent and mysterious. How hot it was—even in the shade. She felt more than a little sleepy.

"I see you are interested in the Sur-Réalistes, monsieur."

Julia leapt to her feet, speechless with fright, to see the suave, bony face of the Skeleton behind her. He had approached them in complete silence, and stood leaning on a stick, his thin, bent form dressed in formal black and starched linen.

"So much so, Herr Goetz, that I have been wishing all the morning that a naturally timid disposition did not prevent me from breaking into your house as well as your garden. In fact, if you hadn't turned up, I'm not at all sure that my desire to see your very distinguished collection of paintings wouldn't have got the better of me, and made me attempt to storm your battlements. Excuse me!"

Putting a final touch to the rather abstract version of a laurel bush which adorned his canvas, Benvenuto jumped to his feet, and turning round he bowed to Adolf Goetz. A slightly ironic smile appeared for a moment on the bony face as Goetz inclined his head politely to them both.

"Fortunately, monsieur, such desperate measures are made unnecessary by our meeting," he said. "I shall be proud to introduce my small collection to the possessor of so much talent. But—you have the advantage of me, since you know both my name and my principal hobby, while I—yet one moment. Permit me—" He stepped in front of the canvas and studied it thoughtfully, then slowly nodded his head. "In 1928," he went on, "an English painter, whose name until then was little known in this country, gave an exhibition of his work at a gallery in the Rue de la Boètie in Paris, and caused no little excitement among the critics. His name, if I am not mistaken was—Benvenuto Brown."

Julia looked from one to the other in amazement, and almost pinched herself to see if she was awake. For Benvenuto, she realized, was actually *pleased*, embarrassed in his pleasure like a small boy, as he made some stammering reply to Adolf Goetz. "You idiot," she addressed him mentally, "to be taken in by such an obvious piece of flattery." She looked again at the canvas, in front of which they were both standing, discussing some point of technique: a small square canvas upon which was a collection of what she privately considered eccentric daubs of paint. Yet Goetz had had the effrontery to pretend that from it he could tell the artist's name as plainly as from a visiting-card. And, more amazing still, here was Benvenuto drinking it all in, listening almost reverently to his criticism, completely fooled by a skilful compliment. Yes, Goetz was clever, she decided, shuddering a little as she looked at him—clever and cunning. Obviously he had had them both under his eye, and knew their business. He—but he had turned and was speaking to her.

"Surely," came the precise, carefully modulated, slightly foreign voice, "surely I am right in thinking I have the honour to entertain Miss Julia Dallas?"

"You are no doubt a magician, Herr Goetz—and a very clever one," answered Julia smiling, and praying that Benvenuto's eyes would now be opened to the absurd pretence, "for that certainly is my name. Is it permitted to inquire into the secret of how the magician has come by his knowledge in *my* case?"

A faint answering smile disturbed for a moment the grave ivory mask. "The explanation, Miss Dallas, is a simple—and rather terrible—one, in which magic has no part. I will explain—but please do not linger here in the heat. A few steps in the sunshine, and we shall enter my house, which remains cool in the hottest weather thanks to the defensive instincts of the original builder."

Her heart beating fast Julia walked beside him along the sun-flecked path, and tried to appear calm and collected, and to respond intelligently to Goetz's description of the history of his house. Here, she felt sure, there awaited dangers and adventures which would make her previous escapade pale into insignificance—and she was extremely thankful for the presence of Benvenuto, walking behind them with his canvas. Surely by now he must realize that Goetz was playing them like two foolish fish on a line.

From the brilliant heat of the garden they walked into the cool dimness of a stone-flagged hall. Julia, pausing and looking appreciatively round at ancient carving, the subdued glitter of antique mirrors, and the few heavy chests and armoires standing against the walls, felt that here, had he lived in another age, Goetz would have assembled his men-at-arms and sent them out on errands of pillage and extortion into the surrounding country. As it was, he was leading them politely towards a great staircase, at the foot of which he hesitated.

"It would be true kindness to a solitary being," he said, "if you would stay and lunch with me. Also it would enable you to see my pictures in a leisurely fashion, which always seems to me the only possible way to enjoy them. To hurry over a picture is like hurrying over a good meal—it is not only a crime but one which brings its own punishment in the form of æsthetic indigestion. I cannot offer anything but the simplest lunch, I am afraid, but possibly it would be more palatable than the miserable meal they give you in the village."

Very nicely worded, thought Julia as she accepted, particularly as they were now without doubt his prisoners. Goetz was speaking in German to a bullet-headed man-servant who had shut the heavy doors behind them, and once again Julia glanced round the cool dim hall. Then an insignificant object caught her eye, an object curiously out of place amongst the ancient furnishings, but one which made her spirits rise. It was a telephone.

Meanwhile Benvenuto was placidly examining some carvings above the stairway, and the next moment they all three went up to a picture-hung gallery above the main hall.

Benvenuto gave a low whistle as he looked about him.

"I could stay here," he announced, "for weeks."

"But this," replied Goetz quietly, "is only a prelude."

CHAPTER XVIII
"YOU SEE, I KNOW WHO KILLED HIM"

"Do you like my Douanier Rousseau?"

Slowly Julia took her eyes from the painting in front of which she was standing, and raised them to the man at her side.

"Like is hardly the word, Herr Goetz," she said. "It is beautiful—and terrible—and I don't think I shall ever forget it."

He looked down at her speculatively and slowly nodded his head.

"But you know," she hurried on, "I don't think I see it as you do, or as my cousin does—purely æsthetically. I'm probably far too interested in the subject—and not only because of the—stimulant it was to the painter."

"Miss Dallas, I expect you have been appreciating it in precisely the way the Douanier would have liked you to have appreciated it. Remember, he did not live in Montparnasse or Bloomsbury, was not half-painter, half-critic. He was a customs official with a divine imagination who found his inspiration in coloured post cards and cheap prints. He never saw a jungle in his life—never watched the beasts of the jungle moving stealthily through the strange exotic foliage that he paints, or sat in a safe and æsthetic ecstasy in some tree-top studying the pure colour values of a tiger. And thank God he did not, since he has so unself-consciously created for us the beauty and the terror which you feel. It was a great day for me when I brought this painting home—and planned the decoration of this small room to receive it. And now, I cannot allow you to look at anything else—I am sure you are tired with standing so long, and that a cocktail will mean more to you than any picture ever painted. Let us go down."

Julia walked beside him to the door and turned for one last look at the strange, exciting beauty of the painted tiger, arrested for all time in his path through the green flames of jungle foliage, heraldic, significant and mysterious. Then she followed her host through the long gallery, its walls flowering with the limpid beauties of Renoir and the passion of Van Gogh, and felt she was moving through a fantastic dream-world whose dangers lay hidden somewhere behind the personality of her extraordinary host and his disturbingly beautiful possessions.

What *was* Goetz? Why did he live in this silent fortress, alone, except for his works of art? Watching him among his paintings, Julia's fear of him was replaced by intense curiosity. Of one thing at least she was sure—he must be very wealthy to have amassed so perfect a collection—so wasn't it at least arguable that he might have made his fortune by criminal activities in order to satisfy his ruling passion? The theory, Julia caught herself thinking, had at least the advantage of making Terence Rourke's story seem more probable. She watched Goetz detach Benvenuto from the absorbed contemplation of a Gauguin, and they went down to lunch.

During a delicious meal of iced soup, a truffle omelette, chicken cooked in the Spanish fashion, and northern strawberries, perfectly served by two German men-servants, Adolf Goetz proved himself an excellent host. He entertained them with talk of his experiences in different parts of the world, and incidents in the history of the gradual collection of his paintings, yet never seemed to deliver a monologue but rather stimulated his guests to talk. Julia found herself discussing music and the theatre with Goetz as though she had known him for years, and Benvenuto, sipping his Hermitage '21, seemed completely at peace with the world, and to have found in his host a companion after his own heart. The room in which they sat was broad and lofty, furnished with superb examples of Italian and Provençal furniture which were sufficiently solid and simple to be in keeping with the ancient stone house. Outside was a terrace looking over the mountain slope and the sea, and lunch being over they moved their chairs to the long, open windows, where they were served with coffee, and venerable brandy in huge bubbles of glasses.

Then abruptly Goetz turned to Julia.

"Miss Dallas," he said, "you have with admirable restraint refrained from asking me how I came to recognize you when we met in my garden; and in order to explain myself I shall have to talk of a subject which must be inexpressibly painful to you. I was"—he paused, twisting the stem of his glass in his fingers—"a great admirer, though never to my infinite regret a friend, of your late fiancé, Lord Charles Kulligrew."

What is coming, thought Julia, keeping her eyes on the bony face, which was bent, half in shadow.

"The first time I saw him," Goetz went on, "was before the war when I was staying in Oxford. Kulligrew was an undergraduate, and one night I heard him speak in debate at some University club. The subject was not a particularly stimulating one—it was, I think, the future of aircraft, and I had prepared myself for a dull evening spent in listening to a pseudo-Wellsian debate. Instead of which Kulligrew lifted his audience into the realms of both intellect and romance, challenging equally the minds of the youths and the old men before him. Next day I was shown a poem he had written which had gained for him a much-coveted University prize, and I realized that the debate had been no mere flight of eloquence on the part of some brilliant but shallow mind. The poem was a masterpiece which gave him a place in the great tradition of English literature, and from that time Kulligrew, for me, typified all that was best in your country. I was to have met him that same night—a dinner-party was arranged—and then for some reason he left Oxford and did not return during my visit. But I did meet him—about four years later, and in the most unfortunate of circumstances. One of the tragedies of war is that men who, in ordinary life, might have enjoyed each other's friendship are forced by their loyalty to their country to meet as enemies—and it was thus that I met Charles Kulligrew."

Goetz paused and sighed, his face shadowed by his hands. Julia, watching him intently, could tell nothing of his expression; yet his voice, she thought, was weighted with a deep sincerity.

"I am an old man now," he went on, "and have long since lost any rancour I may once have felt towards the English. After the war I followed Kulligrew's life spasmodically from scraps of news in the papers—read of his Aztec expedition and admired his book on the war, and always I hoped that we might meet as human beings, and not as servants of our country. About six months ago we did meet, here in Monte Carlo, and it seemed as though some malignant fate had staged the episode; for we met as enemies again—this time on account of a woman. I will not tell you of it—sufficient to say that we met and parted without a word, I knowing that I had been the unwilling cause of great bitterness to him, yet unable to follow him and explain. Later I read of his engagement to you, and you may imagine my interest when I saw you together in the theatre—on the first night of *The Lily Flower*—on the night of Kulligrew's foul murder. Ever since that night, Miss Dallas, I have devoted myself to the pursuit of his murderer—for I know that though I could never be Kulligrew's friend while he lived, I can serve him now that he is dead. You see, I know who killed him."

Again Goetz paused, and after a moment of silence, Benvenuto bent towards him.

"Having given us your confidence so far, Herr Goetz, will you not share your knowledge with us? You will realize that this is a serious matter for both of us, not only for Julia but for me, because I am her nearest relative, and because Charles was my very good friend."

He signed swiftly to Julia, who also addressed herself to Goetz's bent head.

"It makes me very happy to meet someone who admired Charles—and—and if you will confide in us still further, I shall indeed be grateful, for I want nothing so much as the punishment of a man who must be unbelievably wicked."

"You are right, Miss Dallas—I believe this man to be a particularly vile criminal, for he was at one time a very close friend of Kulligrew. He is a traitor and a robber as well as a murderer, and his name is—Terence Gale Rourke. He is a man who is clever and cunning, and who conceals his rottenness under a cloak of bluff Irish good humour; conceals it so successfully that, but for my possession of peculiar knowledge, I would never have suspected him, and, but for the fact that he took advantage of Kulligrew's quarrel with a certain lady—a quarrel of which, as I told you, I was the cause—to steal her from him, probably Kulligrew's eyes would never have opened to his true character. As things were, I believe the friendship between them ended for ever after the incident I speak of—perhaps that is the only good turn I ever did Kulligrew, though it must have seemed a left-handed one indeed.

"But to continue—it so happened that after the war, I discovered this man Rourke to be the perpetrator of a number of robberies that were committed in France. He was never, as you probably know, caught—he called himself 'The Tiger,' and was clever enough to curry favour with the peasants, and even unofficially with the police and the press, by giving large sums to disabled soldiers. He created for himself a reputation at once gallant and heroic, all the more attractive for being lawless; humanity is incurably soft-hearted about all adventurers, from Casanova to Dick Turpin, and forgets that they all do pretty well for themselves. What was I to do? I knew the truth—I could have informed against him—but I was a German, and the objects of our adventurer's charity were men who had lost their health and livelihood in fighting my countrymen. The French are slow to forgive their enemies—even now there is a good deal of ill-feeling between the nations. So I held my tongue, but I determined that if ever the Tiger stole more than a man's purse, I would inform against him. Actually his activities ceased after his encounter with me, and the next time I saw him was in Monte Carlo, with Kulligrew. I never spoke with him, and he left for London almost immediately, but I heard from the woman who had been Kulligrew's mistress that Rourke had taken her to England with him. I determined not to lose sight of the gentleman, and I kept myself informed of his movements, and so learnt of his break with Kulligrew.

"Then came that night in the theatre, and something which I saw, something about which I beg you will not question me, told me there was likely to be still more bad blood between the two men. I left the theatre early, for I was leaving for France that night, and you may imagine my horror and distress when

I read of your fiancé's murder in the Paris papers—read, too, of the fact that he was stabbed with a sword, which I knew of course to be Rourke's. I felt, unreasonably, it is true, that I could have prevented the crime—but it had happened, he was dead, and to me it seemed as though I had lost a friend. No thought of helping to denounce his murderer entered my head—I know the efficiency of your police, and naturally concluded Rourke would be brought to justice—and then came the first of the series of outrages at the hands of the Tiger, which seem to have paralysed the police of France with fear. I realized then that Rourke was mad, and I determined that I would spread a net for him. That is why I am here in Monte Carlo at a time when I am usually away in Germany, and living in the strictest seclusion, for I am sure that Rourke will realize I am on his track. So far he has eluded me—but my spies are out on the road day and night; and please God I shall capture him before his madness accounts for another victim. I have reason to believe he is in this neighbourhood—and I do beg you both very earnestly not to drive about at night. It is indeed unfortunate that you should be in the South at this time, for Miss Dallas is an obvious victim for him, since I understand she has inherited Kulligrew's fortune. I have no doubt the Tiger knows you are here."

Julia stared out into the sunny landscape beyond the windows. Goetz's suggestion as to her own danger moved her not at all, but a dumb, inexplicable misery had descended on her. She had come to the chateau hopefully—she realized it now—and had nourished her hope on swift, unreasoning suspicions of Adolf Goetz, on a fabric of imaginary evils which she had deliberately woven round him in order to give the lie to her deep-rooted, unwilling conviction of Rourke's guilt.

Terence Gale Rourke—the name drummed in her ears, savage and menacing like primitive music from the wild places of the jungle. Suddenly she saw herself as something stripped, lewd and evil—something which had broken through the self which she had always known, a civilized, cultivated young woman with an only faintly unconventional code; it stood before her, a coarse creature of savage desires, a gangster's woman, fierce and unmoral, ready to fight for a robber, a traitor, the murderer of Charles.

Her cold, shaking hands covered her face as she struggled, tried to crush the thing that had risen in her, tried to catch back to her the Self she had always known, and when at last she dropped her hands and looked again at the sunlight beyond the cool dim room, the table before her with its silver and coffee-cups, and the thin bluish column rising from her half-smoked cigarette, she was weak and exhausted as though in those few seconds she had been burnt out by a fierce flame, and only a husk was left, lifeless, useless, and emotionless.

Vaguely, as if from a distance in time, she heard Benvenuto explaining to Goetz that they, too, were on the same quest, that in seeking the Tiger they had come South, and were equally determined on his capture. She heard him without any feeling; of course he was right, they were there to destroy the Tiger, to capture him and deliver him to justice. It was all she had left to do, she felt, the only sanity left in a mad, horrible world where men killed each other in bad blood, and where in one's own self evil monsters could raise their heads without warning, unannounced. Bad blood—Goetz had said that, and when he had said it it had linked up with some intangible thing floating in her mind as she had sat there listening, looking out of the window. She looked out again, thinking, rather feebly, that some object within her vision would bring that floating thing back to her, so that she might realize its significance. But there was only the sea, the mountain slope, and, nearer, the terrace and the back of a bronze statue that rose from the stone-work, a statue of a woman facing towards the sea like the figure-head of a ship. She sighed as the thing eluded her, leaving only a vague uneasiness behind, and realized with a start that Adolf Goetz was speaking to her.

"You will both be safer here with me," he was saying, "and you will have the advantage of my system of espionage, for I have men out on the roads hunting for him all the time who have orders to communicate with me by telephone immediately they get news of his whereabouts. Since we are all determined on the same end, why should we not join forces? I shall be more than happy if you will share my home until our work is accomplished, and if you will honour me, Miss Dallas, my car will be ready at any time to take you both down to the town to collect your luggage."

A glance at Benvenuto, and Julia thanked him and said they would be delighted to accept his hospitality—he was very kind. As the two men returned to a discussion of plans she let her mind go back to seeking that intangible something, a memory or an idea—that buzzed like a fly in the back of her brain. Her eyes, staring in front of her, came to rest once more on the statue, and the firm, delicate simplicity of the bronze woman's back. The statue! With a slight exclamation she got to her feet and walked out on to the terrace, followed after a moment by Benvenuto and Goetz. She leant over the edge of the stone balustrade and looked down into the depths below; then slowly with a feeling almost of dread, she looked up into the face of the statue.

It was Louise Lafontaine.

Benvenuto stood beside her, looking broodingly at the moulded bronze.

"That is a very fine thing," he said. "The model must have been a great beauty."

Goetz's voice was gentle as he answered:

"The model is the most beautiful woman I have ever known—and, though she has the beauty of a patrician and the dignity and carriage of a queen, she is of humble origin, for she comes from your London suburbs."

CHAPTER XIX
BIG GAME

SLOWLY JULIA undressed, absent-mindedly stripped off her jewels and her frock, kicked away her shoes, peeled her cobweb stockings, and wandered barefoot round the cool, polished tiles of her bedroom. The room, she thought, had been furnished for a woman, and for a beautiful woman. The faded green curtains of brocaded silk powdered with pink flowers, the slender elegance of Empire furniture, the ample, softly-lighted dressing-table and the multitude of mirrors—Herr Adolf Goetz had never planned so much delicate luxury for himself in a corner of his rough stone fortress. She looked at the bed, a day-bed of voluptuous sophisticated grace that looked as though it might have held Napoleon's Josephine, ran her fingers over the silken canopy, and wondered who had slept there. Louise Lafontaine—Louise, the "Lily Flower"—Julia could almost see her moving round the room, the small perfect oval of her face under its dark hair reflected in the mirror; "Am I never to get away from her?" she thought. For, of course, Louise was the woman over whom Charles and Goetz had met and quarrelled—of course Louise was the woman Rourke had stolen and taken to England.

Julia bit her lips, her cheeks suddenly hot, caught up her nightgown and pulled it over her head, then hesitated beside her bed, frowning into space. She would smoke a last cigarette on the balcony, she thought, for it was too hot to go to sleep; and taking a cushion under her arm she stepped through the curtains into the moonlight. Below her was the garden, the statues ghostly among the trees, the trees themselves a strange and leprous green under the brilliant white light, beneath them shadows of a blackness beyond blackness. Away on the right was the sea, pale and distant, shimmering; in spite of Herr Goetz's warnings she would like to take the car down to the shore and swim, thought Julia. Indeed the Tiger, the peril of the roads, seemed very far away and unreal after an evening spent in the chateau, an evening during which all mention of Rourke had been tacitly avoided.

Adolf Goetz's car had taken them down to Monte Carlo, where they had explained matters to Agatha and the Professor, packed their luggage and come back in time to dress for dinner. The meal had been an affair of wonderful foods and wines, and afterwards they had sat on the terrace talking in the moonlight, until, falling silent, their host had left them, and seating himself at a piano in the *salon*, had played Cesar Franck's Sonata in A major with the touch of a master. Remembering the music that had floated out to her through the open windows, Julia grew calm and forgot the troubled moods that had assailed her all day, allowed the spell of the formal black and white garden to hold her, thought of the great house which sheltered her, each room holding so much beauty; beauty in paint that waited in the darkness for another day to re-create it, beauty of music which had risen in delicate sculptured columns of sound—Now the house seemed to exude peace and repose; she was content to enjoy it, content to leave Benvenuto and Goetz downstairs to discuss tomorrow's activities. Furthermore, she was sleepy, she decided, and bending over the iron railing of her balcony she dropped the stump of her cigarette down on to a paved terrace many feet below her where it lay glowing for a moment, then vanished.

From her bed she looked dreamily round the softly lighted room, then put out her hand and extinguished the electric light. For a moment she was in darkness; then as her eyes gradually accustomed themselves to the change, the various objects in the room became once more apparent in the pale light of the moon—apparent, yet strange and rarefied, like ghosts of their familiar forms and colours. Her closing eyes rested for a moment on the round watery pool of a hanging mirror, then slipped towards the oblong of pallid sky between the curtains as she fell asleep.

• • • • •

What had happened? She was still lying in her bed, but the room was in darkness now. She was lying in taut and frozen stillness, her opened eyes fixed in a terrified stare on the faint oblong of the window, on the silhouetted shapes of the iron balcony, and on something else, something which moved upwards and appeared, in a dark outline against the sky, to be an arm and hand, its fingers clutching at the top rail of the balcony. There was a grunt, the sound of something scraping against the stone wall, and at last a figure pulled itself upward, and, in a final effort, threw one leg over the balcony and remained still, sitting astride on the railing. The figure was that of a man, and to Julia watching in a paralysed silence, he appeared enormous, like some fantastic giant outlined against the sky. She longed to scream, to jump from her bed and run to the door, to do anything except lie there like a rabbit fascinated by a snake, but her throat was contracted, her limbs refused to move. The man, too, was immobile, his face turned towards her, apparently staring into the room. Suddenly he sighed, and as though the sound had released her from a trance, Julia's hand shot out to the electric-light switch at her side, and at one and the same moment she flooded the room with light, and slipped her feet to the floor.

It was Terence Gale Rourke.

His clothes were torn and dusty, his hair in a wilder disarray than usual, his face pale under its tan, and he breathed quickly, his fierce, brilliant eyes seeming to scorch her. A sense of utter panic seized Julia, so that she trembled uncontrollably. There was something stern and incomprehensible about Rourke as he stared at her, no trace of the usual laughter in his face. As if she were impelled by some power outside herself Julia moved slowly across the room towards him, while a voice outside herself seemed to whisper to her that a touch of her hands could save her—a touch of her hands could send Rourke crashing backwards on to the stone terrace below. She was close to him now—so close that she could hear him breathing—so close that one movement would end it—and then she felt herself shrink backwards, recoil in horror from something she could not do. She looked down at her hands, feeling sick and faint, then up again at Rourke's face, for he was speaking.

"Julia!" he whispered, coming towards her, "Julia, are you safe? I saw you from the garden—I was watching for that old divil Goetz to start out on his wickedness—I've been waiting for him every night, but he's been lying low—and then, to-night when I saw you on the balcony and realized he'd got you here in his power—why, I went near crazed with fear. Are you all right?"

Julia nodded her head, trying desperately to collect her scattered wits as he rushed on.

"Then praise be to Heaven. And what has Ben been thinking of to let you out of his sight? But there, we must hurry. 'Tis as safe now as it will ever be, for all the lights have been out an hour since. I've got me car down the road, and once we're out of this house I'll have you back in your hotel in half an hour. Get some clothes on and hasten—"

As he spoke he led her towards the dressing-room, and switching on the light he left her and shut the door.

Julia's eyes gleamed with excitement as she pulled on her clothes. All her weakness was gone—all her fear, and her pity with it, as she braced herself for a battle between Rourke's wits and her own. It was her chance—by pretending to believe in him, in his character of her heroic rescuer, she would succeed where Leech and Goetz and Benvenuto had failed. Already a plan for his capture was forming in her mind, and from her suit-case she took the revolver that Benvenuto had given her and slipped it into her handbag. A hurried glance in her mirror and she quietly opened the door and entered the room.

For a moment Rourke did not see her. He was beside the dressing-table, slipping something into the pocket of his coat, and Julia realized that the small travelling case in which she carried her pearls was gone; the pang of bitterness which she experienced acted as the last spur to her courage.

"I'm ready," she said.

He turned towards her and came forward, his head up and something of his old swagger in his air as he laughed down at her. "I have your trinkets," he announced imperturbably. "No need to leave those for the old villain. Now follow me—and quietly."

He switched off the lights in the room and, softly opening the door, with the aid of a flash-lamp he guided her along the corridor and down the staircase into the great hall. He seemed to tread softly as a cat in spite of his enormous height, and Julia kept pace with him, trying not to shrink from the touch of his hand on her arm.

Near the front door she paused. "Terence," she whispered, "I left my coat in the cupboard there—will you get it for me? I'm cold."

"Why, of course," he answered, and the next moment had opened the door and was searching with his flash-lamp amongst an array of coats and macintoshes that hung round the walls of the small closet.

Julia's heart was racing, almost choking her, as she turned on the hall light.

"And now put your hands up, Mr. Terence Gale Rourke," she said calmly, pointing her revolver at him. "Step a little farther back into the cupboard, will you? That's better—now I can shut the door." She paused, her hand on the door-knob, and laughed, a little hysterically. "I don't know why you should look so startled—surely you didn't think you could fool me again? You are getting over-confident, you know, slipshod in your methods. Why, the way you took my pearls—it was positively amateurish. Still, I suppose you thought I was too dazzled by your Fairbanksian methods to be critical of your technique. By the way, I must apologize for offering you such a small cage, but it won't be for long—I've no doubt Herr Goetz and my cousin will be able to provide you with a fine one with bars, more worthy of so famous a Tiger."

She bowed to the tall figure in front of her, whose hands were held high above his mane of hair, and whose eyes stared at her in ludicrous amazement, and still pointing the revolver at his chest, she stepped backwards and swiftly closed the door, pushing the heavy bolt into place. Then she paused, listening. For from behind the door, muffled by the thick wood, came a roar of laughter, mocking her. She clenched her teeth, her breath coming quickly, and turning round she ran across the hall and up the staircase, her hands over her ears. The long gallery at the top was in darkness, and she hunted frenziedly for a switch, small dry sobs fighting their way into her throat as the echo of that horrible mad laughter pursued her. At last she found the light and stumbled on towards Benvenuto's room, gasping with relief as she opened the door and saw him standing by his bed pulling on a dressing-gown over his pyjamas.

"Julia! My good woman, for God's sake point that gun away."

"Ben—don't—it's serious. Please get Herr Goetz quickly—I want you both, downstairs. I've got—something for you. Don't stand there staring at me—go and fetch him now, at once."

"What on earth—all right, all right, I'll fetch him, though it's hardly etiquette on the part of a guest. May I be permitted to put on some slippers? Probably the poor old gentleman is already awake considering the noise that's been going on in the hall. I was just coming to investigate. Ah—here he is."

In the doorway stood Adolf Goetz, his gaunt form hung with a Jaeger dressing-gown, and an expression of puzzled anxiety on his face.

"My dear Miss Dallas," he began, when Julia swept past him, her eyes blazing with excitement, now completely mistress of herself.

"Please come with me, Herr Goetz—and you too, Ben—I want you to take charge of my prisoner."

Revolver in hand she hurried towards the staircase and down into the hall, the two men following her. No sound came from the cupboard; she paused, her heart beating painfully, and raised her gun to the door.

"Please stand beside me, Herr Goetz—and will you unbolt the door, Benvenuto?"

The next moment she heard a gasp from the old man as, with his arms folded across his chest, and his head thrown proudly back, the Tiger emerged from his captivity, and stood facing them. Then as his eyes fell on Goetz, his face went dark with fury, and it seemed to Julia that the two men were about to spring upon each other; when suddenly the silence was broken by the loud shrilling of the telephone bell. The absurd sound, commonplace and insistent, coming from a table by their sides, broke the electric atmosphere in the hall, and the various actors hesitated, relaxed, and looked at each other in confusion. The first move was made by Benvenuto who stepped forward, slipped his hand through the arm of Terence Rourke, and nodded Goetz towards the telephone. The old man, after a momentary glance at Julia, standing at his side with the gun still pointing at Rourke, crossed swiftly to the instrument and lifted the receiver.

"Hullo—hullo! Oui, c'est moi. What do you say—on the road between Cagnes and Vence—fifteen minutes ago—fifteen minutes—impossible! What—what—the woman is unconscious, you say? Yes—yes—Hotel des Pins—yes—I will come at once. Do all you can for her."

He dropped the receiver and faced the three people who in intense perplexity were watching him. His face was frozen and incomprehensible, and when at last he spoke his words dropped slowly into the silence.

"Fifteen minutes ago the Tiger held up a car on the road between Vence and Cagnes—at least forty miles from here—and robbed and wounded a woman. Then he escaped."

"Fifteen minutes—fifteen minutes ago"—Julia's voice rose hysterically as she faced Terence Rourke—"you were— in my room."

His eyes mocked her as he bowed his agreement.

CHAPTER XX
BEAUTY AND THE BEAST

JULIA LEANT over the balustrade of the terrace and stared, unseeing, into the peerless blue of a Mediterranean morning. A light breeze from the distant Alps made the air cool and delicious; the sea, already dotted with the white sails of yachts, sparkled in the sunshine, and on the terrace of the old house the pleasant and comforting fragrance of coffee came from a breakfast-table laid for two, and mingled with the scent of the lilies and carnations which grew in stone jars. But Julia, waiting for her host, looked pale and unhappy, and had no thought for her surroundings; Benvenuto and Terence Rourke had disappeared in the Bugatti on the previous night immediately after the arrival of the telephone message, leaving her in the care of Adolf Goetz, and promising to send word to the chateau at the first possible opportunity. They would return, they said, when they had captured the Tiger, and not before. Julia had gone to bed miserable and ashamed after her night's adventures, and, contrary to her expectations, had slept, to awaken to a morning laden with anxiety and depression. Now she turned eagerly to greet her host, who was emerging from the open french windows of the dining-room.

"Have you any news?" she asked quickly.

He shook his head.

"You must not worry, Miss Dallas. There is no reason at all to be distressed—you must realize that by now your cousin and Mr. Rourke may be hundreds of miles away in their search for this bandit; it seems to me most probable that they will be making inquiries in remote mountain villages from which there is no telephonic communication with the outer world. Furthermore, this is not England or Germany—it is the Midi, where the telephone service is, to say the least, erratic, and we cannot expect your cousin to waste precious time in trying to get through to us. Ours is a waiting part, and there is nothing we can do, except be as philosophical about it as possible." He smiled at her. "Now let us breakfast—it is always difficult to philosophize on an empty stomach—and when you are fortified with coffee there is much that I want to learn from you."

Julia seated herself at the table and poured coffee from a silver pot, trying to school herself into a more reasonable frame of mind as she talked to her host. She was, she decided, as she peeled and sliced her peach, a failure; since leaving England she had done nothing at all to help Benvenuto, had indeed definitely hindered him with her ridiculous adventure with Carrado, and now there was her idiotic exploit of last night, which, whenever she remembered it, sent hot blushes into her cheeks. She could at least put her mind to entertaining Adolf Goetz, who was no doubt as anxious and mystified as herself; and with this resolve she managed to turn breakfast into a pleasant and conversational meal. At last it was over, the table carried away by the silent-footed German butler, and Herr Goetz, having provided Julia with a cigarette and lit one himself, turned to her gravely and said:

"Miss Dallas, you will relieve my confusion of mind a great deal if you will tell me what you know of Rourke's motives in coming here last night. I thought I understood them only too well until that amazing telephone message, of which I could never have believed the truth had I not recognized the voice of my own trusted servant who has been on the watch for the Tiger during the past week."

Julia laughed bitterly. "It never occurred to me to doubt the message, Herr Goetz, for I realized from your voice there was no room for doubt. Terence Rourke came here last night to rescue me—he waited in the garden for hours, after seeing me on the balcony, and then in the dark he climbed up the stone-work to my room. Heaven knows why he did not kill himself doing it."

She paused, shuddering, as she remembered her inspection that morning of the scene of Rourke's midnight climb, and the old man bent towards her, his expression mystified.

"But, Miss Dallas, he came to rescue you—from what?"

"From you!" Julia threw him a brief mischievous smile before continuing. "It's a long story, Herr Goetz, but if you will be patient I can make you understand the whole thing."

Gradually she recapitulated for him all the events from the night in the theatre, the discussion in Benvenuto's studio, and the journey abroad, to the meeting with Rourke in Lyon, his story, his disappearance, the unfortunate affair of Uncle Edward, and finally, the events at the farm-house and the journey to Monte Carlo.

Adolf Goetz heard her almost in silence after his first shock of surprise, though when she told him, as gently as she could, Rourke's account of the war incident, he bowed his head and said: "Yes, that is true—all true"—as though to a very bitter memory. When she ended they both fell silent, until at last Goetz spoke.

"It is a strange story of blind and obstinate conviction on the part of two men, a conviction founded, I suspect, on deep-rooted temperamental dislike. Rourke and I could never be friends, however impeccable we believed each other's motives, for there is something in his tempestuous personality which arouses antagonism in me. And now, in pursuing an end which we both want to attain, in trying to avenge Kulligrew, we have both allowed ourselves to be blinded by instinctive antagonism, while the murderer goes free. The Tiger, the peril of the roads, is without doubt a common robber unknown to both of us—while the murderer of Kulligrew—I wonder—I wonder."

He had been speaking half to himself, and now impulsively he turned to Julia.

"Tell me, Miss Dallas—tell me—what is your true opinion of Terence Rourke?"

She looked at him, wide-eyed and troubled. Then: "I—I don't know," she stammered. "I don't know what to believe. Oh, my God! I hate him, *hate* him." Now her hands were covering her face, and between her fingers she felt her hot tears trickling. She jumped to her feet and turned and ran across the terrace, down the stone steps and away into the garden, away where no one could see her.

Perhaps ten minutes later, pale and self-controlled, she walked slowly back towards the terrace, rehearsing in her mind the excuses she would make to Goetz. "I was tired," she heard herself saying; "it has all been so upsetting, and I'm worried—about Benvenuto—" But at the top of the garden steps she paused. Goetz had gone, the terrace was empty, and she sat down in a chair and began to look through the pages of an illustrated paper.

Presently the butler came to her and handed her a note which she took eagerly; perhaps it was from Benvenuto. Then she saw to her disappointment that the handwriting was unknown to her, crabbed and old-fashioned.

MY DEAR MISS DALLAS [she read]

Most regrettably I am called away on urgent business. I trust I shall not be away for more than a few hours and that in my absence you will make yourself comfortable, and treat my house and garden as your own.

With my apologies
Cordially,
ADOLF GOETZ.

As she finished reading there came from the court-yard the sound of an engine accelerating, and running to the top of the steps she saw the long grey car move down the drive and disappear through the big gates, which were held open by a man-servant. Feeling more forlorn and forsaken than ever, she turned back, and after a moment's hesitation entered the house, deciding to go up to her room and write some letters. The house was silent and dim, closed against the sun, and arriving in her room she flung open the shutters and looked down into the garden, which lay arid and tremulous in the heat. Against her will her eyes were drawn to the stone pavement below her balcony where Rourke might so easily have fallen the night before, and shivering suddenly in spite of the sun, she turned away and sat down determinedly at the writing-table. A cheque to her dressmaker—instructions to her maid—a line to her lawyer giving him her address at the chateau, and then she thought of Agatha and the Professor, who would be worrying unless they heard from her.

"Dearest Uncle Edward," she began, then hesitated. What had she to tell him that could ease his mind? That she was alone at the château—that Benvenuto had gone, she knew not where—that Rourke was innocent—but was he? Across her mind came the memory of Uncle Edward, sitting in the bedroom of his hotel. "If only," he had said, "if only I could remember where I put the sword."

Throwing down her pen she jumped to her feet, and deciding she would go to the village to post her letters and forget all her problems in exploring the countryside, she took a hat from her dressing-room and went down into the garden. Walking along the drive the heat was intense, but she welcomed the physical discomfort as an escape from her mental struggles and hurried on. At the big gates she had difficulty with the fastening and bruised her fingers against the iron lock, then stood aside as she saw the German butler rapidly approaching her from the house. At the gates he stopped and faced her, bowing respectfully.

"Madame wishes any commission made for her in the village?" he suggested in French, his small piggy eyes roving over her face.

"No, thank you," returned Julia, "I am going for a walk and can post my own letters."

"The Herr's letter-bag goes to the village every day," said the man, and paused. "Very pleasant walk in the gardens," he went on, the respect in his voice tinged with authority. Julia made a step forward and stopped, the blood rushing to her face, for the German had raised his arm and was barring her way.

She was, she realized, a prisoner.

She pulled herself together and turned aside. "Perhaps you are right," she agreed; "the garden is the best place in the heat of the morning," and handing him her letters she strolled off down a shady path.

Reaching the laurel grove where Benvenuto had made his painting, only—was it possible?—the day before, she sank down on a stone seat to consider things. Her own position, she found, amused her somewhat; from being on the staff of the attacking army she found herself instead a prisoner of war—and then, as the full significance of her plight dawned on her, she was stilled with terror. If she was Goetz's prisoner then Benvenuto and Terence Rourke were the victims of a trap, and were now undoubtedly in his power. The telephone call was faked—a last desperate throw made by the Tiger when he found himself faced by Terence Rourke, and one which had succeeded only too well; Terence had been right all along, Goetz was the real villain, the terror of the road, and, she saw it all now, the murderer of Kulligrew—and Terence had risked everything to save her from him. His face swam before her, his face resolute and tender, then amazed, then laughing, mocking her. She shut her eyes, trying to escape from him. It was her fault—all her fault. But for her Benvenuto and Terence would between them have outwitted their enemy, and now they were both in his power. Was there nothing she could do to help them? She sat up and dried her eyes, trying to find a gleam of hope in the situation. Why had Goetz kept up his pretence of innocence with her that morning unless—She clutched at the idea joyfully—unless he were still unsure of himself—still doubtful of their having fallen into his trap. While there remained that hope her part was plain—she must behave as though nothing had happened, as though she trusted him implicitly. Probably she still had a few hours alone in which to fortify herself against Goetz's return, and meanwhile his servants must notice nothing of her fear.

A sudden thought occurring to her, she jumped to her feet. The telephone—she could ring up the police, or, better still, the British Consul at Monte Carlo, and ask them to trace the Bugatti. She could get in touch with Leech. She hurried towards the house, and pushed open the front door. Was it chance that the German butler was standing by the telephone table, arranging some flowers in a bowl?

"Lunch is in ten minutes, madam," he said.

She went upstairs to wash her hands and powder her face, and frowned when she caught sight of her pallor in the glass. Presently when she went down the man was still there at the foot of the stairs and he followed her politely to the dining-room.

The long hours of that hot afternoon were fantastic and unreal as a dream, a dream in which she wandered aimlessly through the great dimly-lit rooms of a strange house looking for she knew not what, waiting for she knew not what. Sometimes she found, herself walking up and down the paths of the desolate walled garden, and once or twice was brought back to reality by coming upon the stolid figure of the German servant, his small, expressionless eyes fixed on her. It was evident that he was under orders to watch her.

At last the sun sank and the day grew cool, and Julia roused herself from her despairing apathy. It was nearly seven o'clock—nine hours since Goetz had left the château, and there was, she felt, at least a possibility that his plans had miscarried. She determined on clinging to her last shred of optimism, and decided she would go to her room and dress carefully for dinner. It would occupy her and make her feel more normal and civilized. She took a bath, lingered meticulously over her nails and her hairdressing, selected her smartest frock and was amazed at the change of spirits she experienced. She would go down and ask Hans for a cocktail, she decided, and before the evening was over something, surely, would happen.

The *salon* was empty, softly lighted by shaded lamps, the windows were open, and Julia's eyes were drawn to the terrace where the statue of Louise stood, silhouetted sharply against the evening sky. Then she caught her breath—for beside the statue, silent and still as the bronze itself, was Adolf Goetz, leaning over the parapet, staring broodingly down into the valley.

CHAPTER XXI
THE EAGLE

> "He clasps the crag with crooked hands,
> Near to the sun in lonely lands,
> Ringed by the azure world he stands.
> The wrinkled sea beneath him crawls,
> He watches from his mountain walls,
> And like a thunderbolt, he falls."

THE WORDS threaded through Julia's mind as she stood quite still, watching him. He's not like a tiger, she thought, he's like a bird of prey—an eagle, with his thin, bent face, bony and angular. And she—what was she—his helpless prey? For the first time that day real fear for herself gripped her, and she clung to a chair beside her, trembling. Oh, God! Why had Terence abandoned her?

Suddenly Goetz turned and came towards her, not seeing her, his face dark and frowning.

"My dear Miss Dallas—I must have startled you. Please forgive me."

The frown had gone now, his face was softened into a kindly smiling mask as he took her hand. "I fear you have had a lonely day, and I must ask you to forgive me for that too. Myself, I have passed a busy day, though a useless one I fear."

He sighed, and all at once she thought he looked old and tired and quite unfrightening. She took a cocktail from a tray the butler handed her, and sat down on a divan near the window. She felt confident, able to deal with him.

"Have you any news?" she asked.

He shook his head. "I was about to ask you the same question. You have had no word from your cousin?"

"Nothing. Tell me, Herr Goetz, what you think about it all. You look worried."

"I think"—he smiled at her—"I think you must trust in Benvenuto Brown, and not distress yourself."

"But *you* are worried. You suspect something, I'm sure. Please tell me what it is."

(She was being rather good, she thought. He would never guess what she knew.)

He looked at her earnestly and came and sat down beside her.

"I think you are a brave woman, and I will share my fears with you. I had wished to spare you my thoughts, but you see through me. Ever since I let your cousin go with Rourke last night I have been afraid—I have been afraid it was a trap. The Tiger is known to have had a confederate—let us, with this fact in view, consider the possibilities. Suppose I have been right all the time—suppose Terence Gale Rourke is the Tiger; and that he realizes that both Benvenuto Brown and I are on his track, and that it is only a question of time before we have him. He learns that we have joined forces—he knows that my men are on the roads in wait for him, and he plans one last desperate coup. He stages a hold-up—by his confederate—at a place where he knows my men are watching for him, and makes his own dramatic entrance into my house at a time which forbids his having been present during the Tiger's attack. He plans to persuade you to escape with him, and as a last stroke of audacity says that it is from *me* that he is protecting you. He does not care whether you believe him or not, for his whole aim is to be caught by Brown and myself—to establish his alibi. Unwittingly you fall in with his plans to the extent of effecting his capture yourself. Indeed, luck is with him all the way, for the telephone call from my servant comes at the moment when he is faced by us, and he is able to profit by it to the extent of accompanying Brown—*Brown, who is his chief enemy, his chief danger*—on a supposed hunt for the Tiger. Miss Dallas—I am afraid—I am terribly afraid for your cousin, for, if I am right in my belief, Rourke is a desperate man who will not spare his enemies. He cannot afford to—he is fighting for his own life. And I did not see—I let him go."

Goetz's voice broke, and he looked at her with tragic eyes. Julia stared back at him, deathly pale. Her thoughts raced aimlessly through her tired and frightened brain, her convictions of a few moments before shattered by even more terrible possibilities. Now she was hopeless, helpless, a bird in a trap not knowing where to turn.

Whom was she to believe—what was she to believe?

Suddenly she remembered—she had been kept a prisoner all day. Goetz must be lying; then, as though he could read her thoughts, the old man went on.

"I have something else to tell you, Miss Dallas—a confession to make. I told my servants not to let you leave the grounds in my absence, not to let you out of their sight, and though you have not known it you have been virtually a prisoner all day. You see, I was so afraid that devil might come back for you, deceive you and carry you away. Will you forgive me?"

Julia nodded, speechless, and rising to her feet she took and lit a cigarette to hide her face from him in case he should see her misery of doubt and indecision.

"All day I have been scouring the country," he went on, "hoping to trace your cousin, but without success. I visited the hotel where the victim of last night's robbery is lying, but the poor lady is still unconscious, and my own man who I expected to find there had gone without leaving a word. Still, we must not despair. I have great faith in the courage and cleverness of Benvenuto Brown, and I cannot give up hope. Come, Miss Dallas!" Rising, he offered his arm and led her through into the dining-room.

Through dinner he talked to her gently, intelligently, as though they were two friends who had met to enjoy good conversation, good food and good wine. Julia responded as best she could, studying him across the table. He looked old and tired and haggard, his curious face grave and mysterious. Whom was she to believe—what was she to believe? She felt herself beating impotently against the mask of his age and his experience, felt herself an ignorant, defenceless fool, futile and powerless.

She wished desperately for Benvenuto, his good-humoured, intelligent face, his reassuring presence. Would she ever see him again? Of Rourke she could not think.

Slowly the meal went on, gradually the food and wine which she consumed gave her new strength. She caught sight of herself in a mirror on the opposite wall, her face and her bare throat very white above her black dress. Her hand went to her throat as she thought of her pearls, and Rourke, slipping her jewel case into his pocket.

Suddenly she jumped to her feet and faced Goetz across the table, tense and passionate with a new-found strength.

"I am going—now, at once. I shall go to the consul and the police and get help."

He looked at her in amazement and rose. "But—I have done everything, Miss Dallas, everything possible. At this moment the police and my own men are searching the country for your cousin. Please calm yourself."

"How can I tell—how can I know what to believe? I must go and look for him." Her voice rose shrilly.

He came round the table and put his hand on her arm. "Please—you are overwrought. Now drink this glass of wine. My dear, I cannot let you go from here at night while there is danger of Rourke or his men being on the roads. It is impossible. I assure you that your cousin—"

"I will not be kept a prisoner!" She knocked the wine-glass to the floor, trembling with rage; but Goetz, folding his arms, looked down at her coldly, and then, his voice hard and distinct, said, "You shall not go."

For a moment they remained still, facing each other defiantly, Julia's eyes blazing up into his inscrutable face, and then each turned with a start as if to meet some physical presence when the telephone bell sounded sharply from the hall. In an instant Goetz was at the door, Julia beside him; another moment, and the bell was silenced as he lifted the receiver from the instrument.

"Oui—oui—c'est moi qui vous parle—ah! c'est vous, Karl—comment?—oui—Monsieur Brown—au Café de Paris—a neuf heures et demi—bon—bon—c'est entendu. Au revoir."

Goetz's face was expressionless and his hand trembled slightly as he turned to Julia.

"Your cousin wishes us to meet him at the Café de Paris in Monte Carlo at half-past nine."

Silently they walked back to the dining-room.

CHAPTER XXII
CABARET

THE DRIVE DOWN to Monte Carlo was, for obvious reasons, rather a silent affair. Julia, sitting back in a corner of the big car, looked out into the darkness and felt profoundly ashamed of her outburst in Goetz's dining-room. At once ashamed and defiant, for after all what grounds had she for the feeling of reassurance which pervaded her now? The telephone call, one half of which she had overheard—might not that, too, have been pre-arranged for her benefit? What guarantee could she possibly have of the sincerity of Adolf Goetz? Her state of mind, she thought, alighting from the car and preceding Goetz into the brightly-lit Café de Paris, was very similar to that of Uncle Edward during his famous bedroom scene; indecision and doubt were the predominating emotions in her being.

She looked expectantly round the crowded café, peering anxiously through the couples on the small dance floor. There were English tourists in plenty, drinking coffee and liqueurs at the marble-topped tables, Germans drinking beer, dark and oily-looking gentlemen with brightly coloured syrups in front of them, but never a sign of Benvenuto—or—Julia's thoughts wavered—or of Terence Rourke.

Presently, sitting opposite Adolf Goetz, she drank a glass of the excellent champagne he had ordered, and looked across at him broodingly. He was talking of music—of the relation of music and architecture. Suddenly she could bear it no longer, and her overstrained nerves seeking some kind of relief, her longing to approach the problems which beset her overcoming her, she burst out: "Louise Lafontaine is coming to Monte Carlo. Martin Pitt has written to tell us so."

Perfectly calm and expressionless, Goetz inclined his head. "So I understand. I heard from her this morning. You know her, Miss Dallas?"

"I—I have met her."

The bony face was suddenly transfigured as he bent towards her, softened and subdued into tenderness and humanity. "Is she not beautiful?" he said, and not waiting for her reply he went on—"So beautiful and so much of an artist that none of the ordinary conventions of life can be applied to her. She is above them and beyond them, a rare and vivid creature whose nature demands complete freedom, a life overflowing with richness and variety. I am an old man, I understand her now, though I passed through a period of great bitterness before I could do so. Charles Kulligrew never understood her, and so never fully appreciated the infinite variety of her mind and soul. Round the beautiful body of Louise he created a phantom woman, a woman built perhaps in his own image; he clothed the pagan in the Puritan's dress, and then, when the dress was stripped away, thought his dream was a vulgar and wanton reality. I know better—but it is my everlasting regret that I was the unconscious and unwilling means of destroying Kulligrew's happiness in her. It is true the thing was bound to end sooner or later—but it so happened that at the time when my relations with Louise came to his knowledge and shocked him into a passionate quarrel with her, she was not only his mistress, but the great inspiration in his literary work. I went away and travelled round Europe—there was nothing I could do—and then I heard from Louise that Kulligrew had left her, and that she had gone to London with Terence Rourke. Whatever one may think of *his* part in the affair, one cannot but be glad of the result—the production of *The Lily Flower* with Louise in the name part. I fear I am boring you, Miss Dallas— it is but rarely I speak of Louise and she means a great deal to me; she always has and always will."

Julia did her best to seem sympathetic, her thoughts racing bitterly through her mind. Louise, Louise, Louise. Would she ever get away from her? She tried to dismiss her as an old man's infatuation, but that would not do. There were Charles—and Martin Pitt—and—Terence Rourke.

The fierce, strong music of a tango came to an end, and couples drifted away from the floor. Then suddenly the lights were lowered, and from the orchestra came the rattle of drums announcing a cabaret turn, while the circle of watching faces at the tables turned pale in the reflection of a cold white spot-light. Languidly Julia watched the floor where an ostrich-plumed girl had appeared and was executing an eccentric dance; then her interest quickened a little as the main doors of the restaurant swung wide and a man's figure dressed in a blue shirt and a pair of white trousers appeared, carrying something on his shoulder, something which on closer inspection looked like a trussed-up body. Evidently it was an apache turn, rather well put on. The man with the burden advanced slowly towards her, swaying in time to the music, and as he neared the middle of the floor the spot-light illumined him from the waist downwards, showing on the white trousers most realistic patches of blood. The be-feathered dancer was backing away from him in a well-simulated fear, thought Julia, who the next moment had leapt from her seat, and pushing past Adolf Goetz, was facing the chief character of the cabaret drama. Suddenly the trussed-up bundle was dropped at her feet, and the man in the blue shirt, bending down, kissed her hand. Julia stood paralysed, heard as in a dream the rich Irish voice saying, "It's sorry I am, Miss Dallas, to give you nothing but an imitation Tiger," watched him take a glass of champagne from the table and drink it down, and then, almost before she realized what was happening, Terence Rourke waved to the assembled company and was gone.

The bundle on the floor was kicking and struggling, trying to free itself of a black hood which was over its head, but Julia, staring out of the door through which the tall figure of Rourke had just disappeared, paid no heed to it. Only one thing she wanted, for him to come back. Come back, come back, please come back, she prayed. It was the one thought which emerged clearly from the tangled emotions which filled her.

Soon she was brought back to reality by a crowd of comic-opera policemen in white uniforms and plumed helmets who appeared to have sprung from nowhere and to be filling the café. One man in mufti who seemed to be directing them ordered a space to be cleared round the struggling body on the floor, and gradually the crowd was pushed back until only Goetz and Julia remained at the scene of action, their table being against the wall. Then Julia remembered—it was *her* prize down there at her feet. What had Terence Rourke brought her—who was the Tiger, the robber and murderer?

Two uniformed men advanced self-importantly towards the bound figure, and kneeling down commenced to loosen his bonds. First the legs were freed and the figure jerked to its feet, then while a man held him by each arm a third man cut the cords which held in place the hood of black cloth, and Julia found herself looking into the face of Count Carrado, the Casanova of Annécy.

He blinked round in the sudden light, his hair ruffled over his forehead, his face grimy, and wearing the look of a trapped animal; then catching sight of Julia something of his old assurance returned to him, and he bowed to her. The man in mufti was giving orders to his men. "Take him to the commissionaire—and look out. It is the Tiger, otherwise Gambetta the Italian murderer. A slippery devil."

As the prisoner was led out the crowd pressed round him, and the café was filled with an excited murmur—"Le Tigre! Le Tigre!"

Julia sank back in her chair and turned to Adolf Goetz, who had watched the proceedings silently. "The Tiger—Carrado—Terence Rourke. Oh, I wish Benvenuto were here to tell us what it's all about," she said despairingly.

"We aim to please," came Benvenuto's voice in her ear. "I've been here since the beginning of the amateur theatricals, only you didn't notice me. And now, since the Captains and the

Kings have departed, suppose you come along with me to the Royalty bar and I'll give you the low-down on the situation."

CHAPTER XXIII
"THE FORESTS OF THE NIGHT"

BENVENUTO, finishing his brandy and soda, lit a cigarette and looked amusedly at his expectant listeners. The Royalty bar was filled with a buzz of conversation, which came in a variety of tongues from groups of people leaning on the bar or seated in corners over the last drinks of the day. At the next table the occupants were lost in the vagaries of poker dice which they were throwing for "high-balls," and Benvenuto was as much alone with his audience of two as though on a mountain-top. He gave an order to Francis the barman, who approached smiling and efficient, then looked across at Julia.

"I was as pleased as Punch when you captured Rourke, my dear. I wanted him badly, though not for the reasons either of you supposed. I'd realized for a long time, of course, that he wasn't the modern Tiger, but I wanted some information from him, and he kept disappearing like the 'Vanishing Lady.' Well, when he found up at the chateau last night that *you* couldn't be the Tiger, Herr Goetz, he felt he'd made a fool of himself, and his one idea was to rush off and hunt the brute down at once. I was not particularly keen on big game of this kind, but my one chance of keeping in touch with Terence, and I wasn't going to lose him again, was to go out hunting too—and get my information in the lucid intervals, so to speak. As it turned out the lucid intervals have been few, as you'll see.

"Now, before I go on, I think I'd better tell you, Julia, Rourke's explanation of his disappearance that night at Lyon, after he'd told us the story of his life; you, Herr Goetz, can probably verify it. After he'd said good night to us, he went out to the garage to get his bag out of the car. Just as he got there he saw *your* car pass, leapt into his own, had it filled with petrol, threw a hundred francs to the man, and was after you like a shot, quite forgetting all our arrangements in his excitement."

"Yes," said Goetz slowly, "it is true enough. He followed me, very fast, along the Avignon road. But my car is faster. I won. I thought it was the Tiger, after my blood and pocket-book, and for a certain reason I was not, at that moment, prepared to deal with him. We had a thrilling race, and I, by a stratagem, shook him off near Orange."

"To find him later on in your hall cupboard with a woman policeman on guard over him," said Benvenuto, winking at Julia.

"If he is not the Tiger," said Goetz, bending forward earnestly, "he is almost certainly the murderer of his friend Kulligrew. See! He has vanished once more."

"This time," said Benvenuto, slowly, "he has vanished with my knowledge, help, and approval."

Julia sat up quickly, sensing something electric in the atmosphere. "Now, Ben, you're to tell me at once how you and Mr. Rourke captured the Tiger. I can't bear to wait another moment," she said.

"The game was given away by his lady-love, my poor Julia; 'Ruined by a Woman,' or 'Put not your trust in Blondes.' Well, to begin.

"Rourke and I set off at a great pace towards Nice, just as if we were going to catch a train. When we got to Eze, however, he drew up, and said, 'Ben, what exactly are we going to do?' This was precisely what I was wondering myself. Useless to go to the scene of the hold-up—the Tiger would be miles away. Besides, we had to proceed without the help of the police, because of Terence, of course. He was, at that moment, utterly without a plan in his head. The ground had crumbled beneath his feet, and his realization that you, Herr Goetz, were not the Tiger left him as helpless as a child, though full of ferocious energy against *someone*. So I said to him, 'Terence, there's just one hope. We must find Blind Pasquale.' Now, Blind Pasquale is an old friend of mine, a wandering guitar player, and he sees more than most people with eyes. What he doesn't know about this part of France isn't worth a sou. What he does know would ruin thousands if he liked to turn blackmailer. I felt it was just on the cards that he might be able to give us a tip about the Tiger. I explained all this to Terence, and he agreed, though really he wanted to fight someone at once, and off we went again. We dropped down into Nice, and raked the all-night cafés. He wasn't there. Someone said he might be in Toulon, someone else had heard of him in St. Antoine. We left Nice full of drinks from the cafés and drove that night along the coast to Toulon, deciding we would if necessary search through all the coast towns next day. At Toulon we slept for three hours, got up, and started looking for Pasquale. Again, nothing doing. Finally, to cut it short, we ran him to earth in St. Tropez, having a late lunch after guitaring to the glittering mob. That's the place where they all dress up like artists and go about in Rolls-Royces and million-dollar yachts.

"I took him into a corner and told him what I wanted. I said, 'Pasquale, I've never asked you for anything.' He hesitated for a moment, and then said in a low voice, 'Cherchez La Chloryse,' and added, 'Hotel Luxuria, à Cannes.'"

"Ben! how thrilling," murmured Julia, who had forgotten to drink her liqueur.

"We went off like a shell from a gun to Cannes, booked rooms at the Luxuria, washed and shaved, and turned into the lounge for tea. To think that was only this afternoon! We didn't know who La Chloryse was or what the hell she had to do with the Tiger, but a large tip to the maître d'hôtel and a simple journalistic expression soon got us in touch with her. She was pointed out to us, reclining in a cosy corner of the lounge, taking tea with an American. What a woman! A super-blonde, fully charged with scent and sex-appeal, real pearls and imitation passion. Voluptuous on the outside, and hard as nails. In short, a 'poule de luxe.' I said to Terence, 'If Pasquale is right, that lady is the Tiger's bait, and a very juicy bit too.'"

"Don't be disgusting, Ben," said Julia.

"Sorry," he replied. "I forgot for the moment that tigers are your pets. Well, we had nothing but this assumption to go on; and from it arose the possibility that the American, a genial-looking cove with a moneyed air, was being gently drawn towards the fangs. Pure guess-work, but we acted on it; it was all we could do. When he rose we followed him upstairs to his room and knocked at the door. He let us in, and I realized that the best thing to do was to be quite frank with him. He was that sort. He didn't say anything till I'd finished my little story, then he looked me and Terence up and down. 'Boys,' he said, 'I like my little girl downstairs, but I didn't take her for Florence Nightingale or the Spirit of Spring, as you guys seem to think. Have a cigar. Well, I'm willing to try out your theory. If you're right we'll have gotten this gangster. If you're wrong, you buy my girl friend a diamond handcuff. Is that O.K?' This made Terence laugh, and after sending for some whisky we made a plan. The American, whose name by the way is Hotton, was a sport, and insisted on being fair to both sides. He wouldn't say whether La Chloryse had been pumping him or not, but he agreed to go down and mention to her casually that he was going to drive to Monte Carlo that evening with a big wad of money, to gamble in the Salles Privées. We went down, and I, from a discreet distance, watched the scene at the tea-table; Terence had gone out to buy a couple of guns.

"La Chloryse did what I was expecting, hoping, she would do. She got up and went to the writing-room, and presently emerged with a letter, which she gave quite openly to the chasseur. I followed the chasseur to a café, where he delivered the letter to a young man in plusfours. He read it, paid for his drink, went out and mounted a motor-bike, and vanished towards Nice. The trap was set—"

"You had luck as well as judgment," remarked Goetz.

"More than our share," agreed Benvenuto, "as you will soon see." He resettled himself in his chair and took a drink.

"Terence and I had some food at a small restaurant and then went round to Hotton's garage, as we had arranged. His car was a Cord limousine, large, powerful, and sparkling. After a bit he joined us, and we pushed off slowly out of Cannes, Hotton driving, Terence and I sitting on the floor at the back grasping our death-dealing weapons. It was just getting dark. I couldn't see out of the windows, but before long I realized we were passing the lights of Nice. As you know, there are three ways from Nice to Monte Carlo; the Lower, the Moyen and the Upper Corniche, and after a whispered conversation we decided to take the upper, it being the best road and the most usual.

"It's a long climb up the hill, and near the top in a pretty lonely and desolate spot we felt the Cord slowing down; Hotton turned round and whispered, 'Here he is, boys.' It was a tense moment, I can tell you. Our plan was to keep quiet until the Tiger was engaged in rifling the American's pockets and then rush him; so we kept quiet. The car stopped.

"The next thing was a voice out of the darkness, saying in French, 'Pardon, monsieur, but I have run out of petrol. Would you have the gentillesse to lend me some?' I peeped over the front of the seat. There was a car by the side of the road, and I could see a man in motor-goggles talking to Hotton. I said to Terence, *'Now!'* We slid very quietly out of the door facing away from the two men, and crept round the back of the car, got on either side of the bandit, covered him with our guns, and then Terence said very fiercely, 'Haute les mains!'

"I've never seen anyone so surprised in my life. The wretched fellow sank on his knees to the ground and put his hands up like a German prisoner."

Well, said Julia, "that *was* a tame ending."

Benvenuto laughed. "It was tame, but it wasn't an ending. We'd trapped a kitten instead of a tiger. The poor fellow was perfectly genuine, and it took us ten minutes to explain to him that we weren't a bunch of Tigers ourselves. Hotton and I saw the joke—but poor Terence was furious. To be mistaken for the Tiger again! Well, we apologized to our victim, gave him some petrol, and weighed anchor, feeling rather small.

"We'd just passed Eze when the fun began. A motor-bike passed us at a furious pace, and in the light of our head-lamps I recognized the back view of the gentleman who'd received the letter from La Chloryse at Cannes. Another kilometre or so, and Hotton said, 'Watch out, boys.' I looked over the front seat again, and saw the words 'Sens Obligatoire' and an arrow pointing to the left, stretched on a rope across the road. It was exactly like an official notice, and any motorist would have been taken in. Without a moment's hesitation Hotton swung round to the left, and we prepared for action. We got it.

"The car bumped over what felt like a log, and stopped. Terence and I squatted on the floor, one facing each door. Nothing happened for a moment, then we heard a voice say 'Stick 'em up.' Hotton managed to get an excellent tremor into his reply. 'What's this—a hold-up? Want my wad, eh?' he said, and things began to move. A hand with a flash-lamp came over the top of my door, and I grabbed it, got to my feet, and dived out of the window on top of someone whose gun went off beside my ear. We were on the edge of a ditch, and with a sudden effort the man under me, whom I had by the wrists to prevent him using his gun, managed to upset me; and down the bank we rolled, this time with me underneath. I still had hold of his gun-hand though, and by a bit of luck managed to bring off an old trick. I brought my knee up sharply and got him under the chin with it. This rattled him considerably, but he was still on top of me, and he managed to get his knee on my wind. I was on the point of giving in when he sprang up and ran for his life; I could have shot him as he went, but—I didn't.

"I crawled to the top of the ditch again and, panting for breath, looked to see how the battle went.

"In the full glare of the car's head-lamps, two men were clasped in each other's arms. For a moment, being a bit dazed, I thought it was some kind of a dance. One of them was Rourke; the other, a man just as tall, had a black mask over his face. They swayed slightly backwards and forwards, and I heard their joints cracking. Two yards away stood Hotton, judicially, a lighted cigar in his mouth.

"The two men were pretty evenly matched and the clinch continued in silence, broken only by their own grunts and gasps. Then I noticed blood running down Terence's leg and remembered I had heard another shot go off while I was busy with my sparring partner. I was just standing by to intervene when suddenly a kind of Irish war-howl came from Terence— the Tiger, it appeared later, had bitten him on the arm—and the two of them disengaged. The Tiger's hand went like a flash to his belt for a knife, but before it got there Terence's left caught him under the jaw, and he went down like a tree struck by lightning. Terence sat on him, while Hotton solemnly counted him out."

Involuntarily Julia clapped her hands. "Why, oh, why didn't I see it? But—Ben, the blood—was he shot?"

"It was nothing—a scratch down the skin. He was lucky all the same, for the Tiger fired at him as he dived out of the car. Another centimetre and there might have been no fight, and no capture."

"This Mr.—er—Hotton seems to have taken an exceedingly passive part in the affray," remarked Adolf Goetz.

Benvenuto nodded. "I give him full marks for that, for he looks a tough old warrior himself. He realized that Terence was keen to bring his own bird down, and so didn't butt in; I think he was standing by for action, all the same."

"When did you discover that the Tiger was—Carrado?" asked Julia; reddening a little.

"I should very much like," replied Benvenuto, "to say that I discovered it while we were sitting by the roadside in the dark outside Castellane. But I didn't. Only I did think it rather curious that the gentleman should have given you so accurate an account of Terence in the part of the Tiger—I knowing to my perfect satisfaction that he *wasn't* the Tiger—until I realized that Carrado's answers were inspired by your questions. At the moment I put it down to a natural desire to embellish an imaginary adventure which he'd invented 'pour épater les femmes,' and yet when Terence pulled away the black cloth from the face of the fallen Tiger I wasn't entirely amazed to recognize the handsome features of young Casanova. That lad is certainly a good looker and a good fighter, and had he been able to develop his talents during, say, the Italian Renaissance, he'd probably have been a popular hero instead of rather a nasty little gangster.

"Well, there isn't much more to tell you. As soon as Terence had got his breath he insisted that he must lay the Tiger at your feet, so we tied him up and bundled him into the car. By the way, he didn't of course know that Carrado was—er—a pal of yours, and I—didn't tell him."

"Thank you, Ben," murmured Julia, her face scarlet.

"We drove on to Eze in the car," went on Benvenuto, his eyes tactfully lowered to his glass, "and sent you a telephone message from there; then, after a little first-aid work and a drink we came down here, leaving a note for the police on the way explaining matters, and saying they'd find something to their advantage on the floor of the Café de Paris."

Julia drew a deep breath and relaxed in her chair. "Tiger, Tiger, burning bright," she murmured. But she was not thinking of Carrado.

Goetz and Benvenuto had drawn their chairs closer and were talking, and she heard their voices as a murmur from a long distance.

"Terence insisted he must lay the Tiger at your feet," Benvenuto had said. Was he mocking her with his prize? Her eyes stared unseeing over the smoke-filled room, as she thought of a tall figure striding towards her across the Café de Paris, a bundle dropped at her feet, a swift glance from the fierce bright eyes as he lowered his head to kiss her hand. In that moment he had not mocked her, she told herself. She could almost see him, his blue shirt, his bloodstained trousers, his mane of hair, white-streaked, above his young sunburnt face.

Suddenly her eyes widened, and her cheeks which had been pink grew white, as a realization came to her of what she had been staring at, across the room, through her cloud of memory.

On a high stool at the bar was sitting a woman whose back was towards Julia, a woman with dark curls above a low-cut pink frock—and next to her—turning towards her—the yellow head of Martin Pitt.

Swiftly Julia got to her feet.

"I'm going, Ben, I'll wait for you—in the car."

She hurried out, her hands clenched. Fool, she told herself, fool!

For she had been forgetting Louise.

CHAPTER XXIV
SIX CHARACTERS IN SEARCH OF
A CRIMINAL

THE GREAT HOUSE was alive with hurrying footsteps, servants passed in and out of the brightly-lit rooms and up and down the staircase, preparing for the guests that were soon due to arrive. Adolf Goetz was giving a dinner-party.

Julia, pausing for a moment in the hall on her way to the garden where she wished to be alone until dinner-time, saw a maid go by with a bouquet of flowers for one of the upper rooms—for Louise's room she guessed; and then as the door to the service quarters swung open, she heard for a moment the voice of a peasant, in the kitchens, singing a song. It was almost impossible to believe that Goetz's house, so full of warmth and light and hospitable activity, could have a shadow of tragedy overhanging it. For a moment Julia wanted to run into the kitchens, strip off her satin dress and help the peasants in preparing food, wanted to stay with them and listen to their comfortable laughter and harsh, swift talk until—until it was all over. Then, her chin up, she walked steadily out into the quiet garden. She had to help Benvenuto to-night, had to appear natural and gay and careless. A few moments alone, with still trees and dark, scented flowers round her, and she would find courage to do it.

From the road came the sound of a car mounting the hill in low gear, then a blaze of light as a big limousine entered the drive. Julia, watching from among the trees, saw a brilliant figure alight; Louise, exquisite and graceful in a golden cloak, followed by Martin Pitt—she recognized his yellow head in the lamplight and his slim figure, very neat and elegant in evening dress.

The party had begun.

Slowly the big car crept away from the door, and as it did so the lights of a second came over the hill. This time it was a taxi, noisy and protesting, grinding its way up on bottom gear. It stopped in front of the house and a waiting man-servant held open the door for the guests to alight; Julia felt a pang of pity as she saw the thin figure of the Professor, bent and grotesque in his old-fashioned evening cloak, helping, rather helplessly, the nervously energetic Agatha up the steps. Life, she thought, was too ruthless a business for these two. They had become entangled accidentally in its swift stream, after many years of vague and comfortable unreality.

She must go in, though Julia, and after a last glance at the quiet garden she walked hesitatingly towards the lighted doorway.

From the *salon* came the sound of laughter and voices. It is all a dream, she thought, as she entered the charming panelled room—this is a dinner-party in a country house, not the prelude to a tragedy; and in a moment when she found herself shaking hands with Louise and Martin Pitt, kissing Agatha and the Professor, it was with a feeling of complete unreality that she greeted them. From the fireplace Adolf Goetz smiled at her gravely; while Benvenuto handed her a cocktail and seemed, silently, to offer her encouragement with a glance of his bright narrow-lidded eyes. By no sign did his face convey the responsibility that weighed on him as he turned and began to talk to Louise about a new exhibition of paintings in London.

Soon Julia found herself in the next room, sitting between the Professor and Martin Pitt at a round table, bright with silver and flowers. The sickening falling spasm which would not leave her heart, her moist palms, and her knees which had no strength in them, spelt to her for the first time in her life the real meaning of fear. She had determined on being natural, careless and gay, yet it was more difficult than she had thought. Charles's death had been a shell-burst of swift horror. This was worse. It was the cold-blooded anticipation of she knew not what, for Benvenuto, that morning, had warned her only of a shock which awaited her.

She was glad to be seated, and a spoonful of soup revived her a little. Martin Pitt was saying something to her, asking her questions about their host, "an old friend of Louise's, of course." She replied as intelligently as she could, one half of her mind occupied with the fact that Terence Rourke was absent from the table—there was not even a place prepared for him. She drank her wine, and her glass was immediately refilled by a footman.

Across the table she was conscious of Louise Lafontaine looking at her with dark, painted eyes, and found in the strange secretive regard a challenge which reacted on her more swiftly than the wine. She began to feel more sure of herself—her sick fear had gone, and was replaced by a curious excitement. These people! Her senses quickened, she looked round at the circle of faces, and saw them as six masks, masks which hid, all too effectively, the workings of each one's mind.

Whose mind was it that held the secret knowledge, the fear, the guilt of murder?

She did not know, and now, in her new-found excitement she craved to know.

Adolf Goetz and Benvenuto were discussing wines, and the science of collecting them. Great and beautiful names drifted to her across the table, Hermitage, Romanée-Conti, Chateau Yquem. How lovely they were, she thought, and what kindly deities. Benvenuto was talking brilliantly and well, and for the moment everyone was listening to him; only Julia noticed that his left hand worked quickly, nervously, at the moulding of little pellets of bread. The discussion ended abruptly in bathos as Agatha expressed a wish that they could all taste her parsnip wine which, besides being agreeable to the palate, had great medicinal value.

Professor Milk, looking strangely sinister with his newly sprouting beard and cropped head, addressed Martin Pitt.

"And what are you working at now, my dear boy?"

"A one-act play, Professor," replied Pitt. "And talking of that, do you think, Miss Dallas, I might have the courage to ask Benvenuto Brown to paint a backcloth for it? It is supposed to be going to have a certain importance in the theatrical world, I believe. I think I might dare to say it is the best thing I have yet written."

Success had certainly improved him, thought Julia, just as Charles had predicted. It had made him more solid, more sure of himself, and actually he was not so thin, she told him. This remark, however, was unfortunate, for he turned to speak to Agatha, and Julia felt a little snubbed. Louise Lafontaine meanwhile had endeavoured to make conversation with the Professor, but he, having accidentally upset his wine on to her plate, had not responded with any bonhomie; and she was now talking in a low tone with Benvenuto.

Under the table Julia found the Professor's hand and pressed it for comfort; her nameless fear, for a moment, descended on her like a fog. His dry, thin fingers responded gently to her pressure, but his eyes were fixed, rather anxiously, upon Benvenuto. One by one the diners, as if impelled by some common instinct, followed his example. Agatha, her lips twitching nervously, darted little glances alternately at her brother and Benvenuto, while Adolf Goetz, who had picked up the faint challenge in Pitt's last remark and had been offering him a serious and intelligent appreciation of *The Lily Flower*, hesitated, then fell silent, as both he and Pitt looked across to the silent figure sitting beside Louise.

Benvenuto raised his eyes from the table and looked round the circle of suddenly expectant faces. His own face was grave and seemed drawn, and suddenly older; Julia's heart was beating violently, painfully, as in a quiet voice he began to speak:

"It was I who persuaded Herr Goetz to ask you all here tonight—though without, let me add, any difficulty. My reason for doing so was that you were all present in the theatre on the first night of *The Lily Flower*, on the night of poor Charles Kulligrew's death—and you are all, as his friends, intensely interested in the mystery of that tragic death. Ever since that night I have been working in a sense for all of you, in my efforts to follow up various clues which I believed might lead me to a solution. I am here now to make a confession to you.

"I have not succeeded.

"To-night, before you all, my investigation comes to an end."

Abruptly his voice ceased, and with a hand which seemed to Julia's watching eyes to be nervously unsteady, he picked up his glass and raised it to his lips.

In the complete silence which held the table Julia's mind seemed to stagger under the unexpectedness of Benvenuto's speech, to stagger and then recover in new-born relief and hope. Was this the tragedy she had awaited with such fear and horror—was this the end? Where Benvenuto had failed no one would succeed. Almost she could have cried aloud her joy and relief, until with a swift chill round her heart she remembered Terence. Why was he absent? What did it mean? Painfully her eyes sought Benvenuto's across the table, but he was looking at Adolf Goetz, who had been the first to break the silence.

The precise, faintly foreign voice was offering courteous sympathy, building up a polite defence for Benvenuto's failure. Gradually each guest joined in, until Benvenuto was the silent recipient of a kind of chorus of excuse and condolence.

"Without the equipment of the superb machinery of a modern police force, the solitary investigator is a boxer with one hand tied behind his back," heard Julia. Then: "It was too much to expect, Benvenuto, my dear boy, that you should succeed in routing an organized gang of criminals, as I have no doubt they were," from Agatha, and her voice, though sympathetic, seemed to have in it a note of exultancy, as though she too shared the relief that had swept over Julia a few moments before.

As the chorus died away, Martin Pitt leant forward and addressed Benvenuto.

"There is one question, Brown, that has been troubling me for a long time, but which I haven't dared to ask. Now, however, that you have taken us into your confidence I'm going to pluck up courage to do so. What of the Mystery Man—what of Terence Rourke?"

Before Benvenuto could reply the voice of Louise came swiftly, passionately, across the table.

"No one who knows Terence Rourke as I know him could for one moment associate him with the guilt of murder!"

For an instant, through her bitterness and fear, Julia's eyes caught and held those of Louise in a glance that had no enmity. The next moment she had risen and was facing Adolf Goetz.

"Let us have our coffee in the next room," he said.

CHAPTER XXV
"THE PLAY'S THE THING"

LOUISE, SEATED on an Empire couch with Benvenuto and Martin Pitt, seemed as though she wished to atone for her outburst at the end of dinner. Julia stood looking out on to the terrace, the dark night and the distant sea. Already a cold and hesitant suggestion of pallor was painting the sky where the moon would shortly rise, though on the terrace the darkness was emphasized by two yellow roads of light cast from the open glass doors of the dining-room and *salon*. Between them, high up and impressive, rose the bronze statue of Louise, surmounting the low stone balustrade like some noble figure-head of a ship, and Julia stared at the vague silhouette while, half unconsciously, she listened to the beautiful voice of the original, behind her in the lighted room. How rich and musical was that voice, thought Julia, and how well she controlled it, like a skilful player on an instrument. A few moments before she had heard it ring out across the table, passionate, almost harsh in its emphatic defence of Rourke; now it was low and cool like falling water, persuasive, caressing.

They were discussing, once again, *The Lily Flower*, and Louise, with rare humility, was explaining to Benvenuto and Pitt a doubt which had perplexed her since the beginning of the play's run—a doubt as to her interpretation of certain lines.

"I am afraid my chief concern in the disappearance of Terence Rourke," she was saying, "was because of my inability to ask his opinion on those lines, after my first performance. He is a great producer—certainly the greatest producer I have ever worked for, and I would trust his judgment beyond anyone else's—even beyond *yours*, Martin. You must forgive me for that—authors are proverbially incompetent in the production of their own plays!"

Martin Pitt laughed. "Don't mention it. Any little confidence I may once have cherished in my ability to speak my own lines was destroyed long ago by Terence's barely concealed disdain. And I admit he was invariably right—he is, as you say, a great producer. But might the mere author inquire which part of the play it is which troubles you?"

She nodded. "You certainly might, my dear." She pondered for a moment, seeming to murmur her lines below her breath. By now Julia had turned round and was watching them, saw the quick, impatient gesture of Louise's hands and the apologetic smile she threw to the two men beside her.

"It is the scene where I am alone on the stage, before my suicide—but forgive me, without the context I am dumb, I can get no emotion into it, and could not explain to you what I mean. Some other time, when we are alone, Martin, I will run through the scene."

"Why not here and now?" suggested Benvenuto. "This room is the perfect substitute for a theatre. See—there is your stage, in the dining-room, beyond the open doors—and here we can sit in opulent ease occupying stalls more sumptuous than those of a picture palace de luxe. It would be a privilege for us—and might help you to arrive at a conclusion."

She looked at him doubtfully, and Martin Pitt jumped up and took her hand.

"Do, Louise—I beseech you. And when you've finished I might even dare to offer a criticism, free as I am here from the terrors of professional producers."

After a momentary hesitation she rose to her feet.

"Very well—on your own heads be it! But I have one condition, Martin—and that is that you read the part yourself when I have finished. Your own rendering might—I don't say it would, but it *might*—solve the problem for me. I must go and change this gaudy frock. You arrange the stage—you know how it goes. I'll enter there."

She pointed to a door leading from the dining-room into the hall, and hurried out of the room, singing to herself. "She certainly has the most amazing charm," thought Julia, following the gold-clad figure with her eyes.

In a moment the long room had woken to life. Benvenuto, having explained to their host and to Agatha and the Professor that they were to see a private performance of *The Lily Flower*, had put them into a pleasurable flutter, and they all seated themselves in a row facing the open doors of the dining-room. Here the servants were clearing away the last of the meal, while Martin Pitt busily arranged the furniture into a semblance of the suburban sitting-room where the tragedy was played. Benvenuto went to the electric switches and plunged the *salon* into darkness, at the same time turning up all the dining-room lights so that the stage was vividly illuminated. The servants finished their work and went out, and Martin Pitt retired to the back of the stage, as the door slowly opened and Louise came in.

She had taken off her golden dress and was wearing a white wrapper, drawn closely round her, and giving her an air of statuesque purity. Julia, watching her from the darkness, bit her lips with sudden pain, so forcibly was she taken back to that first night in the theatre, which had begun so triumphantly and ended so tragically.

But something was wrong. Louise's air of high tragedy was swiftly overlaid by irritation as she looked round the brightly lit room.

"I always play this scene in a half-light," she snapped, and Benvenuto hurried off apologetically to the switches. In a moment the stage was dim and shadowy, the white figure of Louise seen vaguely, unreally. After a pause she began her monologue, and at once the magic of her voice held the six watching people silent and still. Clearly and beautifully it rose, each phrase dropping into the stillness with its perfectly controlled burden of tragedy and despair, then, as she came to the important passage, she paused, before enunciating it very slowly and distinctly:

"'*Long ago they taught me, "Honour thy father and thy mother."*

"'*I'll have to go alone, to find the way. It cannot be more lonely.*'"

Soon the lovely voice ceased and she dropped her head and remained so, still for a moment, before signing to Martin Pitt to give his rendering of the lines. Then she slipped into a seat with the others and sat forward, watching him broodingly as he came on to the stage.

What an ordeal, thought Julia, to follow such perfect acting—even before *us*. But though he hesitated for a moment Martin Pitt spoke the lines well, firmly and clearly, giving them a meaning and significance a little different from Louise's own. He is rather wonderful, thought Julia, watching his curious, beautiful face, rather wonderful to be able to preserve his own point of view in the face of Louise's performance—but then, after all, he is the author. And then, as he ended, her eyes left his face and went swiftly to the door that led through to the hall.

In the dim light she could see it was opening—a man was coming in. He was tall and dark—he walked with a slight characteristic limp. She strained her eyes, peering at him, and half rose from her chair, her heart seeming to have stopped its beating. It was—it must be—Charles Kulligrew. He was speaking—and it was with Charles's voice, Charles's slight nervous hesitation. He was saying, "You are wrong. Louise understands. *I wrote it for Louise.*"

What was happening? What was happening to Martin Pitt? Blindly Julia got to her feet. He was coming towards her, stumbling across the stage. He was pointing at her—Oh, God! no—he was pointing at Charles. A strange strangled noise was coming from his throat which gradually clarified into speech.

"I knew you'd come back—I've been waiting for you!"

Suddenly, horribly, he laughed. "You know—I thought a knife in the back would keep you quiet. But I forgot—I forgot if a man will die for glory he'll come back to life for it, too. You heard all the praise—you saw your success—you knew it was yours—wasn't that enough for you—damn *you—damn you!* And now you've come back to tell them—but they won't believe you—they won't believe a ghost!" His voice was high, shrill, triumphant; then suddenly he stopped, his face working horribly, fear gripping him. "But suppose they did," he muttered. "Suppose they did believe you—" He looked over his shoulder, then turned and dashed across the room, out on to the terrace.

"Stop him!" shouted a voice, and there was the sound of heavy feet running over the paving. A moment later Leech appeared white-faced, in the doorway through which Martin Pitt had run.

"He was too quick for us. He's gone—over the edge."

"Then he's dead," said the voice of Terence Rourke.

The room rocked and swung as Julia caught at her chair—blurred faces rushed before her eyes—she was slipping—slipping away into darkness with voices following her, voices crying, "He's dead—he's dead."

CHAPTER XXVI
AND HOW—

THE TWO FISHERMEN worked by the light of a lantern hung from the mast, splashing about in the water with bare feet that were sunburnt, like seasoned wood. Into the boat they put a jar of oil, a big iron pot, and a basket of fish fresh caught and many-coloured. Strange words caught Julia's ears as the fishermen described to Benvenuto and Terence Rourke how to make a bouillabaisse, their Provençal accent rounding the words, giving them a Mediterranean tang, rich and deep. Roucaou, she heard, Beaudroit, Rascasse.

It was clear and starlit and very warm. Warm enough to bathe at midnight, thought Julia, and perhaps the sea would be phosphorescent and she would feel like a silver fish, swimming in silver fire. She looked across the little port of St. Antoine, past the brightly lit cafés and the high, narrow houses which lined the quay, across the dark sea to the glittering belt of lights which marked the beginning of the *chic* Riviera—Cannes, Antibes, Nice, Monte Carlo. Never, she told herself, did she want to go back there; never could she forget that last horrible night ending in the death of Martin Pitt. It had been Benvenuto's idea that they came to St. Antoine by road next morning, she and Agatha and the Professor and Terence Rourke, and he had been right. The long ride over the dusty sunlit roads of Provence seemed to have separated her by more than miles from the tragedy at the chateau. St. Antoine was simple and sweet, men and women lived near to the earth and the sea, and from their proximity found an instinctive confidence and an acceptance of life which was calming and reassuring—or so it seemed to Julia, listening to the Provençal voices of the fishermen. She raised her eyes and found them caught and held by those of Terence Rourke, his eyes that were bright and troubling and that seemed to-night in the light of the hanging lantern to have lost their fierceness. Quickly she turned and walked up the quay, her new confidence swept away on a stream of shame and unhappiness. Fool, she told herself—fool!

Down the street, arm in arm, came Agatha and the Professor, Agatha's penetratingly English voice rising above the music in the cafés.

"I think him most agreeable," Julia heard her say, "and a perfect gentleman, though foreign of course. We became *quite* intimate. Why, only yesterday I said to him, 'Herr Goetz, I fear you are nothing but a Tease,' whereupon we both laughed immoderately. So I confess, Edward, I am utterly at a loss to understand how he came to invite that actress hussy to stay on at the château. I am convinced it was *pure* kindness of heart, and that he would infinitely have preferred to accompany us here. Ah, my dear, there you are!"

Julia linked her arm in the Professor's and walked back towards the boat. It would be easier now that they had come. In the boat she would sit between them, she decided, and not think of Terence Rourke. Never again would she be able to look him frankly in the face, for always she would have the memory of the night at the chateau when she had suspected him, tricked him, deceived him. Again she felt the hot blood rush to her face and was thankful for the darkness, and the erratic beams of the swaying lantern.

Benvenuto and Terence were on board, busy stowing bottles of wine into the hold.

"Dear me," laughed Agatha, "how this takes me back to my childhood spent in Bournemouth. We used constantly to go for marine excursions, and I remember my dear father saying I was quite a little sailor, though poor Edward was invariably unwell."

The Professor frowned slightly and tilted his panama to a more nautical angle. "Shall we embark?" he inquired, almost with asperity.

Soon the little boat was chugging across the port, towards the lighthouse and the open sea. The six passengers were silent, watching the town of St. Antoine recede across the water, beautiful and unreal as a stage *decor*. It reminded Julia of Picasso's "Pulcinella" with its high, ancient houses and narrow, mysterious streets, while in front, where the orchestra should have been, lay a second town reflected in the water; a town of lights, bright and tremulous.

The younger of the two fishermen, lying across the bow, began to sing in his rough, deep voice a Provençal song, pausing as they rounded the mole to shout greetings to another boat coming in with the evening catch. The moon was not yet risen, but once out in the open sea, they moved through a pale and watery half-light, so that they could see each other's faces, sculptured and colourless.

"Once," said Benvenuto, "I used to make this journey every night, to take food and water to a suspected murderer."

"You're very mysterious, Ben," said Julia. "Where are we going—and who was the murderer?"

"We're going to an island which you'll see as soon as we get out of the bay; as for the story, it's too long to tell you now. I'm saving my energies till after supper, my dear, when I've got another story to tell you—the story which came to an end at Goetz's house. I've promised the Professor to give my version to all of you to-night. Meanwhile, let's have a drink."

It might have come to an end for him, thought Julia, but it hadn't for her—nothing could ever be the same again. Or for Terence Rourke and Louise—Louise, who had believed in him and defended him all the time, she thought bitterly. Soon, she supposed, they would get married. And she—what would she do? Against her will her eyes sought Terence, who, seated on the gunwale of the boat, was uncorking a bottle. On the sea he looked like a muscular pirate, with his bare arms and striped jersey. She turned and began to talk to the Professor.

"Jam paret media fluctu nemorosa Jacynthos!" he exclaimed, and Julia looking over the bow saw that the island had come into view, rising at the end of a chain of smaller rocks, like a great sea beast, followed by its young.

As they drew nearer it seemed impregnable, a bare mountain of rock; but the little boat, turning suddenly, entered a long fiord with high rocky walls from which the noise of the engine echoed loudly. The fisherman bent forward, the noise ceased, and in utter silence they drifted slowly down to a sandy beach.

"You've chosen a most dramatic setting for your story, Ben," said Julia. "How awe-inspiring and mysterious this place is—it looks as though it had been invented by Wagner."

He laughed. "In daylight it's the perfect desert island—grey rocks and sand and blue water and the best bathing in the world; wait till we've got a fire going and you'll see what it looks like."

And in a few minutes, with flames leaping from a bonfire of dry and salted wood, casting moving lights on pine trees and twisted rocks, with the company seated in a wide circle and a savoury smell of garlic and saffron rising from a casserole where the two fishermen were preparing bouillabaisse for supper, Julia forgot her first feeling of awe, and was happy. The wine, cooled in the sea, tasted fresh and delicious, the night was warm and starlit, the saffron-flavoured lobster, when it came, a gastronomic joy; here on the island before the leaping fire it was easy enough to live for the moment. From a few feet away Terence Rourke smiled at her over his wine; he was silent and it seemed, thought Julia, as though the Tiger had for the time being become a lamb. Most of the conversation came from the Professor, who ate and drank in the best of spirits, and who presented the appearance of an ancient Bacchus with a twisted wreath of vine leaves placed round his head by Julia.

"How agreeable it is," he murmured, gesturing vaguely round with the claw of a lobster, "to be seated here, feasting like heroes of antiquity. And now Benvenuto, since you have all finished—I perceive I am the last—will you not allow us to feast our ears upon your account of those mysteries which have surrounded us?"

Benvenuto stretched himself at full length before the fire, and after lighting his pipe, began his story.

"The drama began for me," he said, "on the evening of that other drama—*The Lily Flower*; but it began before the murder of poor Charles Kulligrew.

"I had once seen a play by Martin Pitt produced at the Guild Theatre, and had, in a way, admired it. A kind of transcendental ecstasy, an impossible idealism, an extravagant cynicism showed through the piece which, as a play, as drama, was poor stuff.

"At the end of the first act of *The Lily Flower*, I *knew* that whoever had written it, it wasn't Martin Pitt. Allowing that the human mind is contradictory and inconsistent, I felt that there were limits to one man's points of view; and here I heard, let us say for the sake of argument, a Shelley speaking with the tongue of Donne,

"Many things are possible, but that is not possible.

"Martin Pitt's mind was the mind of a man who lived in a heaven, or a hell, of his own. In a word, he learnt nothing, nothing at all, from life. He was slightly mad. He was not even a genius, which would have saved him.

"The man who wrote *The Lily Flower* knew almost all about life that it is possible to know and distilled it in his brain to pure poetry. He was a genius, and I drink to his memory.

"During the second act I said to myself—if Charles had written this, I shouldn't be so surprised. I knew Charles's mind, and I could imagine that he might have been capable of it. What was more, he was the admirer, he had been the lover, of Louise—and here was the perfect part created for her—apparently by someone else!

"It is the truth—I am not boasting—that at the end of the second act I believed that Charles had written the play and had given it to Pitt.

"What actually happened it is impossible to say—they are both dead. Charles, I think, must have written it when he was stimulated by passion for Louise. Later, as we know, he left her. He, oddly enough, greatly admired Pitt's work, and it is probable that he gave Pitt the play to read. Let us imagine what happened. Pitt is enthusiastic, and offers to get the play produced. Charles always shy as a nervous racehorse and disillusioned (mistakenly, as it happens) about Louise, yet wanting to see her in the name part, persuades his friend to accept the play as a gift and stage it as his own. Pitt accepts, at first through pure friendship.

"Terence produced the play and can tell us what happened next."

Benvenuto paused, and threw a log on the fire.

"To begin with," said Terence Rourke, "Martin brought the play to me, and I read it. It was a damned good play and I hit him on the back and said, 'Martin, me boy, it's a damned good play.' I remember thinking at the time that Charles might have given him a helping hand with it, but that wasn't my affair. He said he'd like Louise to play the name part, and that was about the only intelligent thing he did say. He made other suggestions during the rehearsals, weak suggestions, and when I showed him he was wrong, he left it to me; sort of shrugged his shoulders."

"Well," said Benvenuto, "I wasn't the only one who realized that Pitt hadn't written it—isn't that so, Professor? During the performance I saw you were disturbed about something, and then, in Chamonix, when you spoke of the mystery of *The Lily Flower*, I felt sure that *you* hadn't been deceived."

The Professor fingered his beard nervously.

"I knew, Benvenuto, my dear boy, that *The Lily Flower* could not have come from the brain of Martin Pitt, and I was very distressed—very worried and distressed. Indeed, I feared I was losing my reason, confusing the minds of those two poor boys. But I must explain that I never for one moment connected my idea about the play with Charles's murder—indeed I still do not see—"

"Let me try to explain.

"To begin with I am sure the crime was not premeditated. It was the sudden impulse of a man mad with jealousy, confronted with opportunity in the shape of a sword-stick left leaning up against the wall, by *you*, Professor."

"Edward cannot be blamed for *that*," said Agatha, sharply. "He has always been forgetful from a schoolboy, and it's no use *your* trying to alter him, Benvenuto."

"It all comes back to me now," murmured the Professor. "Pray continue, my dear boy."

"Martin Pitt had always been told," went on Benvenuto, "that he was a genius. At Oxford he was the brilliant poet, the Rupert Brooke, the coming man. 'A young Apollo, golden-haired, stands dreaming . . .' and so forth. He acted the part excellently, and thought very well of himself. In London, after he came down, he continued to think well of himself, and by the strength of his curious personality he succeeded in making a fair number of other people think well of him. But London was the acid test—too acid for his mediocre talent—and his two plays were damned with faint praise. Even so, he had a fair personal success—he *looked* so like the real thing, and Charles, for one, continued to believe in him.

"To be a failure! That was what he dreaded, and only that.

"Well, on the opening night of *The Lily Flower* he tasted for the first time real, intoxicating success. London was at his feet; the most important people accepted him for—what he was not, what he could never be. Aren't you, in a way, sorry for him? His cup was poisoned, poor fellow.

"I don't think for a moment he killed Charles, as someone suggested, for money reasons, so that the profits of the play should be his. No. I think he killed Charles because he could not bear one man to exist in the world who knew that he was a fraud. He killed Charles—because he was insane with jealousy.

"The rest is quickly told. We don't know why he went into the box, but go he did. It was empty except for Charles, the Professor had just left, the lights were low.

"Pitt looked at Kulligrew's back, and saw the sword-stick ready to his hand. A moment later he was gone—and Charles was dead."

"Then—then," said Julia, "when I met him in the corridor—it was a moment after—he said he was looking for Uncle Edward—he'd just come from the box." She stared into the fire and went on in a low voice. "I spoke to Charles—and hated him for not answering. And he was dead."

A silence fell. Benvenuto looked at her kindly, and went on.

"Imagine, if you can, Martin Pitt's emotions during that last act. Leech tells me he left the theatre and walked round Golden Square. But he came back. Trembling, dazed, full of fear and horror, he came back. He knew he *had* to come back."

"Why, exactly?" asked Terence Rourke.

"To make his speech, and *to be the first to discover the murder, in full view of five hundred people.* When Pitt did that he was almost a genius. A criminal genius. And a damned good actor. Five hundred people, the cleverest in London, their eyes fixed on his face, watched him as he spoke; saw him falter, stare, point at Charles's dead face, and fall forward in a faint. A most brilliant bluff, and wonderfully done. He was not suspected for a moment. How could he be?"

"Except by you," put in the Professor.

"Except by me," agreed Benvenuto. "And I could not be sure. Now, Pitt had an extraordinary piece of luck, and that was—the disappearance of Terence Rourke. But it was in his endeavour to profit by this piece of luck that he made his one fatal mistake. He told me that Rourke was in the box with Charles when he, Pitt, went in to look for the Professor—knowing full well that Rourke had disappeared and could not correct him. As soon as I found you, Terence, and heard your story that night in Lyon, I knew that Pitt had lied, and felt that my theories—my beliefs, were justified. Furthermore, Pitt did his best, very cleverly and subtly, to increase our suspicions of you, and of Louise, whilst appearing to defend you both warmly."

"The poor mean-hearted deceiving divil, God rest his soul," murmured Terence.

"Tell me, Ben," broke in Julia, "when exactly did you *know* Martin Pitt was the murderer?"

"In my studio, when I told him I was going to search for Rourke, the pupils of his eyes dilated. At that moment my instinct became, for me, knowledge. But it wasn't evidence. I couldn't get any real evidence, try as I would. To Scotland Yard, Pitt's word about not being alone with Charles in the box would have been as good as, and a great deal better than, the word of a mad, disappearing Irishman, who was already suspected of every crime in the legal code. They'd have hanged you on your past, Terence, me boy, on your shady, privateering, racketeering, piratical past."

"You saved me from the gallows, so I'll not be knocking you down to-night," growled Rourke, waving his cigar amiably.

"Well, my search for evidence proving pretty hopeless and Terence's position becoming every day more dangerous, I had to try other tactics, and it was only the goodwill and intelligence of Detective-Inspector Leech that enabled me to carry them out. I took him into my confidence after I'd found him in Terence's farm-house at Castellane, and told him of the last throw I was about to make. He agreed to postpone proceeding against Terence, and to stand by to watch the result of my experiment. I had, as you know, decided to stage a rehearsal of *The Lily Flower* at Goetz's house, and to bring Pitt face to face with his victim. To do this I had of course to take Louise and Terence into my confidence—and it was on Terence that the success of the whole thing depended. If he had failed in his impersonation of Charles he'd have set Martin Pitt free and condemned himself to death. But he didn't fail. Louise, too, was magnificent; it was a big thing to ask of her and she behaved superbly. She had loved Charles.

"So, you see—I gambled on Pitt's nature—with the help of those two, I won."

"Then Inspector Leech knew all about it too?" said Julia.

"Yes, he was waiting on the terrace to overhear Pitt's confession, if my plan came off, and to arrest him."

"But he wasn't quick enough," remarked Agatha acidly. "I always told you the man was nothing but a fool."

"Perhaps," replied Benvenuto, "his bad judgment was the least harmful example of bad judgment that has occurred in the whole affair. God knows there's been enough of it, what with Goetz and Terence each firmly convinced that the other was the criminal, to say nothing of the Professor being more than half convinced that he'd done it himself. By the way, Agatha, I'd like to congratulate you publicly on the masterly way you hid your own suspicions of the Professor's guilt."

"*Benvenuto!*" Agatha sat up violently, her face red. "I will not sit here and be insulted! Never for one instant did I doubt my poor brother; and in any case, supposing anyone had so far have forgotten themselves as to suspect Edward, they would naturally have realized that he had done it with the best possible motives."

"Exactly," said Benvenuto.

"And as for that old divil Goetz," remarked Terence Rourke, "he was prejudiced against me. All this time the old boy has been labouring under the delusion that I ran off with Louise after she'd quarrelled with Charles—whereas there were never two people with less personal sympathy than Louise and meself! For me she was a terrible fine actress, and also at that time a woman with a heart half breaking for Charles—so I took her to London and started her off in a show, knowing there was nothing like hard work for curing a broken heart."

Benvenuto nodded. "All the same I doubt if you and Herr Goetz could ever be exactly soul-mates. And now, for God's sake let's have a drink and sing something coarse and honest—I'm tired of crime. Come on, Terence:

"'A platter and can for every man
What more can the quality want?'"

As they sang, one of the fishermen in the boat began to play a tentative accompaniment on a guitar, and then as the song ended Benvenuto called across to him, "Chantez, mon vieux."

Over from the boat came the notes of the guitar, low and plaintive, and then a deep sweet southern voice singing an old song, "*Le Temps des Cerises*." The moon had risen, painting a silver path on the water in which the little boat rocked gently, pouring a silver pallor over the shore and seeming to cool the dying embers of the fire.

Julia wandered down to the edge of the sea. She sat on a ledge of rock, sat very still and tried to calm the wild, joyful beating of her heart. "Good-bye, Louise, good-bye," she murmured to herself. "You were never there at all, never where I thought you were, close beside Terence. You'll never be in my world any more."

And it seemed as though her world had changed, as if by magic; it was a treasure-house now, unexplored. The voice of the sea whispering at her feet held no melancholy; it caressed her, murmured promises to her; the moonlight on the water had no cold and deathly pallor, it was a path of dancing brilliance. Softly she began to sing "*Le Temps des Cerises*."

Turning her head she could see the dull glow of the fire illuminating faintly the four people who sat round it, Agatha and the Professor close together, still and peaceful; Benvenuto with the smoke of his pipe forming a cloud round his head; and there, between them, with his back to her, the mane of hair and the broad shoulders of Terence Rourke.

He can never forgive you, never, said a cold voice inside her. You doubted him—you tricked him—what can he think of you?

As she watched, he rose to his feet and walked down the beach towards her. Her heart beating, she looked out across the sea, and he came and sat down beside her and was silent.

"I—I rather thought I'd go for a swim," said Julia.

"Take care," he answered. "There must be sea-monsters out there, watching you, waiting to carry you off. Aren't you afraid?"

"No," she said, "I'm not afraid."

"You weren't even afraid of me, when you thought I was a Tiger. I don't want anyone to carry you off, so may I come with you—shall we go together?"

"Yes," said Julia, "let's go—together."

THE END

Lightning Source UK Ltd.
Milton Keynes UK
UKOW02f0715130117
292010UK00013B/163/P